THE STORY OF SAPHO

THE
OTHER VOICE
IN
EARLY MODERN
EUROPE

A Series Edited by Margaret L. King and Albert Rabil Jr.

RECENT BOOKS IN THE SERIES

Madeleine de Scudéry

THE STORY OF SAPHO

෨

*Translated and with an introduction
by Karen Newman*

THE UNIVERSITY OF CHICAGO PRESS
Chicago & London

Madeleine de Scudéry (1607–1701)

Karen Newman is University Professor and professor of comparative literature and English at Brown University. Her previous books include *Fashioning Femininity* and *English Renaissance Drama* (1991), published by the University of Chicago Press.

The University of Chicago Press, Chicago 60637
The University of Chicago Press, Ltd., London
© 2003 by The University of Chicago
All rights reserved. Published 2003
Printed in the United States of America
12 11 10 09 08 07 06 05 04 03   1 2 3 4 5

ISBN: 0-226-14398-8 (cloth)
ISBN: 0-226-14399-6 (paper)

Library of Congress Cataloging-in-Publication Data

Scudéry, Madeleine de, 1607–1701.
    [Artamène. English. Selections]
    The story of Sapho / Madeleine de Scudéry ; translated and with an introduction by Karen Newman.
        p.   cm.—(The other voice in early modern Europe)
    Includes bibliographical references and index.
    ISBN 0-226-14398-8 (cloth : alk. paper)—ISBN 0-226-14399-6 (pbk. : alk. paper)
    I. Newman, Karen, 1949–   . II. Title. III. Series.
PQ1922.A8 E5   2003
843'.7—dc21   2002043558

⊚ The paper used in this publication meets the minimum requirements of the American National Standard for Information Sciences—Permanence of Paper for Printed Library Materials, ANSI Z39.48-1992.

For Jonathan

CONTENTS

ACKNOWLEDGMENTS

I was prompted to undertake this translation by the work of Joan DeJean, whose *Tender Geographies* first moved me to read Scudéry's novels. I subsequently wanted to teach them but found to my dismay that not only have there been no translations into English since the mid-seventeenth century when the novels first appeared; there is still no modern edition of Scudéry's novels in French. When Albert Rabil wrote to me for advice about what work of Scudéry's might reasonably be translated for The Other Voice series that he and Margaret King edit for the University of Chicago Press, I not only suggested the *Histoire de Sapho* but offered to translate it myself. At the time, I was chairing the Department of Comparative Literature at Brown, a task that made it virtually impossible to pursue other kinds of scholarly work, most notably a book on London and Paris that was well under way, but still incomplete.

Translating has been an unexpected pleasure. Every translation is, of course, a reading, but the pleasure for me was taking up a few pages at a time, in odd moments, when there was no time for the focused development of argument and evidence demanded by other kinds of critical writing. And yet translation offers, nonetheless, all the pleasures of close reading that in turn prompt writing: engagement with language and style, preoccupation with diction and figure, reflection on nuance, and for the comparatist, lessons in the incommensurability of two linguistic and literary traditions at the very moment one is yoking them together.

Not only did Joan DeJean's work prompt the initial reading of Scudéry that eventuated in this translation, but my introduction owes a great debt to her work and learning, a debt I acknowledge here and in the introduction itself. She also took time from a sabbatical to read and offer comments and suggestions on the translation. Keith Waldrop and Lewis Seifert were excellent readers of early sections, and I thank them. Jonathan Goldberg generously read and commented on the entire manuscript. For the occasional obscure reference, thanks to Steve Thompson and Karen Bouchard of the Rockefeller Library at Brown and my Brown colleagues in Classics and Comparative Literature, Alan Boegehold, David Konstan, and Michael Putnam. I am especially grateful to my friend and colleague Michel-André Bossy for his generosity and patience in helping with occasional difficult and tricky moments in the French text. Thanks also to the press's reader, Patricia Francis Cholakian, for many helpful suggestions. As convention has it, mistakes are my own. This translation is dedicated to Jonathan Goldberg, with whom I have long exercised the art of conversation that is so much the subject of the *Histoire de Sapho*. That Sapho's history is also about friendship between men and women, between men, and between women, makes this dedication all the more fitting.

Karen Newman

THE OTHER VOICE IN
EARLY MODERN EUROPE:
INTRODUCTION TO THE SERIES

Margaret L. King and Albert Rabil Jr.

THE OLD VOICE AND THE OTHER VOICE

In western Europe and the United States, women are nearing equality in the professions, in business, and in politics. Most enjoy access to education, reproductive rights, and autonomy in financial affairs. Issues vital to women are on the public agenda: equal pay, child care, domestic abuse, breast cancer research, and curricular revision with an eye to the inclusion of women.

These recent achievements have their origins in things women (and some male supporters) said for the first time about six hundred years ago. Theirs is the "other voice," in contradistinction to the "first voice," the voice of the educated men who created Western culture. Coincident with a general reshaping of European culture in the period 1300–1700 (called the Renaissance or early modern period), questions of female equality and opportunity were raised that still resound and are still unresolved.

The other voice emerged against the backdrop of a three-thousand-year history of the derogation of women rooted in the civilizations related to Western culture: Hebrew, Greek, Roman, and Christian. Negative attitudes toward women inherited from these traditions pervaded the intellectual, medical, legal, religious, and social systems that developed during the European Middle Ages.

The following pages describe the traditional, overwhelmingly male views of women's nature inherited by early modern Europeans and the new tradition that the other voice called into being to begin to challenge reigning assumptions. This review should serve as a framework for the understanding of the texts published in the series The Other Voice in Early Modern Europe. Introductions specific to each text and author follow this essay in all the volumes of the series.

TRADITIONAL VIEWS OF WOMEN, 500 B.C.E. – 1500 C.E.

Embedded in the philosophical and medical theories of the ancient Greeks were perceptions of the female as inferior to the male in both mind and body. Similarly, the structure of civil legislation inherited from the ancient Romans was biased against women, and the views on women developed by Christian thinkers out of the Hebrew Bible and the Christian New Testament were negative and disabling. Literary works composed in the vernacular language of ordinary people, and widely recited or read, conveyed these negative assumptions. The social networks within which most women lived—those of the family and the institutions of the Roman Catholic Church—were shaped by this negative tradition and sharply limited the areas in which women might act in and upon the world.

GREEK PHILOSOPHY AND FEMALE NATURE. Greek biology assumed that women were inferior to men and defined them merely as child bearers and housekeepers. This view was authoritatively expressed in the works of the philosopher Aristotle.

Aristotle thought in dualities. He considered action superior to inaction, form (the inner design or structure of any object) superior to matter, completion to incompletion, possession to deprivation. In each of these dualities, he associated the male principle with the superior quality and the female with the inferior. "The male principle in nature," he argued, "is associated with active, formative and perfected characteristics, while the female is passive, material and deprived, desiring the male in order to become complete."[1] Men are always identified with virile qualities, such as judgment, courage, and stamina, and women with their opposites—irrationality, cowardice, and weakness.

Even in the womb, the masculine principle was considered superior. The man's semen, Aristotle believed, created the form of a new human creature, while the female body contributed only matter. (The existence of the ovum, and with it the other facts of human embryology, was not established until the seventeenth century.) Although the later Greek physician Galen believed that there was a female component in generation, contributed by "female semen," the followers of both Aristotle and Galen saw the male role in human generation as more active and more important.

In the Aristotelian view, the male principle sought always to reproduce itself. The creation of a female was always a mistake, therefore, resulting

1. Aristotle, *Physics* 1.9.192a20–24, in *The Complete Works of Aristotle*, ed. Jonathan Barnes, rev. Oxford trans., 2 vols. (Princeton, 1984), 1:328.

from an imperfect act of generation. Every female born was considered a "defective" or "mutilated" male (as Aristotle's terminology has variously been translated), a "monstrosity" of nature.[2]

For Greek theorists, the biology of males and females was the key to their psychology. The female was softer and more docile, more apt to be despondent, querulous, and deceitful. Being incomplete, moreover, she craved sexual fulfillment in intercourse with a male. The male was intellectual, active, and in control of his passions.

These psychological polarities derived from the theory that the universe consisted of four elements (earth, fire, air, and water), expressed in human bodies as four "humors" (black bile, yellow bile, blood, and phlegm) considered, respectively, dry, hot, damp, and cold, and corresponding to mental states ("melancholic," "choleric," "sanguine," and "phlegmatic"). In this schematization, the male, sharing the principles of earth and fire, was dry and hot; the female, sharing the principles of air and water, was cold and damp.

Female psychology was further affected by her dominant organ, the uterus (womb), *hystera* in Greek. The passions generated by the womb made women lustful, deceitful, talkative, irrational, indeed—when these affects were in excess—"hysterical."

Aristotle's biology also had social and political consequences. If the male principle was superior and the female inferior, then in the household, as in the state, men should rule and women must be subordinate. That hierarchy did not rule out the companionship of husband and wife, whose cooperation was necessary for the welfare of children and the preservation of property. Such mutuality supported male preeminence.

Aristotle's teacher Plato suggested a different possibility: that men and women might possess the same virtues. The setting for this proposal is the imaginary and ideal Republic that Plato sketches in a dialogue of that name. Here, for a privileged elite capable of leading wisely, all distinctions of class and wealth dissolve, as do, consequently, those of gender. Without households or property, as Plato constructs his ideal society, there is no need for the subordination of women. Women may, therefore, be educated to the same level as men to assume leadership responsibilities. Plato's Republic remained imaginary, however. In real societies, the subordination of women remained the norm and the prescription.

The views of women inherited from the Greek philosophical tradition became the basis for medieval thought. In the thirteenth century,

2. Aristotle, *Generation of Animals* 2.3.737a27–28, in *The Complete Works*, 1:1144.

the supreme Scholastic philosopher Thomas Aquinas, among others, still echoed Aristotle's views of human reproduction, of male and female personalities, and of the preeminent male role in the social hierarchy.

ROMAN LAW AND THE FEMALE CONDITION. Roman law, like Greek philosophy, underlay medieval thought and shaped medieval society. The ancient belief that adult, property-owning men should administer households and make decisions affecting the community at large is the very fulcrum of Roman law.

About 450 B.C.E., during Rome's republican era, the community's customary law was recorded (legendarily) on twelve tablets erected in the city's central forum. It was later elaborated by professional jurists whose activity increased in the imperial era, when much new legislation, especially on issues affecting family and inheritance, was passed. This growing, changing body of laws was eventually codified in the *Corpus of Civil Law* under the direction of the emperor Justinian, generations after the empire ceased to be ruled from Rome. That *Corpus*, read and commented on by medieval scholars from the eleventh century on, inspired the legal systems of most of the cities and kingdoms of Europe.

Laws regarding dowries, divorce, and inheritance pertain primarily to women. Since those laws aimed to maintain and preserve property, the women concerned were those from the property-owning minority. Their subordination to male family members points to the even greater subordination of lower-class and slave women, about whom the laws speak little.

In the early republic, the paterfamilias, or "father of the family," possessed *patria potestas*, "paternal power." The term *pater*, "father," in both these cases does not necessarily mean biological father but, rather, head of household. The father was the person who owned the household's property and, indeed, its human members. The paterfamilias had absolute power— including the power, rarely exercised, of life or death—over his wife, his children, and his slaves, as much as his cattle.

Male children could be "emancipated," an act that granted legal autonomy and the right to own property. Those over fourteen could be emancipated by a special grant from the father or automatically by their father's death. But females could never be emancipated; instead, they passed from the authority of their father to that of a husband or, if widowed or orphaned while still unmarried, to a guardian or tutor.

Marriage in its traditional form placed the woman under her husband's authority, or *manus*. He could divorce her on grounds of adultery, drinking wine, or stealing from the household, but she could not divorce him. She could neither possess property in her own right nor bequeath any to her children upon her death. When her husband died, the household property passed not to her but to his male heirs. And when her father died, she had no claim to any family inheritance, which was directed to her brothers or more remote male relatives. The effect of these laws was to exclude women from civil society, itself based on property ownership.

In the later republican and imperial periods, these rules were significantly modified. Women rarely married according to the traditional form but according to the form of "free" marriage. That practice allowed a woman to remain under her father's authority, to possess property given her by her father (most frequently the "dowry," recoverable from the husband's household in the event of his death), and to inherit from her father. She could also bequeath property to her own children and divorce her husband, just as he could divorce her.

Despite this greater freedom, women still suffered enormous disability under Roman law. Heirs could belong only to the father's side, never the mother's. Moreover, although she could bequeath her property to her children, she could not establish a line of succession in doing so. A woman was "the beginning and end of her own family," said the jurist Ulpian. Moreover, women could play no public role. They could not hold public office, represent anyone in a legal case, or even witness a will. Women had only a private existence and no public personality.

The dowry system, the guardian, women's limited ability to transmit wealth, and total political disability are all features of Roman law adopted by the medieval communities of western Europe, although modified according to local customary laws.

CHRISTIAN DOCTRINE AND WOMEN'S PLACE. The Hebrew Bible and the Christian New Testament authorized later writers to limit women to the realm of the family and to burden them with the guilt of original sin. The passages most fruitful for this purpose were the creation narratives in Genesis and sentences from the Epistles defining women's role within the Christian family and community.

Each of the first two chapters of Genesis contains a creation narrative. In the first "God created man in his own image, in the image of God he created him; male and female he created them" (Gen. 1:27 NRSV). In the second, God created Eve from Adam's rib (2:21–23). Christian theologians relied principally on Genesis 2 for their understanding of the relation between man and woman, interpreting the creation of Eve from Adam as proof of her subordination to him.

The creation story in Genesis 2 leads to that of the temptations in Genesis 3: of Eve by the wily serpent and of Adam by Eve. As read by Christian theologians from Tertullian to Thomas Aquinas, the narrative made Eve responsible for the Fall and its consequences. She instigated the act; she deceived her husband; she suffered the greater punishment. Her disobedience made it necessary for Jesus to be incarnated and to die on the cross. From the pulpit, moralists and preachers for centuries conveyed to women the guilt that they bore for original sin.

The Epistles offered advice to early Christians on building communities of the faithful. Among the matters to be regulated was the place of women. Paul offered views favorable to women in Galatians 3:28: "There is neither Jew nor Greek, there is neither slave nor free, there is neither male nor female; for you are all one in Christ Jesus." Paul also referred to women as his coworkers and placed them on a par with himself and his male coworkers (Phil. 4:2–3; Rom. 16:1–3; 1 Cor. 16:19). Elsewhere, Paul limited women's possibilities: "But I want you to understand that the head of every man is Christ, the head of a woman is her husband, and the head of Christ is God" (1 Cor. 11:3).

Biblical passages by later writers (although attributed to Paul) enjoined women to forgo jewels, expensive clothes, and elaborate coiffures; and they forbade women to "teach or have authority over men," telling them to "learn in silence with all submissiveness" as is proper for one responsible for sin, consoling them, however, with the thought that they will be saved through childbearing (1 Tim. 2:9–15). Other texts among the later Epistles defined women as the weaker sex and emphasized their subordination to their husbands (1 Peter 3:7; Col. 3:18; Eph. 5:22–23).

These passages from the New Testament became the arsenal employed by theologians of the early church to transmit negative attitudes toward women to medieval Christian culture—above all, Tertullian ("On the Apparel of Women"), Jerome ("Against Jovinian"), and Augustine ("The Literal Meaning of Genesis").

THE IMAGE OF WOMEN IN MEDIEVAL LITERATURE. The philosophical, legal, and religious traditions born in antiquity formed the basis of the medieval intellectual synthesis wrought by trained thinkers, mostly clerics, writing in Latin and based largely in universities. The vernacular literary tradition that developed alongside the learned tradition also spoke about female nature and women's roles. Medieval stories, poems, and epics also portrayed women negatively—as lustful and deceitful—while praising good housekeepers and loyal wives as replicas of the Virgin Mary or the female saints and martyrs.

There is an exception in the movement of "courtly love" that evolved in southern France from the twelfth century. Courtly love was the erotic love between a nobleman and noblewoman, the latter usually superior in social rank. It was always adulterous. From the conventions of courtly love derive modern Western notions of romantic love. The phenomenon has had an impact disproportionate to its size, for it affected only a tiny elite, and very few women. The exaltation of the female lover probably does not reflect a higher evaluation of women or a step toward their sexual liberation. More likely it gives expression to the social and sexual tensions besetting the knightly class at a specific historic juncture.

The literary fashion of courtly love was on the wane by the thirteenth century, when the widely read *Romance of the Rose* was composed in French by two authors of significantly different dispositions. Guillaume de Lorris composed the initial four thousand verses about 1235, and Jean de Meun added about seventeen thousand verses—more than four times the original—about 1265.

The fragment composed by Guillaume de Lorris stands squarely in the tradition of courtly love. Here the poet, in a dream, is admitted into a walled garden where he finds a magic fountain in which a rosebush is reflected. He longs to pick one rose, but the thorns around it prevent his doing so, even as he is wounded by arrows from the god of love, whose commands he agrees to obey. The rest of this part of the poem recounts the poet's unsuccessful efforts to pluck the rose.

The longer part of the *Romance* by Jean de Meun also describes a dream. But here allegorical characters give long didactic speeches, providing a social satire on a variety of themes, including those pertaining to women. Love is an anxious and tormented state, the poem explains; women are greedy and manipulative, marriage is miserable, beautiful women are lustful, ugly ones cease to please, and a chaste woman, as rare as a black swan, can scarcely be found.

Shortly after Jean de Meun completed *The Romance of the Rose*, Mathéolus penned his *Lamentations*, a long Latin diatribe against marriage translated into French about a century later. The *Lamentations* sum up medieval attitudes toward women and provoked the important response by Christine de Pizan in her *Book of the City of Ladies*.

In 1355, Giovanni Boccaccio wrote *Il Corbaccio*, another antifeminist manifesto, although ironically by an author whose other works pioneered new directions in Renaissance thought. The former husband of his lover appears to Boccaccio, condemning his unmoderated lust and detailing the defects of women. Boccaccio concedes at the end "how much men naturally surpass women in nobility" and is cured of his desires.[3]

---

3. Giovanni Boccaccio, *The Corbaccio; or, The Labyrinth of Love*, trans. and ed. Anthony K. Cassell, rev. ed. (Binghamton, N.Y., 1993), 71.

WOMEN'S ROLES: THE FAMILY. The negative perceptions of women expressed in the intellectual tradition are also implicit in the actual roles that women played in European society. Assigned to subordinate positions in the household and the church, they were barred from significant participation in public life.

Medieval European households, like those in antiquity and in many non-Western civilizations, were headed by males. It was the male serf (or peasant), feudal lord, town merchant, or citizen who was polled or taxed or who succeeded to an inheritance or had any acknowledged public role, although his wife or widow could stand as a temporary surrogate for him. From about 1100, the position of property-holding males was enhanced further: inheritance was confined to the male, or agnate, line—with depressing consequences for women.

A wife never fully belonged to her husband's family, nor was she a daughter to her father's family. She left her father's house young to marry whomever her parents chose. Her dowry was managed by her husband and normally passed to her children by him at her death.

A married woman's life was occupied nearly constantly with cycles of pregnancy, childbearing, and lactation. Women bore children through all the years of their fertility, and many died in childbirth before the end of that term. They also bore responsibility for raising young children up to six or seven. That responsibility was shared in the propertied classes, since it was common for a wet nurse to take over the job of breast-feeding and for servants to perform other chores.

Women trained their daughters in the household duties appropriate to their status, nearly always tasks associated with textiles: spinning, weaving, sewing, embroidering. Their sons were sent out of the house as apprentices or students, or their training was assumed by fathers in later childhood and adolescence. On the death of her husband, a woman's children became the responsibility of his family. She generally did not take "his" children with her to a new marriage or back to her father's house, except sometimes in artisan classes.

Women also worked. Rural peasants performed farm chores, merchant wives often practiced their husband's trade, the unmarried daughters of the urban poor worked as servants or prostitutes. All wives produced or embellished textiles and did the housekeeping, while wealthy ones managed servants. These labors were unpaid or poorly paid but often contributed substantially to family wealth.

WOMEN'S ROLES: THE CHURCH. Membership in a household, whether a father's or a husband's, meant for women a lifelong subordination to others.

In western Europe, the Roman Catholic Church offered an alternative to the career of wife and mother. A woman could enter a convent, parallel in function to the monasteries for men that evolved in the early Christian centuries.

In the convent, a woman pledged herself to a celibate life, lived according to strict community rules, and worshiped daily. Often the convent offered training in Latin, allowing some women to become considerable scholars and authors as well as scribes, artists, and musicians. For women who chose the conventual life, the benefits could be enormous, but for numerous others placed in convents by paternal choice, the life could be restrictive and burdensome.

The conventual life declined as an alternative for women as the modern age approached. Reformed monastic institutions resisted responsibility for related female orders. The church increasingly restricted female institutional life by insisting on closer male supervision.

Women often sought other options. Some joined the communities of laywomen that sprang up spontaneously in the thirteenth century in the urban zones of western Europe, especially in Flanders and Italy. Some joined the heretical movements that flourished in late medieval Christendom, whose anticlerical and often antifamily positions particularly appealed to women. In these communities, some women were acclaimed as "holy women" or "saints," while others often were condemned as frauds or heretics.

In all, although the options offered to women by the church were sometimes less than satisfactory, sometimes they were richly rewarding. After 1520, the convent remained an option only in Roman Catholic territories. Protestantism engendered an ideal of marriage as a heroic endeavor and appeared to place husband and wife on a more equal footing. Sermons and treatises, however, still called for female subordination and obedience.

THE OTHER VOICE, 1300–1700

When the modern era opened, European culture was so firmly structured by a framework of negative attitudes toward women that to dismantle it was a monumental labor. The process began as part of a larger cultural movement that entailed the critical reexamination of ideas inherited from the ancient and medieval past. The humanists launched that critical reexamination.

THE HUMANIST FOUNDATION. Originating in Italy in the fourteenth century, humanism quickly became the dominant intellectual movement in Europe. Spreading in the sixteenth century from Italy to the rest of Europe,

Series Editors' Introduction

it fueled the literary, scientific, and philosophical movements of the era and laid the basis for the eighteenth-century Enlightenment.

Humanists regarded the Scholastic philosophy of medieval universities as out of touch with the realities of urban life. They found in the rhetorical discourse of classical Rome a language adapted to civic life and public speech. They learned to read, speak, and write classical Latin and, eventually, classical Greek. They founded schools to teach others to do so, establishing the pattern for elementary and secondary education for the next three hundred years.

In the service of complex government bureaucracies, humanists employed their skills to write eloquent letters, deliver public orations, and formulate public policy. They developed new scripts for copying manuscripts and used the new printing press for the dissemination of texts, for which they created methods of critical editing.

Humanism was a movement led by males who accepted the evaluation of women in ancient texts and generally shared the misogynist perceptions of their culture. (Female humanists, as will be seen, did not.) Yet humanism also opened the door to a reevaluation of the nature and capacity of women. By calling authors, texts, and ideas into question, it made possible the fundamental rereading of the whole intellectual tradition that was required in order to free women from cultural prejudice and social subordination.

A DIFFERENT CITY. The other voice first appeared when, after so many centuries, the accumulation of misogynist concepts evoked a response from a capable female defender: Christine de Pizan (1365–1431). Introducing her *Book of the City of Ladies* (1405), she described how she was affected by reading Mathéolus's *Lamentations:* "Just the sight of this book . . . made me wonder how it happened that so many different men . . . are so inclined to express both in speaking and in their treatises and writings so many wicked insults about women and their behavior."[4] These statements impelled her to detest herself "and the entire feminine sex, as though we were monstrosities in nature."[5]

The rest of the *Book of the City of Ladies* presents a justification of the female sex and a vision of an ideal community of women. A pioneer, she has not simply received the message of female inferiority but, rather, she rejects it. From the fourteenth to the seventeenth century, a huge body of literature accumulated that responded to the dominant tradition.

---

4. Christine de Pizan, *The Book of the City of Ladies*, trans. Earl Jeffrey Richards, foreword by Marina Warner (New York, 1982), 1.1.1 (pp. 3–4), 1.1.1–2 (p. 5).

5. Ibid., 1.1.1–2, p. 5.

The result was a literary explosion consisting of works by both men and women, in Latin and in the vernaculars: works enumerating the achievements of notable women; works rebutting the main accusations made against women; works arguing for the equal education of men and women; works defining and redefining women's proper role in the family, at court, in public; works describing women's lives and experiences. Recent monographs and articles have begun to hint at the great range of this movement, involving probably several thousand titles. The protofeminism of these "other voices" constitutes a significant fraction of the literary product of the early modern era.

THE CATALOGS. About 1365, the same Boccaccio whose *Corbaccio* rehearses the usual charges against female nature wrote another work, *Concerning Famous Women*. A humanist treatise drawing on classical texts, it praised 106 notable women, ninety-eight of them from pagan Greek and Roman antiquity, one (Eve) from the Bible, and seven from the medieval religious and cultural tradition; his book helped make all readers aware of a sex normally condemned or forgotten. Boccaccio's outlook, nevertheless, was unfriendly to women, for it singled out for praise those women who possessed the traditional virtues of chastity, silence, and obedience. Women who were active in the public realm—for example, rulers and warriors—were depicted as usually being lascivious and as suffering terrible punishments for entering into the masculine sphere. Women were his subject, but Boccaccio's standard remained male.

Christine de Pizan's *Book of the City of Ladies* contains a second catalog, one responding specifically to Boccaccio's. Where Boccaccio portrays female virtue as exceptional, she depicts it as universal. Many women in history were leaders, or remained chaste despite the lascivious approaches of men, or were visionaries and brave martyrs.

The work of Boccaccio inspired a series of catalogs of illustrious women of the biblical, classical, Christian, and local past, among them Filippo da Bergamo's *Of Illustrious Women*, Pierre de Brantôme's *Lives of Illustrious Women*, Pierre Le Moyne's *Gallerie of Heroic Women*, and Pietro Paolo de Ribera's *Immortal Triumphs and Heroic Enterprises of 845 Women*. Whatever their embedded prejudices, these works drove home to the public the possibility of female excellence.

THE DEBATE. At the same time, many questions remained: Could a woman be virtuous? Could she perform noteworthy deeds? Was she even, strictly speaking, of the same human species as men? These questions were debated over four centuries, in French, German, Italian, Spanish, and English, by authors male and female, among Catholics, Protestants, and Jews, in ponderous volumes and breezy pamphlets. The whole literary genre has been called the *querelle des femmes,* the "woman question."

The opening volley of this battle occurred in the first years of the fifteenth century, in a literary debate sparked by Christine de Pizan. She exchanged letters critical of Jean de Meun's contribution to *The Romance of the Rose* with two French royal secretaries, Jean de Montreuil and Gontier Col. When the matter became public, Jean Gerson, one of Europe's leading theologians, supported de Pizan's arguments against de Meun, for the moment silencing the opposition.

The debate resurfaced repeatedly over the next two hundred years. *The Triumph of Women* (1438) by Juan Rodríguez de la Camara (or Juan Rodríguez del Padron) struck a new note by presenting arguments for the superiority of women to men. *The Champion of Women* (1440–42) by Martin Le Franc addresses once again the negative views of women presented in *The Romance of the Rose* and offers counterevidence of female virtue and achievement.

A cameo of the debate on women is included in *The Courtier,* one of the widely read books of the era, published by the Italian Baldassare Castiglione in 1528 and immediately translated into other European vernaculars. *The Courtier* depicts a series of evenings at the court of the duke of Urbino in which many men and some women of the highest social stratum amuse themselves by discussing a range of literary and social issues. The "woman question" is a pervasive theme throughout, and the third of its four books is devoted entirely to that issue.

In a verbal duel, Gasparo Pallavicino and Giuliano de' Medici present the main claims of the two traditions. Gasparo argues the innate inferiority of women and their inclination to vice. Only in bearing children do they profit the world. Giuliano counters that women share the same spiritual and mental capacities as men and may excel in wisdom and action. Men and women are of the same essence: just as no stone can be more perfectly a stone than another, so no human being can be more perfectly human than others, whether male or female. It was an astonishing assertion, boldly made to an audience as large as all Europe.

THE TREATISES. Humanism provided the materials for a positive counterconcept to the misogyny embedded in Scholastic philosophy and law and inherited from the Greek, Roman, and Christian pasts. A series of humanist treatises on marriage and family, education and deportment, and the nature of women helped construct these new perspectives.

The works by Francesco Barbaro and Leon Battista Alberti—*On Marriage* (1415) and *On the Family* (1434–37), respectively—far from defending female equality, reasserted women's responsibility for rearing children and managing the housekeeping while being obedient, chaste, and silent. Nevertheless, they served the cause of reexamining the issue of women's nature by placing domestic issues at the center of scholarly concern and reopening the pertinent classical texts. In addition, Barbaro emphasized the companionate nature of marriage and the importance of a wife's spiritual and mental qualities for the well-being of the family.

These themes reappear in later humanist works on marriage and the education of women by Juan Luis Vives and Erasmus. Both were moderately sympathetic to the condition of women without reaching beyond the usual masculine prescriptions for female behavior.

An outlook more favorable to women characterizes the nearly unknown work *In Praise of Women* (ca. 1487) by the Italian humanist Bartolommeo Goggio. In addition to providing a catalog of illustrious women, Goggio argued that male and female are the same in essence, but that women (reworking from quite a new angle the Adam and Eve narrative) are actually superior. In the same vein, the Italian humanist Maria Equicola asserted the spiritual equality of men and women in *On Women* (1501). In 1525, Galeazzo Flavio Capra (or Capella) published his work *On the Excellence and Dignity of Women*. This humanist tradition of treatises defending the worthiness of women culminates in the work of Henricus Cornelius Agrippa *On the Nobility and Preeminence of the Female Sex*. No work by a male humanist more succinctly or explicitly presents the case for female dignity.

THE WITCH BOOKS. While humanists grappled with the issues pertaining to women and family, other learned men turned their attention to what they perceived as a very great problem: witches. Witch-hunting manuals, explorations of the witch phenomenon, and even defenses of witches are not at first glance pertinent to the tradition of the other voice. But they do relate in this way: most accused witches were women. The hostility aroused by supposed witch activity is comparable to the hostility aroused by women. The evil deeds the victims of the hunt were charged with were exaggerations of the vices to which, many believed, all women were prone.

The connection between the witch accusation and the hatred of women is explicit in the notorious witch-hunting manual The *Hammer of Witches* (1486), written by two Dominican inquisitors, Heinrich Krämer and Jacob Sprenger. Here the inconstancy, deceitfulness, and lustfulness traditionally associated with women are depicted in exaggerated form as the core features of witch behavior. These traits inclined women to make a bargain with the devil—sealed by sexual intercourse—by which they acquired unholy powers. Such bizarre claims, far from being rejected by rational men, were broadcast by intellectuals. The German Ulrich Molitur, the Frenchman Nicolas Rémy, and the Italian Stefano Guazzo all coolly informed the public of sinister orgies and midnight pacts with the devil. The celebrated French jurist, historian, and political philosopher Jean Bodin argued that because women were especially prone to diabolism, regular legal procedures could properly be suspended in order to try those accused of this "exceptional crime."

A few experts raised their voices in protest, such as the physician Johann Weyer, a student of Agrippa's. In 1563, he explained the witch phenomenon thus, without discarding belief in diabolism: the devil deluded foolish old women afflicted by melancholia, causing them to believe that they had magical powers. Weyer's rational skepticism, which had good credibility in the community of the learned, worked to revise the conventional views of women and witchcraft.

WOMEN'S WORKS. To the many categories of works produced on the question of women's worth must be added nearly all works written by women. A woman writing was in herself a statement of women's claim to dignity.

Only a few women wrote anything before the dawn of the modern era, for three reasons. First, they rarely received the education that would enable them to write. Second, they were not admitted to the public roles—as administrator, bureaucrat, lawyer or notary, or university professor—in which they might gain knowledge of the kinds of things the literate public thought worth writing about. Third, the culture imposed silence upon women, considering speaking out a form of unchastity. Given these conditions, it is remarkable that any women wrote. Those who did before the fourteenth century were almost always nuns or religious women whose isolation made their pronouncements more acceptable.

From the fourteenth century on, the volume of women's writings crescendoed. Women continued to write devotional literature, although not always as cloistered nuns. They also wrote diaries, often intended as keepsakes for their children; books of advice to their sons and daughters; letters to family members and friends; and family memoirs, in a few cases elaborate enough to be considered histories.

A few women wrote works directly concerning the "woman question," and some of these, such as the humanists Isotta Nogarola, Cassandra Fedele, Laura Cereta, and Olympia Morata, were highly trained. A few were professional writers, living by the income of their pens—the very first among them being Christine de Pizan, noteworthy in this context as in so many others.

In addition to *The Book of the City of Ladies* and her critiques of *The Romance of the Rose*, she wrote *The Treasure of the City of Ladies* (a guide to social decorum for women), an advice book for her son, much courtly verse, and a full-scale history of the reign of King Charles V of France.

WOMEN PATRONS. Women who did not themselves write, but encouraged others to do so, boosted the development of an alternative tradition. Highly placed women patrons supported authors, artists, musicians, poets, and learned men. Such patrons, drawn mostly from the Italian elites and the courts of northern Europe, figure disproportionately as the dedicatees of the important works of early feminism.

For a start, it might be noted that the catalogs of Boccaccio and Alvaro de Luna were dedicated to the Florentine noblewoman Andrea Acciaiuoli and Doña María, first wife of King Juan II of Castile, while the French translation of Boccaccio's work was commissioned by Anne of Brittany, wife of King Charles VIII of France. The humanist treatises of Goggio, Equicola, Vives, and Agrippa were dedicated, respectively, to Eleanora of Aragon, wife of Ercole I d'Este, duke of Ferrara; to Margherita Cantelma of Mantua; to Catherine of Aragon, wife of King Henry VIII of England; and to Margaret, duchess of Austria and regent of the Netherlands. As late as 1696, Mary Astell's *Serious Proposal to the Ladies, for the Advancement of Their True and Greatest Interest* was dedicated to Princess Anne of Denmark.

These authors presumed that their efforts would be welcome to female patrons, or they may have written at the bidding of those patrons. Silent themselves, perhaps even unresponsive, these loftily placed women helped shape the tradition of the other voice.

THE ISSUES

The literary forms and patterns in which the tradition of the other voice presented itself have now been sketched. It remains to highlight the major issues around which this tradition crystallizes. In brief, there are four problems to which our authors return again and again, in plays and catalogs, in verse and letters, in treatises and dialogues, in every language: the problem of chastity, the problem of power, the problem of speech, and the problem of knowledge. Of these the greatest, preconditioning the others, is the problem of chastity.

THE PROBLEM OF CHASTITY. In traditional European culture, as in those of antiquity and others around the globe, chastity was perceived as woman's quintessential virtue—in contrast to courage, or generosity, or leadership, or rationality, seen as virtues characteristic of men. Opponents of women charged them with insatiable lust. Women themselves and their defenders—without disputing the validity of the standard—responded that women were capable of chastity.

The requirement of chastity kept women at home, silenced them, isolated them, left them in ignorance. It was the source of all other impediments. Why was it so important to the society of men, of whom chastity was not required, and who, more often than not, considered it their right to violate the chastity of any woman they encountered?

Female chastity ensured the continuity of the male-headed household. If a man's wife was not chaste, he could not be sure of the legitimacy of his offspring. If they were not his and they acquired his property, it was not his household, but some other man's, that had endured. If his daughter was not chaste, she could not be transferred to another man's household as his wife, and he was dishonored.

The whole system of the integrity of the household and the transmission of property was bound up in female chastity. Such a requirement only had an impact on property-owning classes, of course. Poor women could not expect to maintain their chastity, least of all if they were in contact with high-status men to whom all women but those of their own household were prey.

In Catholic Europe, the requirement of chastity was further buttressed by moral and religious imperatives. Original sin was inextricably linked with the sexual act. Virginity was seen as heroic virtue, far more impressive than, say, the avoidance of idleness or greed. Monasticism, the cultural institution that dominated medieval Europe for centuries, was grounded in the renunciation of the flesh. The Catholic reform of the eleventh century imposed a similar standard on all the clergy and a heightened awareness of sexual requirements on all the laity. Although men were asked to be chaste, female unchastity was much worse: it led to the devil, as Eve had led mankind to sin.

To such requirements, women and their defenders protested their innocence. Furthermore, following the example of holy women who had escaped the requirements of family and sought the religious life, some women began to conceive of female communities as alternatives both to family and to the cloister. Christine de Pizan's city of ladies was such a community. Moderata Fonte and Mary Astell envisioned others. The luxurious salons of the French *précieuses* of the seventeenth century, or the comfortable English drawing rooms of the next, may have been born of the same impulse. Here women not only might escape, if briefly, the subordinate position that life in the family entailed, but they might make claims to power, exercise their capacity for speech, and display their knowledge.

THE PROBLEM OF POWER. Women were excluded from power: the whole cultural tradition insisted on it. Only men were citizens, only men bore arms, only men could be chiefs or lords or kings. There were exceptions that did not disprove the rule, when wives or widows or mothers took the place of men, awaiting their return or the maturation of a male heir. A woman who attempted to rule in her own right was perceived as an anomaly, a monster, at once a deformed woman and an insufficient male, sexually confused and, consequently, unsafe.

The association of such images with women who held or sought power explains some otherwise odd features of early modern culture. Queen Elizabeth I of England, one of the few women to hold full regal authority in European history, played with such male/female images—positive ones, of course—in representing herself to her subjects. She was a prince, and manly, even though she was female. She was also (she claimed) virginal, a condition absolutely essential if she was to avoid the attacks of her opponents. Catherine de' Medici, who ruled France as widow and regent for her sons, also adopted such imagery in defining her position. She chose as one symbol the figure of Artemisia, an androgynous ancient warrior-heroine who combined a female persona with masculine powers.

Power in a woman, without such sexual imagery, seems to have been indigestible by the culture. A rare note was struck by the Englishman Sir Thomas Elyot in his *Defence of Good Women* (1540), justifying both women's participation in civic life and their prowess in arms. The old tune was sung by the Scots reformer John Knox in his *First Blast of the Trumpet against the Monstrous Regiment of Women* (1558), for him rule by women, defects in nature, was a hideous contradiction in terms.

The confused sexuality of the imagery of female potency was not reserved for rulers. Any woman who excelled was likely to be called an Amazon, recalling the self-mutilated warrior women of antiquity who repudiated all men, gave up their sons, and raised only their daughters. She was often said to have "exceeded her sex" or to have possessed "masculine virtue"—as the very fact of conspicuous excellence conferred masculinity even on the female subject. The catalogs of notable women often showed those female heroes dressed in armor, armed to the teeth, like men. Amazonian heroines romp through the epics of the age—Ariosto's *Orlando Furioso* (1532) and Spenser's *Faerie Queene* (1590–1609). Excellence in a woman was perceived as a claim for power, and power was reserved for the masculine realm. A woman who possessed either was masculinized and lost title to her own female identity.

THE PROBLEM OF SPEECH. Just as power had a sexual dimension when it was claimed by women, so did speech. A good woman spoke little. Excessive speech was an indication of unchastity. By speech, women seduced men. Eve had lured Adam into sin by her speech. Accused witches were commonly accused of having spoken abusively, or irrationally, or simply too much. As enlightened a figure as Francesco Barbaro insisted on silence in a woman, which he linked to her perfect unanimity with her husband's will and her unblemished virtue (i.e., her chastity). Another Italian humanist, Leonardo Bruni, in advising a noblewoman on her studies, barred her not from speech but from public speaking. That was reserved for men.

Related to the problem of speech was that of costume—another, if silent, form of self-expression. Assigned the task of pleasing men as their primary occupation, elite women often tended toward elaborate costume, hairdressing, and the use of cosmetics. Clergy and secular moralists alike condemned these practices. The appropriate function of costume and adornment was to announce the status of a woman's husband or father. Any further indulgence in adornment was akin to unchastity.

THE PROBLEM OF KNOWLEDGE. When the Italian noblewoman Isotta Nogarola had begun to attain a reputation as a humanist, she was accused of incest—a telling instance of the association of learning in women with unchastity. That chilling association inclined any woman who was educated to deny that she was, or to make exaggerated claims of heroic chastity.

If educated women were pursued with suspicions of sexual misconduct, women seeking an education faced an even more daunting obstacle: the assumption that women were by nature incapable of learning, that reasoning was a particularly masculine ability. Just as they proclaimed their chastity, women and their defenders insisted on their capacity for learning. The major work by a male writer on female education—that by Juan Luis Vives, *On the Education of a Christian Woman* (1523)—granted female capacity for intellection but still argued that a woman's whole education was to be shaped around the requirement of chastity and a future within the household. Female writers of the following generations—Marie de Gournay in France, Anna Maria van Schurman in Holland, Mary Astell in England—began to envision other possibilities.

The pioneers of female education were the Italian women humanists who managed to attain literacy in Latin and a knowledge of classical and Christian literature equivalent to that of prominent men. Their works implicitly and explicitly raise questions about women's social roles, defining problems that beset women attempting to break out of the cultural limits that had bound them. Like Christine de Pizan, who achieved an advanced education through her father's tutoring and her own devices, their bold questioning makes clear the importance of training. Only when women were educated to the same standard as male leaders would they be able to raise that other voice and insist on their dignity as human beings morally, intellectually, and legally equal to men.

THE OTHER VOICE. The other voice, a voice of protest, was mostly female, but it was also male. It spoke in the vernaculars and in Latin, in treatises and dialogues, in plays and poetry, in letters and diaries, and in pamphlets. It battered at the wall of prejudice that encircled women and raised a banner announcing its claims. The female was equal to (or even superior to) the male in essential nature—moral, spiritual, intellectual. Women were capable of higher education, of holding positions of power and influence in the public realm, and of speaking and writing persuasively. The last bastion of masculine supremacy, centered on the notions of a woman's primary domestic responsibility and the requirement of female chastity, was not as yet assaulted—although visions of productive female communities as alternatives to the family indicated an awareness of the problem.

During the period 1300–1700, the other voice remained only a voice, and one only dimly heard. It did not result—yet—in an alteration of social patterns. Indeed, to this day they have not entirely been altered. Yet the call for justice issued as long as six centuries ago by those writing in the tradition of the other voice must be recognized as the source and origin of the mature feminist tradition and of the realignment of social institutions accomplished in the modern age.

We would like to thank the volume editors in this series, who responded with many suggestions to an earlier draft of this introduction, making it a collaborative enterprise. Many of their suggestions and criticisms have resulted in revisions of this introduction, although we remain responsible for the final product.

PROJECTED TITLES IN THE SERIES

Laura Battiferra, *Selected Poetry, Prose, and Letters*, edited and translated by Victoria Kirkham

Giulia Bigolina, *Urania*, edited and translated by Valeria Finucci

Elisabetta Caminer Turra, *Writings on and about Women*, edited and translated by Catherine Sama

Maddalena Campiglia, *Flori*, edited and translated by Virginia Cox with Lisa Sampson

Rosalba Carriera, *Letters, Diaries, and Art*, edited and translated by Shearer West

Madame du Chatelet, *Selected Works*, edited by Judith Zinsser

Christine de Pizan et al., *Debate over the "Romance of the Rose,"* edited and translated by Tom Conley with Elisabeth Hodges

Christine de Pizan, *Life of Charles V*, edited and translated by Charity Cannon Willard

Christine de Pizan, *The Long Road of Learning*, edited and translated by Andrea Tarnowski

Gabrielle de Coignard, *Spiritual Sonnets*, edited and translated by Melanie E. Gregg

Vittoria Colonna, *Sonnets for Michelangelo*, edited and translated by Abigail Brundin

Vittoria Colonna, Chiara Matraini, and Lucrezia Marinella, *Marian Writings*, edited and translated by Susan Haskins

Marie Dentière, *Epistles*, edited and translated by Mary B. McKinley

Marie-Catherine Desjardins (Madame de Villedieu), Memoirs *of the Life of Henriette-Sylvie de Molière*, edited and translated by Donna Kuizenga

Princess Elizabeth of Bohemia, *Correspondence with Descartes*, edited and translated by Lisa Shapiro

Fairy Tales by Seventeenth-Century French Women Writers, edited and translated by Lewis Seifert and Domna C. Stanton

Isabella d'Este, *Selected Letters*, edited and translated by Deanna Shemek

Moderata Fonte, *Floridoro*, edited and translated by Valeria Finucci

Moderata Fonte and Lucrezia Marinella, *Religious Narratives*, edited and translated by Virginia Cox

Francisca de los Apostoles, *Visions on Trial: The Inquisitional Trial of Francisca de los Apostoles*, edited and translated by Gillian T. W. Ahlgren

Catharina Regina von Greiffenberg, *Meditations on the Life of Christ*, edited and translated by Lynne Tatlock

Annibal Guasco, *Discourse to Lady Lavinia His Daughter concerning the Manner in Which She Should Conduct Herself at Court*, edited and translated by Peggy Osborn

Louise Labé, *Complete Works*, edited and translated by Annie Finch and Deborah Baker

Madame de Maintenon, *Lectures and Dramatic Dialogues*, edited and translated by John Conley, S.J.

Lucrezia Marinella, *L'Enrico; or, Byzantium Conquered*, edited and translated by Virginia Cox

Lucrezia Marinella, *Happy Arcadia*, edited and translated by Susan Haskins and Letizia Panizza

Chiara Matraini, *Selected Poetry and Prose*, edited and translated by Elaine MacLachlan

Olympia Morata, *The Complete Writings of an Italian Heretic*, edited and translated by Holt N. Parker

Isotta Nogarola, *Selected Letters*, edited and translated by Margaret L. King and Diana Robin

Jacqueline Pascal, *"A Rule for Children" and Other Writings*, edited and translated by John Conley, S.J.

Eleonora Petersen von Merlau, *Autobiography (1718)*, edited and translated by Barbara Becker-Cantarino

Alessandro Piccolomini, *Rethinking Marriage in Sixteenth-Century Italy*, edited and translated by Letizia Panizza

In Praise of Women: Italian Fifteenth-Century Defenses of Women, edited and translated by Daniel Bornstein

Madeleine and Catherine des Roches, *Selected Letters, Dialogues, and Poems*, edited and translated by Anne Larsen

Oliva Sabuco, *The New Philosophy: True Medicine*, edited and translated by Gianna Pomata

Margherita Sarrocchi, *La Scanderbeide*, edited and translated by Rinaldina Russell

Madeleine de Scudéry, *Orations and Rhetorical Dialogues*, edited and translated by Jane Donawerth with Julie Strongson

Justine Siegemund, *The Court Midwife of the Electorate of Brandenburg* (1690), edited and translated by Lynne Tatlock

Gabrielle Suchon, *"On Philosophy" and "On Morality,"* edited and translated by Domna Stanton with Rebecca Wilkin

Sara Copio Sullam, *Sara Copio Sullam: Jewish Poet and Intellectual in Early Seventeenth-Century Venice*, edited and translated by Don Harrán

Arcangela Tarabotti, *Convent Life as Inferno: A Report*, introduction and notes by Francesca Medioli, translated by Letizia Panizza

Francesco Buoninsegni and Arcangela Tarabotti, *Menippean Satire: "Against Feminine Extravagance" and "Antisatire,"* edited and translated by Elissa Weaver

Arcangela Tarabotti, *Paternal Tyranny*, edited and translated by Letizia Panizza

Laura Terracina, *Works*, edited and translated by Michael Sherberg

Katharina Schütz Zell, *Selected Writings*, edited and translated by Elsie McKee

VOLUME EDITOR'S INTRODUCTION

THE OTHER VOICE

Ridiculed for her plainness, derided for her Saturday salon, scorned for her infamous map of love, belittled for her relationship with a younger man, sneered at for her lengthy romance novels, and mocked for her ideas about love, marriage, and the education of women, Madeleine de Scudéry has suffered at the hands of the literary establishment of her own time and of ours. Yet her novels were bestsellers in her day and well into the eighteenth century. Contemporary readers were apparently willing to pay for single sheets before an entire print run was completed; booksellers inflated their profits by dividing her ten volume *Clélie* into even smaller sections and selling them separately; English readers across the channel managed to secure the last volumes of perhaps her most popular novel, *Artamène; ou, Le grand Cyrus,* (1649–53) within weeks of its publication even in the midst of the French civil uprising known as the Fronde. Demand was such that her printer was obliged to increase the print run for later volumes and to reprint the early volumes in 1650 and again in 1654; a complete fourth edition appeared in 1655.

Like so many women writers, Scudéry was enormously popular in her own day and thereafter forgotten. No modern edition of her romance novels exists in French, nor have they been translated into English since the seventeenth century, despite a recent revival of interest in her work among feminist critics and literary historians. In short, Scudéry's work deserves not only critical reconsideration, but to be made available in translation to the English reader.

LIFE AND WRITINGS

Born in the French provincial port of Le Havre in 1607 and orphaned at an early age like her fictional namesake, the legendary Greek poet Sappho,

Madeleine de Scudéry moved to Rouen, where she was educated under the auspices of an uncle with an extensive library and relatively emancipated ideas about women's education. As the daughter of a member of the lesser nobility (her father had been governor of Le Havre), she was instructed in the feminine arts of dancing, drawing, painting, and music. She learned Italian and Spanish and to write and spell correctly in French, an unusual skill in women of the time and one that provokes considerable discussion in the *Histoire de Sapho* among Sapho and her circle. Her interests were broad and included gardening and botany, herbal medicine and cooking, as well as literature and history. Although she apparently knew no ancient language, her novels show considerable knowledge of ancient history, literature, and geography and thus demonstrate her wide reading and collaboration with others more familiar with classical materials.[1]

Scudéry moved to Paris in her thirties where she lived with her brother, Georges de Scudéry, a practicing, lesser dramatist and writer under whose name her novels initially appeared. In Paris, she frequented what we now term the "salon" of Madame de Rambouillet, where she met many of the leading literary and political figures of her day. Except for three years in Marseilles with her brother during his service as a provincial governor, Scudéry, who never married, spent the rest of her life in Paris where she held a salon of her own known by the day of the week on which it took place, thus her *samedis*, from the French word for Saturday. At Scudéry's *samedis*, contemporaries read aloud and discussed literature, invented and played literary games, and apparently collaborated—Scudéry's famous *carte de tendre* (Fig. 1), which presents a psychology of love as movement through geographical space, is said to have originated out of a game or *jeu d'esprit* among her friends. Like Sapho, Scudéry presided over her "court," guided its conversations, and was its arbiter of taste.

Her first novel, *Ibrahim; or, The Renowned Bassa* (*Ibrahim; ou, L'illustre Bassa*), which appeared in 1641, is a heroic action tale filled with adventures set in exotic places; in the same year she published an epistolary collection modeled on Ovid's *Heroides* entitled *Lettres amoureuses de divers auteurs de ce temps*. In 1642, she published *Les femmes illustres; ou, Les harangues héroïques*, an example of the so-called women worthies tradition.[2] Joan DeJean has written eloquently of Scudéry's impact on the genre: instead of "third person biographies of

---

1. On collaboration and the question of authorship, see Joan DeJean, *Tender Geographies* (New York: Columbia University Press, 1991), 71 ff.

2. Natalie Zemon Davis, "'Women's History' in Transition: The European Case," *Feminist Studies* 3 (1976): 83.

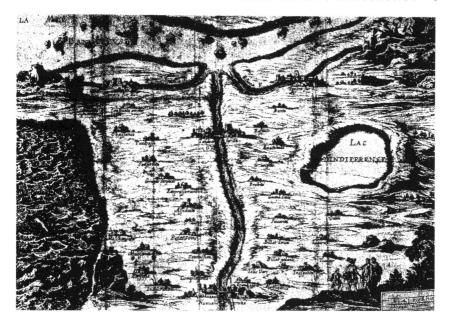

Figure 1. *La Carte de Tendre*, from *Clélie, histoire romain* (1654) by Madeleine de Scudéry.

illustrious women," she imagines "first person 'autobiographical' accounts of those she views as having been neglected by previous chroniclers."[3] Each *harangue* includes an "Argument," a prefatory and concluding poem, the oration or *harangue* itself, and a moral or brief statement of its "effect." Among the illustrious women she includes are Cleopatra, Mariam, Cloelia (Clélie), and Sappho, who, in the twentieth and final *harangue* translated here, exhorts her friend Erinne to write. The ten volumes of her most popular novel, *Artamène; ou, Le grand Cyrus*, followed in 1649–53, and *Clélie, Histoire romaine*, also in ten volumes, followed *Artamène* in 1654–60. Later, when the vogue for romance novels had mostly passed, she wrote collections of conversations, beginning with her *Conversations sur divers sujets* (1680), many of which are taken from the earlier novels;[4] she also wrote a guide to the gardens at Versailles dedicated to the king. She outlived most of her contemporaries and died at the age of ninety-three on June 2, 1701, in Paris.

Scudéry's novels were widely read and admired, but also vilified and

---

3. DeJean, *Tender Geographies*, 32.

4. On changing literary taste and contemporary politics, see Jean Mesnard, "Mademoiselle de Scudéry et la société du Marias," *Mélanges offerts à Georges Couton* (Presses Universitaires de Lyon, 1981), 169–89.

attacked in the culture wars of the seventeenth century known as the *Querelle des Anciens et des Modernes*. Joan DeJean argues that the exclusion of Scudéry's novels from the literary history of the French novel can be traced to this early-modern "battle of the books." Nicolas Boileau, sometimes called Despréaux, a self-appointed defender of the ancients and admirer of those contemporary writers whose work has long been associated with neoclassicism—Racine, Molière, and La Fontaine—was perhaps Scudéry's most well-known foe. In his *Dialogue des héros de roman*, usually dated 1664–66, which followed his failure to win official patronage, but while Scudéry's novels remained popular, he attacks the modern genres, especially *Artamène* and Scudéry herself, and seeks to discredit the form through parody.

In the nineteenth century, a "key," now lost, was reputedly discovered at the Arsenal library in Paris that matched the novel's various characters with their seventeenth-century counterparts. In an advertisement that appeared on the publication of the nineteenth-century French critic Victor Cousin's book on Scudéry, we learn that his key "renders *Le grand Cyrus* interesting, making us forget the boredom and tedium of its descriptions by seeking out and authenticating what is historically accurate and showing us that however unrealistic the varied intrigues may appear, the characters themselves are real." The advertisement for Cousin's book exemplifies the critical judgment of Scudéry's romance novels, which were sometimes termed *romans de longue haleine*, what we would call long-winded.

Scholars have faulted Scudéry's novels not only for their length, but for their supposed *invraisemblance*, that is, for being unrealistic and unbelievable. They were said to produce in their readers what in French is termed *dépaysement*, a sense of rootlessness or displacement due to a putative lack of specificity with regard to place that displaces readers in both time and space. Her three novels, *Ibrahim*, *Artamène*, and *Clélie*, are set, respectively, in the Mediterranean from Monaco to Constantinople, in Persia and Greece, and in the ancient Roman world. Long maligned for roving flagrantly through fantasy space, Scudéry's novels have been shown by recent commentators to demonstrate scholarly care and precision in their presentation of ancient history and place. They draw rigorously on what was known about Greek geography, culture, and, in the *Histoire de Sapho*, about the legendary poet from Lesbos, Sappho.[5] Only recently have critics begun to read and reevaluate Scudéry's fiction and its place in the evolution of the French novel.

5. On historical documentation in Scudéry's fiction, see René Godenne, *Les Romans de Mademoiselle de Scudéry* (Geneva: Droz, 1983); Joan DeJean, "Female Voyeurism: Sapho and Lafayette,"

Best known, perhaps, as the favorite reading matter of Molière's provincial, aspiring *précieuses* in *Les précieuses ridicules*, Scudéry's *Artamène; ou, Le grand Cyrus* appeared in the early days of the rebellion against the French monarchy known as the Fronde. Long before the discovery of Cousin's key, the novel was recognized as a *roman à clef* of the Fronde years: contemporaries were said to have lobbied to appear as characters in its pages, and it is acknowledged that the main characters, Cyrus and Mandane, represent the great Condé and his sister, the Duchesse de Longueville, instigators and principal actors in the revolt. Scudéry dedicated all the volumes of *Artamène* to the Duchesse de Longueville who, along with several of her compatriots, exercised power during the Fronde years not behind the scenes, as women often have, but on the ramparts:

> The great, now incredible images of the Fronde are centered on the women who were its principal instigators. The Princesse de Condé marches on Bordeaux and convinces its citizens to defend the *frondeurs* against their king—even at the risk of losing the grape harvest for that year. The Duchesse de Longueville leads the Spanish army on the road to Paris, manipulates all the great rebel leaders from Condé to La Rochefoucauld—and when Anne of Austria and Mazarin [of the king's party] try to imprison her to put an end to her intrigues, disguised as a man she rides for days on end and sleeps in bars and haystacks along the English Channel until she is able to bribe a fisherman to take her to Holland, whence she immediately rides back to France to rejoin her forces.[6]

Perhaps the best known of the Amazonian *frondeuses* is the Duchesse de Montpensier, known as La Grande Mademoiselle, who, with the gates of Paris closed to Condé and the rebel army, orders that they be opened to allow the rebel forces entry and turns the Bastille artillery against the royal troops. During the Fronde years, women exercised power in venues from which they were ordinarily excluded. As Jonathan Dewald has argued, "the novel and the printing press transformed the particulars of aristocratic personality and experience into a public commodity." Scudéry's *Artamène* turned the *frondeur* leaders into aesthetic objects for a broad public eager to consume and criticize.[7]

Rivista de litterature moderne et comparate (1987), 40: 201–15, and idem, *Fictions of Sappho, 1546–1937* (Chicago: University of Chicago Press, 1989).

6. DeJean, *Tender Geographies*, 37.

7. Jonathan Dewald, *Aristocratic Experience and the Origins of Modern Culture: France, 1570–1715* (Berkeley: University of California Press, 1993), 200, 202.

The opening volumes of *Artamène, ou, Le grand Cyrus* record and commemorate the energy of the Fronde years and, particularly, women's heroism. But Scudéry herself seems to have been simultaneously loyal to the *frondeurs* and to the king. DeJean argues that following the defeat of the rebel forces, Scudéry recognized that women would be required to exercise power not through action on the battlements, but indirectly, in interior spaces, through conversation. Thus the later volumes of *Artamène* shift from heroic action to conversation and, in *Clélie*, to the other acknowledged feature of Scudéry's style, the verbal portrait.

SAPHO

Artamène, ou, Le grand Cyrus recounts the history of Cyrus the Great and his Persian empire; the *Histoire de Sapho* is the longest and most ambitious of its numerous intercalated stories. It appears in the tenth and final volume after nine volumes of "characters who fight battles and cross continents—always driven by the form of closure traditional to the early novel, marriage";[8] it introduces a narrative and characters, with one exception, previously unmentioned. Scudéry's Sapho is a woman writer who deems marriage slavery and who is conventionally identified with Scudéry herself. Sapho's story is told by Democedes, who appears in *Artamène* and figures importantly in the tale as the brother of Sapho's closest friend, Cydnon, as well as one of the accomplished young men who frequent Sapho's "salon." The story of Sapho is addressed to another character in the novel, the Queen of Pontus, traces of whom remain in moments of direct address as "Madam." Although Sapho's story has a narrative with a beginning, middle, and end, it is more importantly a series of conversations on *civilité* and is related to the long tradition of dialogues and treatises concerned with the definition and education of a courtier or prince. Sapho and her circle debate, discuss, and define the nature of *galanterie*, the question of female beauty, what constitute appropriate topics of conversation, the nature of marriage, the education of women, love and courtship, and right conduct or *bienséance*.

Although it recounts the trials of the woman writer, the great subject of the *Histoire de Sapho* is love; it is concerned throughout with the conduct of love and affairs of the heart, with *galanterie*. *Galanterie* and its adjectives, *galant(e)*, have a range of meanings that include flirtation and gallantry, but also amorous conduct and love affairs. Sapho resists her feelings for Phaon

---

8. DeJean, *Tender Geographies*, 48.

because she fears he will disappoint her, because, as she tells him, she expects so much from a lover that no man can achieve her ideal. The love she would wish, were she to wish for love, is impossible. Not surprisingly, the tale ends with the lovers' voluntary exile: the ideal of love Sapho articulates, which owes a great deal to Bembo's famous discourse on love in Book IV of Castiglione's *The Book of the Courtier*, is finally not of this world.

In his powerful articulation of the civilizing process, *Power and Civility*, Norbert Elias argues that *civilité* and all it entails—the refinement of manners and speaking, dress, speech, and social behaviors—represented ways in which the elite, increasingly denied a political role in the post-Fronde years, sought to preserve its status by designating new sorts of behaviors as the means of differentiating themselves from their inferiors.[9] Self-restraint, the regulation and control of drives, and the pursuit of activities requiring such restraint, including reading and writing, were part of this civilizing process. Scudéry's *Histoire de Sapho* can be read as one articulation of that process in its valuation of conversation, *lettres*, and love over heroic action, politics, and marriage, but one that was ultimately rejected because it accorded power to women. Scudéry's *Histoire de Sapho* is in part a defense of Scudéry herself, whose learning and literary aspirations and achievements some of her contemporaries satirized. Scudéry is careful to distinguish her namesake from the pedantic learned lady or *savante*, Damophile, a ridiculous, yet potent double, a *précieuse* whom Scudéry satirizes long before Molière. Scudéry provides Damophile as a foil for Sapho and to vindicate her own kind of learning, conversation, and behavior. Sapho encourages women's learning, but within the strict confines of conduct deemed appropriate to her sex. Like the courtier who must seem always to perform and succeed without apparent effort, so Sapho is never seen to read, study, or write. Damophile's cardinal sin is that she advertises her learning; in contemporary parlance, she is a show-off, always seeking to be seen with erudite men and to discuss learned topics. She is so anxious to emulate Sapho that she encourages the attentions of a suitor only in order that he write verses for her that she can pass off as her own.

Sapho, on the other hand, hides her learning, discourages those who would praise it, and presents her verses as no more than an amusement. Nevertheless, the space of writing in the *Histoire de Sapho* is a privileged one, the only arena in which affect may be expressed and thus a space outside

---

9. Norbert Elias, *The Civilizing Process*, translated by Edmund Jephcott, 3 vols. (New York: Pantheon Books, 1978).

the ordinary constraints imposed on women. The *Histoire de Sapho* constitutes spaces and registers that women control and in which they excel: the
cabinet, the salon, the promenade, and, finally, the utopian country of the
Sarmatae, associated with the Amazons, a place where love and constancy,
not politics and property, are the object of judicial oversight. There Sapho,
who has earlier called marriage slavery, forestalls Phaon's suit to oblige her
to marry him by successfully pleading her case before the Sarmatian judges.

But Scudéry's utopia is utopian only for its recognized elite who, having been approved of for entry and having forfeited the right to leave, are
mysteriously allotted sufficient means to live according to their status. In
short, the land of the Sarmatae is a utopia for some, but not for others. It
should come as no surprise that the *Histoire de Sapho* does not end *Artamène, ou,
Le grand Cyrus*. Instead of Sapho's story, or the political intrigues and battles
of the earlier volumes, the novel ends with Cyrus the Great's coronation
and ascent to the throne, a compliment to Louis XIV, whose reign would
last into the next century and whose majority the publication of the final
volume commemorated.

Perhaps because Sapho is widely acknowledged to be a self-portrait, critics
have often overlooked the care and precision with which Scudéry used what
was known of the legendary Greek poet Sappho in her *Histoire de Sapho*.
Scudéry spells Sapho's name with one *p*, as it was frequently spelled in
seventeenth-century France, and thus marks her difference from Sappho.
She uses what little was known of Sappho—that she was born on Lesbos,
was orphaned young, was dark and not known for her beauty, and quarreled with her brother Charaxus. But instead of following the tradition that
claimed Sappho committed suicide after being abandoned by Phaon/Faon,
she ends her story with the lovers' voluntary exile to a protofeminist utopia,
the land of the Sarmatae. Scudéry's Sapho has close women friends, but
Scudéry might at first seem to have eschewed the tradition that associates
Sappho with sapphism, or the love between women. And yet that tradition
is inscribed in Scudéry's text in Sapho's rejection of marriage, her refusal of
Phaon's proposals and, it would seem, of sexual relations, but perhaps most
powerfully in Phaon's extraordinary jealousy prompted by his reading of her
poems to her women friends. Phaon cannot believe that Sapho could know
such intensity of feeling and desire for her women friends and thus concludes
that she either has been in love with a man in the past or that she is in love
with one now. The text is careful to make clear that these poems predate
Sapho's meeting with Phaon and thus cannot be attributed to her love for
him. In other words, Scudéry writes the love of women for women into her

text through the intensity of Phaon's jealousy and suffering. Throughout the *Histoire de Sapho,* there is a certain slippage or ambiguity around desire and sexual object choice, a slippage to be found as well in the Sapphic odes, as commentators have noted, particularly the "Ode to Aphrodite."

Also translated in this volume is an oration or *harangue* from Scudéry's collection *Les femmes illustres; ou, Les harangues héroïques* (1642). In this *harangue* from Sapho to Erinne, the twentieth and final one of the volume, Sapho extols the talents and abilities of women and exhorts Erinne to write. Linked to the so-called *de claribus* tradition proclaiming women's achievements and to the rhetorical exercises on a topic (should a man marry?), the *harangue* debates the question, should a woman write? Sapho argues that women should not be defined by beauty, which is fleeting, but advocates their participation and even superiority in the study of arts and letters. Finally, she admonishes Erinne to write. Each *harangue* ends with an account of its effects—in this case, we learn that Erinne followed Sapho's counsel and excelled her in the writing of hexameters. The final line of the *harangue* presents Scudéry's text as a "triumphant arch" to the glory of her sex. Sapho's defense of writing in the *harangue* makes explicit what is concealed in the *Histoire de Sapho.*

TRANSLATION

Scudéry's text presents a number of challenges to the translator, some similar to those posed by other seventeenth-century writing, some specific to this text. In his own notes on the problems of translation in his introduction to *The Princesse de Clèves,* Terence Cave writes of the imaginary relation of French to neoclassicism and its putative clarity and precision:

> Recent work on the style and semantics of French neoclassicism has shown that the meaning of words and phrases central to the self-conception of the age—*esprit, mérite, honnêteté, galanterie,* to name only a few—is shifting, even shifty; abstraction, far from connoting conceptual lucidity, goes hand in hand with ambivalence.[10]

These same terms pose similar problems of translation in Scudéry's text and have no simple equivalent in English. That problem is posed from the

---

10. From Cave's introduction to his translation of Madame de Lafayette's *The Princesse de Clèves* (Oxford: Oxford University Press, 1992), xxvii; see also Peter Bayley, "Fixed Form and Varied Function: Reflections on the Language of French Classicism," *Seventeenth-Century Studies* 6 (1984): 6–21.

outset, even in the French title *L'histoire de Sapho*, for *histoire* in French means both story and history and thus makes of Scudéry's text at once fiction and history. Another shifty example is *honnête homme*, which I have mostly translated "gentleman," while recognizing the inadequacy, even error, of that choice. To illustrate the problem, consider an example from Molière. At an important moment in *The Would-Be Gentleman (Le bourgeois gentilhomme)*, the young protagonist in love with the would-be gentleman's daughter is called upon to declare himself a gentleman if he is to win the hand of his beloved. M. Jourdain will entertain no suitors who are not gentlemen. Cléonte declares his status in an important speech in which he asserts that he will not claim to be a gentleman because pretense and imposture are unworthy of an *honnête homme*. Gentlemen can be *honnêtes hommes*, but there can be gentlemen who are not, just as there are *honnêtes hommes* who are not gentlemen. *Honnêteté* includes a range of meanings from virtuous and courteous to noble and cultured. And yet gentleman, which has a broader range of meanings in English than the French *gentilhomme*, is the best, if in some ways nevertheless inadequate, equivalent. *Honnêteté*, along with a series of other words such as *mérite* and *vertu*, seem to be words implying moral worth, but often turn out to be linked to social distinctions. Again, like Cave, in attempting to do justice to the French text, I have made use of "equivalents in English which, while not wholly archaic, survive from a parallel cultural tradition familiar to literate readers through, say, eighteenth-century English texts or the novels of Jane Austen."[11]

Esprit is especially challenging because of its range of meanings and its use in forms like *bel esprit*. Although I have often chosen to translate it as "wit," at other times "intelligence" or "mind" or "conceit" seemed better choices. Words to denote forms and stages of amorous attachment and feeling including "inclination," "reconnaissance," "passion," "agitation," and "trouble" posed difficulties as does the whole range of words associated with *galanterie*. I have provided notes indicating a range of meanings for the initial occurrence of many of these terms; a note is sometimes repeated elsewhere at moments where it might prove helpful. Cave notes in his discussion of style in *La Princesse de Clèves* that Madame de Lafayette uses what he terms "the rhetoric of appearances";[12] Scudéry, too, insists on words like *sembler, voir, paraître*, and their synonyms to call attention to the problem of point of view and of reading others, their behaviors, motives, and meanings, but in the case of *voir*, to

11. Ibid., xxviii.
12. Ibid., xxix.

the rhetoric of Petrarchan love as well. For Phaon, love depends on seeing, on presence, on being in sight of his beloved. What does it mean, Scudéry asks, to be seen, to be in or out of sight, to be the object of admiration, to be proverbially out of sight and out of mind?

Scudéry's text provides no paragraphing, but endless sentences made up of clauses yoked with "and" that I have rendered more readable to our modern eye and syntactic ear. Similarly, I have tried to render French pronouns, repeated *il* and *elle*, and the indirect pronouns that alert us to who is watching, judging, seeing, into idiomatic English constructions. My aim has been to provide a readable English text that gives a sense of the original and will, I hope, prompt some readers to tackle the French for themselves.

THE STORY OF SAPHO

To praise the admirable Sapho, Madam, I must begin by praising her native land, since it is natural to praise those things in which we ourselves have an interest, and her native land is also my own. To make you understand the advantages of her birth, you must learn something about one of the most pleasing places on earth, the isle of Lesbos, the loveliest and most fertile that the Aegean Sea can boast. The island is so large that in many places you can imagine yourself on the mainland, but it is not so mountainous that you think it is nothing but a mass of cliffs rising from the sea, nor is it so flat that it offers no heights or seems always about to be engulfed by the surrounding waves. Instead, the Isle of Lesbos offers all the variety to be found in those kingdoms that are not islands: mountains and large forests gird its eastern coast, while on the opposite coast are prairies and plains. The air is pure and bracing, the earth is abundantly fertile, trade is active, and the continent is so close to Phrygia that you can reach a foreign court in a mere two hours. Mytilene, the principal city, is so excellently built with two such beautiful ports that visitors inevitably admire it and delight in staying there. Here Sapho was born, Madam, while the wise Pittacus ruled and attracted to his kingdom innumerable accomplished persons.[1] His son Tisander, one of the worthiest gentlemen in the world, made any visit to Mytilene amusing, but since he has long since died, I won't pause to speak of him even though he was one of Sapho's admirers.

---

1. The French expression is *honnêtes gens; honnête* has a range of meanings from virtuous, sincere, and courteous to honorable, noble, civilized, and cultured. In the next sentence, Tisander is described as an *honnête homme,* an expression that appears frequently throughout the *Histoire de Sapho* and that I have generally translated as "gentleman," but which has the wider range of meanings indicated here.

Having told you of the birthplace of this extraordinary person, I must tell you something about her family: she was the daughter of a man of quality named Scamandrogine, who was of such noble blood that no house in all Mytilene had ancestors stretching back so far or a more illustrious and undisputed lineage. Both Sapho's father and mother were intelligent and virtuous, but she had the bad fortune to lose them at an early age. Since she was only six when they died, she received from them only her earliest inclination toward virtue. They left her in the care of a relation named Cynegire, who possessed all the qualities necessary for raising a child; they also left her with a fortune considerably less than her merits warranted but nevertheless sufficient to make her independent and let her take her rightful place in the world. Sapho had a brother as well, Charaxus, who was extremely rich because Scamandrogine had divided his wealth unequally between them at his death and left much more to his unworthy son than to his daughter, who deserved to wear a crown.

I do not believe that in all Greece, Madam, anyone can compare with Sapho. I shan't take the time here to recount her childhood since by the age of twelve she was already talked of as a person of such beauty, wit,[2] and judgment that the entire world admired her. I will simply say that there has never been anyone of such noble inclinations or with more capacity to learn whatever she wished to know. However charming Sapho was from the cradle, I want to paint the wit and beauty she now possesses so that you may know her better. I tell you, Madam, that though I speak of Sapho as the most extraordinary and most captivating woman in all of Greece, you must not think she is one of those great beauties in whom even Envy cannot find fault; but you should know, nevertheless, that though her beauty is not of that sort, it is capable of inspiring as great a passion as that of the most noted beauties on earth.

To describe the admirable Sapho, Madam, I will tell you that she speaks of herself as small, when she wants to speak ill of herself, but she is really of average height and as nobly formed and neat of figure as one could ask. As for her complexion, it is not as pale as it might be, but nevertheless it is so radiant that you could call it beautiful. But what Sapho possesses above all else are eyes so beautiful and lively, so full of spirit, that one can neither brave the brilliance of her regard nor turn away from it. Sapho's beautiful eyes

---

2. The French *esprit* has a range of meanings from spirit or soul to mind, thought, intelligence, conceit, liveliness, or mettle. Depending on context, I sometimes translate it as "wit," sometimes as "mind" or "intelligence," and occasionally as "spirit" or as a doublet to indicate its range of meanings.

radiate such penetrating fire, and at the same time such passionate softness, that liveliness and serenity dwell in them in harmony. What makes them striking is the contrast of black and white, which never seems harsh because a certain loving ebullience softens them in so charming a way that I don't believe anyone anywhere has such an awe-inspiring gaze. What's more, she has certain qualities rarely found together, a countenance that is fine and unassuming, yet regal and free. Sapho's face is oval, her mouth small and full, and her hands so lovely that they capture hearts. Or if you wish, you might compare her to that learned young girl so beloved of the Muses whose hands are worthy of gathering the most beautiful blossoms on Parnassus.[3]

But what really makes Sapho admirable, Madam, are the charms of her mind, which far surpass even the charms of her person. The compass of her mind is so large that what she doesn't understand, no one can. She has such facility for learning whatever she seeks to know that though you never hear of her studying, she knows all things. She was born with a predilection for writing poetry, a predilection that happily she has cultivated, with the result that her verse is better than anyone's. She has, in fact, invented meters that even Hesiod and Homer didn't know and which have been so admired that they are named saphics after her. She also writes prose quite well—her works are so tender that the hearts of all who read what she writes are moved. One day I saw her improvise a song that was a thousand times more touching than the most plaintive of elegies—there is a certain loving turn to her mind that seems hers alone. She can describe sentiments difficult to describe with such delicacy, and she knows so well how to anatomize an amorous heart, if I may so describe it, that she is able to rehearse the jealousies, anxieties, impatience, joys, antipathies, sighs, despair, hopes, rebellions—all the tumultuous feelings of love known only to those who feel or have felt them.

Nor does the admirable Sapho know only about love; she knows no less well everything about generosity and how to write and speak of all things so perfectly that nothing whatsoever falls outside her understanding. Don't imagine that her knowledge is simply intuitive—Sapho has seen all that is worth seeing and has taken pains to learn all that merits her curiosity. She also plays the lyre, sings, and dances gracefully. She has even sought to know all those works with which so-called learned ladies entertain themselves. But what is admirable in her, this person who knows so many varied things, is that she knows them without pedantry, without conceit, and without disdain

---

3. The learned young girl beloved of the Muses is the Greek poet Sappho, which makes this comparison playfully self-reflexive, a reminder to the reader of Sapho's link with her poetic namesake.

for those who are unlearned. Her conversation is so natural and easy, so charming,[4] that in general conversation she is never heard to say anything but what someone untutored, but of large understanding, might say. Knowledgeable people know perfectly well that Nature alone cannot have opened her mind without study, but Sapho so desires to behave as befits her sex that she almost never speaks of anything that is not deemed suitable for ladies. Only to her particular friends does she acknowledge her learning.

Don't imagine that Sapho affects a vulgar ignorance in conversation; on the contrary, she understands so well the art of guiding conversation that you never leave her without the sense of having heard countless beautiful and agreeable things. Her confident manner gives her such a command over others that she can say whatever she wishes to say to those around her and yet always seems to please. Her wit is so obliging that she speaks equally well of serious matters and of gallant and frivolous things, so that it is sometimes difficult to believe that one person could possess such divergent talents. Even more commendable in Sapho is the fact that no one in the world is a better person, more generous, less self-interested, less self-important. She is loyal in her friendships, with a soul so tender and a heart so passionate that to be loved by her is doubtless to be supremely happy. She is ingenious at ever finding new means to please those she esteems, to make them know her affection, and, while not seeming to do anything out of the ordinary, to persuade those she loves how dearly she loves them. Incapable of envy, she is just and generous in recognizing merit and takes more pleasure in praising others than in being praised. And beyond all I have just said, she is considerate without being weak, infinitely accommodating and agreeable. If upon occasion she refuses her friends something, she does so with such civility and gentleness that they feel obliged to her nonetheless. Imagine, then, how they feel when she is able to grant her friendship and trust.

Such is the marvelous Sapho, Madam; but her brother has quite different inclinations from his sister. It isn't that Charaxus has no good qualities, it is rather that he has many bad ones. He has courage, but the kind of courage that makes the bull bolder than the stag, not at all the sort of valor that is sometimes confused with magnanimity and that is so indispensable to a gentleman.

Despite her modesty and the care she took to conceal her accomplishments, the marvelous young woman I have just described for you, Madam,

---

4. This is the first use of the word *galant(e)*, which appears repeatedly in both its adjectival form and as the noun *galanterie*. It has a range of meanings from the English gallant, noble, or chivalrous to charming, flirtatious, even amorous.

became the talk of the town. Her renown had in fact bruited her name throughout Greece, and so gloriously that no one of her sex before her had ever achieved such a reputation. All over Greece, the most important men of the day avidly commissioned her verse and then guarded it with as much care as admiration. Even so, her poetry remained a mystery, so rarely given and seemingly held in such low esteem by Sapho herself that it increased her fame all the more. No one was ever able to discover when she wrote: she saw friends constantly and was rarely seen reading or writing. She took the time to do whatever pleased her and planned her time so well that she always had leisure both for her friends and for herself. She was so much mistress of herself that whatever cares troubled her spirit, they never showed in her eyes unless she chose to let them.

I should also tell you, Madam, something about those whom the admirable Sapho honored with her friendship so that you can appreciate her good judgment. Among those who attended her there were four women who could most often be found at her entertainments: first Amithone, then Erinne, next Athys, and finally Cydnon, my sister. Though custom frowns upon our praising those closely related to us, and renders our sincerity suspect when we do so, nevertheless, I believe myself obligated, for Sapho's glory, to praise Cydnon since she has always been Sapho's best friend. It is right, therefore, to justify her choice. I will tell you, to begin my description of these four, that Amithone is tall and finely formed with a fair countenance. Without being particularly beautiful, she attracts and pleases. She is sweet tempered and obliging, correct and well spoken. Without any learning beyond what she has gleaned from the conversation of Sapho and the cultivated people around her, she has a fine comprehension even of those things most difficult to understand. Endowed by the gods with a natural understanding enlarged simply through social intercourse, she speaks judiciously of all things.

As for Erinne, she is quite different. She has cultivated what she possesses of understanding so determinedly that although she does not have the artless understanding of Amithone, Art has so complemented Nature in her that her conversation is always charming. Her imagination has not the scope of Amithone's, but its reach is sure. In fact, she writes quite pleasing verse, which, if Sapho's modesty were to be believed, should be ranked above her own.

The beautiful Athys possesses all that is good in both Erinne and Amithone: she has instinctive understanding, and she has taken the trouble to embellish it with learning and to polish it through conversation with the cultured persons of Mytilene. Sapho has so inspired her with that modest air that makes Sapho herself charming, that Athys cannot abide anyone saying she knows what other ladies do not. She admits only that she judges all things with no other guide than common sense and social custom. And her person is charming—she is well formed, with lustrous chestnut hair so bright and beautiful it is almost blond. Her face is pretty, with a marvelous mouth, a well-made nose, brilliant eyes, and a modest air, and she is exceedingly good-natured. Yet, as admirable and beloved as were these three, Sapho loved Cydnon the most of all.

I am unsure how to render the portrait of my sister, Madam, even though I have promised to do so. Perhaps having sworn that I don't resemble her at all, I may be permitted to praise her as I would another, in order to justify Sapho's choice. I should say that all those whom decorum permits to speak of her beauty find her both beautiful and amiable, though she is petite and brunette. But it isn't by way of her person that she won Sapho's friendship; I must speak of her temperament and wit rather than of her beauty. You should know, then, that Cydnon is naturally gay, gentle, kind, and obliging; she is ready and willing to undertake anything for her friends. What's more, she is knowledgeable enough about the higher things and loves with a tenderness so perfectly attuned to that in Sapho's heart, that they could never agree which one knew best how to love. It's not that the lighthearted aren't generally capable of great attachment, but that her gaiety is never excessive and never descends to mockery unless in innocent fun.

These four were not only from Mytilene, but from Sapho's own neighborhood, and so they were accustomed to being always together. Certainly, they saw other ladies upon occasion, but they did not spend time with them as eagerly as they did with one another. Their bond was so strong that one was not invited to a fête without inviting the others. Judge for yourself, Madam, how this admirable company was sought after by almost all the cultivated and accomplished persons of Mytilene, and there were many of them—few cities in Greece could boast so many, especially in Prince Tisander's day, Pittacus's son, who was enamored of Sapho. This prince was Sapho's first conquest—I fear I will be unable to observe the limits I set out for myself and may be obliged to speak longer than I resolved to do—but since he is no more, I will not stop to describe his merit fully since it would only serve to make you pity his miserable destiny. I will simply say that he was such an admirable gentleman that he had won the esteem of the illustrious Cyrus, who is here listening, and well deserved to be mourned by him after his death.

Tisander was one of the most accomplished of men. In his early youth, when love is especially passionate, there was a large party in Mytilene for the wedding of Amithone, who was marrying an extremely rich man singled out by Pittacus for certain reasons of state. Pittacus honored this fête with his presence, as did his son the prince, and there Tisander spoke for the first time with the beautiful Sapho. Cynegire, careful of her charge's upbringing, rarely allowed her to attend public assemblies, so Tisander had seen her only at church. What surprised him greatly was that she appeared unhappy even though she was at the wedding of a friend. Wondering at the lovely melancholy visible in her eyes, Tisander sought her acquaintance:

"You will find me bold, perhaps, amiable Sapho, to wish to begin my conversation with you by demanding of you a confidence; nevertheless, I cannot refrain from asking why you are more serious today than when I see you in church where I have occasionally had the pleasure of meeting you? I have long wished to have the pleasure of speaking with you," he continued, "and wish to know if I should pity you for some small misfortune; then I might, even from the first moment of our acquaintance, render you some proof of my esteem by the concern I feel for whatever concerns you."

"What you say is so kind," replied Sapho, "that I am obliged to tell you the cause of my sadness, but you may find it so ill founded that you will find it difficult to share my feelings. I must admit to you, my lord, that I have never attended a wedding without sadness; my mind is so peculiar that I cannot share in Amithone's happiness even though she is one of my dearest friends and even though ordinarily I am the most sensitive person in the world to the joys that come to those I love."

"It must be, then," said Tisander, "that you don't consider marriage a good." "It is true," answered Sapho, "I consider it as unending slavery." "So you consider all men tyrants?" rejoined Tisander. "I believe they all may become so once they become husbands," she replied, "and this disagreeable thought always comes to mind when I am at a wedding. Sadness steals upon me in proportion to the interest I take in the happiness of whoever is being married." "What upsets me in what you say, Madam," said Tisander, "is that I fear that the hatred you have for marriage comes from your hatred of men in general; you would be unjust to regard your sex as superior to ours. The truth is," he continued, "were there many women like you, you would be right to do so; were there even two or three others on earth, I would consent to what you say. But charming Sapho, since you are peerless in all the world and have discovered the art of uniting all the virtues and excellent qualities of both sexes in your singular person, be content to be admired or envied by all women and to be adored by all men, but without hating them more generally, as I believe you do."

"Since I am not unjust," she replied, "I know well that I mustn't pay attention to these praises you offer me; furthermore, I know there are men who are truly accomplished, who merit all my esteem and who might even secure a share of my friendship. But I will say it again, the moment I consider them as husbands, I consider them as masters, masters apt to become tyrants, and at that moment, it is impossible not to hate them. I thank the gods for giving me this inclination against marriage." "But if there were some gentleman, happy and accomplished enough to touch your heart," replied Tisander, "perhaps you might change your mind." "I don't know if my feelings will change," she responded, "but I know that unless I lose my reason in love, I will never lose my liberty, and I am resolved never to let my slave become my tyrant." "I can't conceive," said Tisander, "that there could be anyone in the world with the audacity to cease to obey you, nor can I conceive of someone who would dare to command you. Really," he added, "it is impossible to imagine that an admirable young woman, so learned—" "Enough, my lord," interrupted Sapho modestly, "don't go on like this; I know so little, that I am not even sure I am right to speak as I have."

As she was speaking, Pittacus, Prince of Mytilene, sent for Tisander, and he was obliged to leave Sapho, but it must be said that he didn't leave her entirely since he lost his heart in that moment, vanquished by the power of this beautiful lady. His love did not remain long hidden because Tisander was young, with an open disposition unsuited to concealment, so everyone soon knew of his love for Sapho. The day after the wedding of Amithone he appeared first thing at her house and showed her so many favors that no one could doubt but that he was in love with this admirable lady. It was the height of the season in Mytilene, and no day passed without some new amusement. But Tisander was not destined to be loved by the admirable Sapho. Her feelings for him were not what he felt for her—that *je ne sais quoi*[5] that provokes love even more than true merit; she esteemed him and acknowledged his affection, but she was not able to follow the advice of her brother, who wanted her to sacrifice her liberty to her fortune and return the prince's love. But even if she had had the consent of Pittacus to marry the prince, she would not have agreed to marry him, because Sapho hated marriage and did not love Tisander at all. Nevertheless, her brother continually hoped to bend her to his will and gave numerous parties for the entire city.

This little court was so civilized and charming[6]—none could have been

---

5. *Je ne sais quoi* means literally "I don't know what" and is used in English to mean indescribable or beyond words.

6. The French is *galante*. See note 2 above.

more so. The admirable Sapho inspired in all who encountered her a certain civility that somehow communicated itself even to those who had never met her. I was surprised that this civility had not spread throughout Mytilene, let alone throughout the Isle of Lesbos, but it had not. Perhaps half the city was prevented from profiting from Sapho's conversation and that of her circle by envy, ignorance, and resentment. To tell the truth, she lost nothing by not mingling with the kind of people who were frightened by her intelligence and breadth of mind. But it was different with visitors to Lesbos; they had hardly arrived when they headed straight for Sapho's, and they departed completely charmed by her conversation. And this was no surprise, since it was impossible to pass two hours in her company without admiring her enormously and without feeling inclined to love her. Five or six of us young men who were inseparable followed Prince Tisander when he visited Sapho, and we didn't stop even when her severity made him so melancholy that he stopped going there himself.

The ignorant—or rather, envious—cabal that was opposed to ours spoke of us so disparagingly that I can't think back on it without astonishment. They imagined that at Sapho's we conversed about poetic rules, about esoteric questions and philosophy; they might even have said that magic was taught there. The truth is, these professed enemies of reason and virtue were a strange sort; having encountered them myself, I found that the most reasonable of those who shunned Sapho and her friends were young men, merry and rash, who bragged that they could not read; they prided themselves on the sort of militant ignorance that gave them the audacity to censure what they knew nothing about. They had persuaded themselves that men of wit did nothing but talk of things they didn't understand, but they never bothered to find out for themselves how those they shunned so diligently really did talk and converse. They made up the most extravagant stories, which made them ridiculous to everyone of good sense. But in addition to these men who were capable only of an empty, frenetic pleasure that drove them continually from visit to visit without knowing what they were looking for, or what they wanted to do, there were also women of the same type who shunned Sapho and her friends and who mocked them in their own fashion. These were women who believed they need know nothing more than that they were beautiful, that they need learn nothing more than to dress well, women, I tell you, who couldn't talk about anything but fashion and whose charm consisted of nothing more than consuming the dinners their gallants served up all the while spouting foolishness. They complained bitterly when they felt they were not treated royally or with respect.

There was still another sort who held that being virtuous required a lady to know nothing more than how to be a wife to her husband, a mother to her children, and a mistress of her family and her slaves. They thought Sapho and her friends spent too much time in conversation and amused themselves in speaking of things that were not strictly necessary. There were also some men who considered a woman nothing more than the first slave of the household; they forbade their daughters to read anything but prayer books and didn't even want them to sing Sapho's songs. Finally, there were both men and women who shunned us, whom one could justly rank with the grossest sort of people even though they were persons of quality. It wasn't that there weren't some people of intelligence who falsely imagined our society to be as the fools described it, but they didn't seek to enlighten themselves. They believed the lies and didn't bother to disabuse themselves.

The truth is, something strange happened that persuaded them that it was dangerous for women to apply their minds to anything more important than ribbons, shoe buckles, and the trifles of ladies' toilettes. You see, Madam, there was a woman in Mytilene who, having seen Sapho in her youth when she lived nearby, got it into her head to imitate her. She believed she imitated her so well that, having moved to another house, she fancied herself the Sapho of her neighborhood. But in truth, she imitated Sapho badly; in fact, I think there could not have been two people less alike. You remember, Madam, that I said that Sapho knows almost everything that one could know, but she never plays the learned lady[7] : her conversation is natural, witty, and decorous. But this other woman, who was named Damophile, was not at all like her although she tried to imitate Sapho. To portray her, and to help you see the difference between the two, I must tell you that Damophile, having got it into her head to emulate Sapho, didn't attempt to emulate her in every particular, but only in being learned.

Believing that she had found the secret of gaining even more of a reputation, Damophile did everything that Sapho did not do. First, she had five or six masters always in tow, the least learned of which, I believe, taught her astrology; she wrote constantly to men of science and couldn't bring herself to speak with the uneducated. You would always find fifteen or twenty books on her table, and if you walked into her room when she was alone, you found her always holding one. I've been told—and it's true—that there were many more books to be seen in her study than she had read, whereas at

---

7. Were "bluestocking" not anachronistic, it would be the best translation of "savante." Bluestocking as a term of derision for a learned woman of literary interests originated in response to the London salon society of the 1750s.

Sapho's one saw far fewer books than she had read. Damophile always used big words that she pronounced haughtily in a solemn tone, even though she talked of trifles; Sapho, by contrast, used ordinary words to say the most admirable things. Moreover, thinking that learning was incompatible with household affairs, Damophile didn't deign to involve herself in domestic matters, whereas Sapho took care to be informed about even the smallest detail. And Damophile didn't only talk like a book; she also talked constantly about books, citing authors no one had ever heard of in everyday conversation as if she were discoursing in public at some renowned university.

What was really beyond the pale about this woman was that she was suspected of having promised herself to a man in whom her beauty had inspired some tender affection and of having listened favorably to his suit, even though he was quite disagreeable, but on the condition that he would provide her with verse that she could say she had written herself so as to resemble Sapho. Judge for yourself—could the obsession with passing for learned inspire more bizarre behavior than that? But what makes her really boring is that from the first moment you meet her, she seeks tirelessly to make sure you know all she knows or pretends to know. Really, there is so much about Damophile that is tedious, vulgar and disagreeable that, rest assured, just as there is nothing more amiable and charming than a woman who has taken the trouble to educate and adorn her mind with knowledge she knows how and when to use, there is nothing more ridiculous and tiresome than a stupid, pedantic woman.

Damophile being as I have described her, she made those who didn't know Sapho or her friends think that our conversation was like hers, since they knew she sought to copy Sapho. It made them say the most extraordinary things about us, tales that amused us no end. In fact, we considered ourselves lucky, since these rumors about our circle kept people from importuning and troubling us with their presence. Tisander took these foolish rumors to heart since he was in love and suffering from Sapho's rejection, and he was so hard on two or three of these impudent enemies of wit that they were compelled to quit the court. But Madam, without dwelling too long on the prince's love, I can tell you he tried everything to win Sapho's heart, and while he was in despair over her severe views on love and marriage, his friend Prince Thrasibule, having lost his kingdom and his entire fleet, arrived in Mytilene with only two ships. Nevertheless, he had a stout heart, and not much time passed after his arrival in Mytilene before his curiosity prompted him to seek out Sapho, whom he greatly esteemed.

Since Tisander's love isn't the principal subject of Sapho's history, Madam, I won't go on about it. I will say simply that though it seemed as if she ought to love him, she didn't love him at all, and he was so desperate that he resolved to embark with Prince Thrasibule when he left Lesbos, in hopes that absence might cure him. Tisander departed, Madam, but not without bewailing the fact and bidding adieu to the admirable Sapho. Since my sister knew all his secrets and told me after he left Lesbos all that I didn't know about his life, I knew that their parting words were among the most beautiful of all time. Sapho managed it with such skill that she was able to make Tisander understand that she was not to blame for not returning his love; she almost persuaded him that she had tried as hard to force her heart to love him as he himself had sought to win her love. So he left finally without complaint, but he remained the unhappiest of men. When he left Mytilene, he commissioned a man of great wit named Alcæus,[8] a fine writer of verse, to speak of him to the admirable Sapho as much as possible and to record everything that happened during his absence and report it on his return. He couldn't have made a better choice for someone to be always near Sapho; since Alcæus was in love with Athys, who was constantly with her, it was easy for him to be Tisander's loyal spy. He was perfect for the job because he was clever and witty, and quite an intriguer.

Since Sapho esteemed Tisander but didn't love him, his absence didn't detract from her pleasures, and in a day or two our circle amused itself as before, maybe even more, since Tisander's pain sometimes made us all a little melancholy. We were together every day—five or six of us with nothing on our minds but seeing Sapho. It wasn't that we didn't make other visits as well on our own, but to tell the truth we went early and made them short so that we could return speedily to Sapho's, where Amithone, Erinne, Athys, and Cydnon were always to be found. When the weather was good, our fine company would walk together along the beach or the river; when bad weather didn't allow it, we would remain at Sapho's house, which was the most agreeable in the world. She had an anteroom, a bedroom, and a study[9] on the same level overlooking the sea. Truthfully, few men met Sapho without coming to love her, or at least feeling a friendship so tender that it was unlike anything they felt for their other women friends. Although Alcæus was in love with the lovely Athys, I have heard him admit that his friendship with Sapho was not of the same order as what he felt for her even though he

8. Alcæus was a lyric poet of Mytilene in Lesbos whose works include political poems and drinking songs that survive only in fragments. He sometimes uses the Sapphic stanza and was associated with Sappho by seventeenth-century French classicists.

9. The French is *cabinet* meaning a little or inner room, a closet, a private, reserved household space sometimes associated with writing.

loved her dearly. But there is something subtle and intense in Sapho's eyes that warms the hearts even of those she does not set on fire.

Don't think that conversation at Sapho's was formal and reserved; it was free and natural. If there was any constraint, it was the constant temptation to praise Sapho to which we dared not succumb because she didn't wish it. Sometimes we rebelled against her—she didn't want to share or give out her poetry, so we had to resort to all sorts of subterfuges to get it. In my case, I was fortunate because she trusted my sister absolutely and thus I saw everything the admirable Sapho wrote. Sometimes I was so moved by the lovely verses she showed Cydnon and the lack of vanity displayed by my sister's celebrated friend, that I thought it impossible to esteem Sapho enough. Cydnon showed me elegies, songs, epigrams, and many other marvelous things, and I was hard put to understand how it was possible for so young a woman to have written them. Her poetry was so beautiful, her style so apt, the sentiments expressed so noble, the passion so tender, that nothing could compare with them. And nothing she did was done by chance. She wasn't one of those women attracted to poetry who are content to dabble but never bother to perfect their verses. All she wrote was polished to perfection. At the same time, this young girl who knew so much had more modesty than those who know nothing.

One day, as chance would have it, an incident occurred that showed everyone who was there with Sapho and Damophile exactly what I have been saying. To recount to you, Madam, what took place on this occasion, you need to know that Mytilene sponsored an exceptionally fine concert, which was attended by everyone in the city and which was held at the residence of a noblewoman. Sapho and her circle were there as were other ladies, but since it was one of these assemblies open to everyone and where one saw as many as a hundred people you never saw otherwise, and if truth be told, wearisome, annoying people you never wanted to see, Sapho found herself seated next to Damophile and obliged to make conversation with her and her entourage until the concert began. Since Damophile never went anywhere without a suite of at least two or three semi-educated types who work harder at making witticisms than real wits do, Sapho was quite embarrassed and feared the worst, and she was right. Having just sat down, Sapho found herself solicited by one of Damophile's friends on a question of grammar, to which she replied casually, turning away as she spoke, that she couldn't answer since she had learned to speak simply through common usage. At that moment, Damophile, quite full of herself, said in a loud whisper that she wanted to consult with Sapho about a line of Hesiod that she didn't understand. "I swear," replied Sapho smiling modestly, "that you would be better off consulting someone else. I consult only my mirror to know what suits me; there's no point in asking me about such difficult questions."

As she spoke these words, one of those gentlemen who believe that one speaks to writers only about books came bounding across the room and asked her if she had written one of the songs that were going to be sung. "I assure you," said Sapho blushing with irritation, "I have done nothing today but be bored; I am impatient for the concert to begin," she added, continuing, "I have never wished for anything more eagerly." A friend of Damophile's said to her, "As for me, I would much prefer to hear you recite some elegant epigram than to hear the music." Just as Sapho, annoyed, was about to answer him, someone else arrived, copybook in hand, and begged her to be so good as to read an elegy that he presented her and give him advice. Since she much preferred to read someone else's verse rather than suffer hearing in such an outlandish way about her own, she began to read in a low voice, or at any rate, to give the appearance of reading. She was so embarrassed to be put in such a situation that she couldn't have judged the verse if she had tried. But what distracted her even more was that while she had her eyes fixed on the poem, she heard men and women behind her talking about her wit, her poetry, her learning, pointing her out to others and talking about her extravagantly. Some said she didn't give the impression of being all that learned; others insisted they could see from her eyes that she knew more than she let on. There was even a man who said he wouldn't have his wife know as much as she did and a woman who said she wished she knew even half what Sapho knew. Everyone either praised or criticized, as he or she saw fit, while Sapho pretended to read attentively.

Damophile conversed with two or three of her demi-literati nearby, speaking pretentiously without saying anything, so that finally I decided that I wanted to hear a conversation between two people as diametrically opposed as Sapho and Damophile and was the first to urge Sapho to give the elegy back to the man who had presented it so as to force her to take part in the conversation. Sapho, comforted to see me near her and hoping to talk only to me, returned the poem to its maker saying she didn't know enough to dare praise it. Turning to me, she said under her breath, "Am I not unfortunate to find myself so near Damophile and her friends? At least I have one consolation," she added. "You have come to my rescue." "No, no, Madam," I said laughing, "that isn't at all what brought me to your side. I think it will bring you praise if you speak and everyone learns that you don't talk in the least like Damophile." Then I joined the conversation of Damophile and her companions, addressing Sapho repeatedly despite her displeasure. There was one man among those with Damophile who spoke well enough of what he knew, and he began to speak quite eloquently of harmony, and then, on the nature of love.

What was extraordinary, Madam, was to see the difference between Sapho and Damophile; the latter couldn't stop interrupting the man speaking, whether to raise muddled objections or to give new reasons why she didn't understand and no one else could either. She didn't hesitate to say all that she said in a fulsome tone and with an affected air so that you could see how full of herself she was. It was easy to see that half the time she didn't understand at all what she was saying. As for Sapho, she didn't speak except when good manners absolutely required her to respond to a direct question. Though she said repeatedly that she didn't understand what he was talking about, in fact, in saying that, she showed herself to be someone who understood better than those who set out to teach such things. For all her modesty and irritation, for all the simplicity of her words, you couldn't help but see that she knew everything and Damophile knew nothing. Damophile talked a lot but said very little; Sapho said little but was admired for all she said.

At last the gods were satisfied and the concert began. The moment it was over, Sapho, pretending to have pressing business, rose quickly and hastened away from Damophile. But Damophile wouldn't let her get away without mortifying her yet again by saying that no doubt Sapho was leaving because she had left some song that she wanted to perfect unfinished in her study. Sapho heard her but didn't bother to respond; on the contrary, taking the arm I offered, she was soon on the other side of the room where Amithone, Athys, Erinne, and Cydnon were seated. She had hardly joined them when she began to urge them earnestly to leave; in fact, she forced them to be gone sooner than they would have otherwise. "What has happened to make you wish to leave so urgently?" said Cydnon, seeing her flushed and so affected. "I'll tell you all when we get to my rooms," said Sapho. "I need some time to collect myself." Amithone turned to me, "You were there, tell us what happened." Without giving me a chance to answer, Athys said, "I can't imagine," and Erinne added, "Maybe Democedes knows no more than we do." "Pardon me," I said, "I know, but I don't know if our lovely Sapho wishes you to know." Sapho answered, "Not only do I want Amithone, Athys, Erinne, and Cydnon to know; if possible, I want all the world to know how much I detest Damophile and her friends and how it wearies me that there are so many people like them in the world." Sapho said this with such a charming melancholy air that she made me laugh.

As we arrived Alcæus joined us—I think I've mentioned that he was known as a man of some wit in Mytilene, and rightly so—and also a gentleman named Nicanor. Just as we arrived at Sapho's gate, we met a lady called Phylire who came in as well. Hearing all the ladies besiege the admirable Sapho about something Alcæus and Nicanor knew nothing about, they began to ask me what was going on the moment we were seated in Sapho's beautiful room. As soon as Sapho heard them questioning me, she turned toward them and began to speak. "No, no," she said to them, "it isn't up to Democedes to explain my embarrassment because only I know what happened." "Tell us then, we beg you," said Nicanor, who was truly a gentleman with none of the faults of young men of his sort. "What you ask is not so easy to explain as it might seem," replied Sapho. "What's wrong," said Alcæus. "What could be bothering you?" And I added, "You, whom all the world admires." "Because I must tell you," continued Sapho, "I am weary of being a wit and of passing for a learned lady. The way I feel today, I am beginning to think that it would be the height of happiness not to know how to read or write or converse, and were it only possible to forget how to read, write, and converse, I promise you I would be silent from this moment. So appalled have I been by the foolishness of the world and by the persecution that seems inevitably to attend those like me who are so unfortunate as to have a reputation for knowing something more than how to curl hair or choose ribbons, that I will speak no more about my life." Sapho said this with such charming distress and with such spirit, that her amiable indignation only increased the love and friendship felt for her in the souls of everyone who heard her.

"Tell us exactly what happened," Cydnon said to her. "How is it possible that you saw me near Damophile," Sapho replied, "surrounded by those pedants who follow her continually, without commiserating and without knowing that I was having a terrible time?" "If you had been where I was," answered Phylire, smiling, "you would not have been troubled by ladies any too learned." "I assure you," Sapho returned, "I don't know where I would have wished to be today. You were in the midst of four or five women who openly profess their hatred of anyone with wit and who affect such a vulgar ignorance that, had they spoken to me, it would certainly either have displeased or bored me." "Had you been where I was," said Nicanor, "you would have been more comfortable because I had only men around me, and you wouldn't have lacked for praise." "No doubt," she replied, "since there seems to be a rumor making the rounds that I must be praised continually; but truly, that would not have been to my liking. Really Nicanor, most of your sort know so little what one ought to say to someone like me that half the time they infuriate me when they try to please me. With the exception of you here present, I hardly know anyone who hasn't said things that annoyed me, and for all I know there may be someone here who has sometimes angered me," she added. "But I know this at least: I implore you not to instruct everyone you meet how you think I want to be treated. As for Alcæus, I am sure that he shares my feelings more than the rest of you."

"It's true," he said laughing, "that the trade of wit in which people say I engage is doubtless unprofitable enough." "But unprofitable how?" asked Phylire. "What harm can there be in Sapho's great reputation in the world? Shouldn't she be delighted to think that everyone with wit from Athens to Corinth, from Sparta to Thebes, from Argos to Delphi, through all of Greece, speaks of her only with admiration?" "As for those who don't know me," answered Sapho, "I am delighted with whatever they say. But as for most of those whom I see every day, I am less than pleased. If you wish me to enumerate my complaints, I will, so that Nicanor may then instruct the court how to live with persons of wit; so that Phylire can teach the ladies of her neighborhood how to get along with those in ours; and so that Amithone, Erinne, Athys, and Cydnon will stop accusing me of imaginary complaints and troubles. That is why I return to my point once more: there is nothing more troublesome than to be a *bel esprit*,[10] or at any rate, to be treated as if one were, if one has a noble heart and is wellborn. It is indisputable that, if you are singled out from the crowd by a flash of wit and acquire a reputation for having more wit than another, and if you write well enough, whether poetry or prose, to produce books, you lose half your nobility if you have any. You are no longer the equal of someone of the same house and blood who doesn't meddle with writing. People treat you differently; they say you were fated only to amuse others, as if there were a law obliging you to write piece after piece, each more beautiful than the last, and should you wish to stop writing, people no longer feel any obligation to notice you. If you are rich, no one can believe it; if you aren't, nothing could be worse. All things considered, one is treated more kindly when one is not at all a wit than when one is."

"Nonetheless, I see that all the men at court esteem those who dedicate themselves to writing," replied Nicanor. "I assure you," said Sapho, "that they show their esteem in a strange way because the young people at court treat those who dedicate themselves to writing as if they were artisans. These young people think they have offered what merit deserves when they praise some piece of writing in passing, often inappropriately. They demand to know what one is up to, what work is in progress, if it will soon be finished, if it isn't too short. That is their subtlest observation: to say that whatever you show them isn't long enough. No doubt distinctions need to be made

---

10. *Bel esprit* is used frequently throughout the *Histoire de Sapho* and can refer either to someone of wit, spirit, intelligence, and finesse or to a fine conceit or example of wit.

among those who write; to be sure, there are those who write and only their works should be seen; but there are others whose person is to be preferred to their writings. And those we call men and women of the world confuse the two and don't speak at all to those who write as they speak to those who don't meddle with writing, even though the former may be the more worthy. I agree that the learned who can't take part in ordinary conversation should not be admitted to such conversations even though we should respect them, or excuse them, if they deserve it. But for those who know how to converse as well as they know how to write, I think they should be spoken to as if they didn't write. They shouldn't be beset by continual demands for their works. I know only too well that there are those who importune them, who never cease persecuting those they are with about these productions of their wit. Truly, I don't know who is most set upon, those who encounter one of these authors who oppress everyone they meet with their continual recitations, or the writer of birth and sensibility, who at every encounter with a person of quality must talk about nothing but what he or she is writing. For myself, I swear that what displeases me most is when people come to me out of the blue to talk of the verse I occasionally write to amuse myself."

"But doesn't it balance out," said Amithone, "because the indifferent never praise what you write at all?" "But those I put up with never stop!" replied Sapho. "One man comes to me demanding an elegy, another wants me to write him a song, and still another wants to know if I wrote a certain epigram. How can I bear it when people don't speak to me as they do to others? I only want to be like everyone else—I can't endure it when I am singled out in such a bizarre manner. No one speaks to me as they do to the rest of the world; to excuse themselves for not visiting me, they say they were afraid of interrupting my work; they accuse me of dreaming and then say no doubt I am never better than when I am alone; if I should say merely that I have a headache, there is always someone ready with the conventional cliché that a headache is the malady of fair wits. Even my doctor, when I complain of some minor indisposition, tells me that the same temperament that makes me a wit makes me suffer. Really, I am so pestered for my poetry, learning, and wit that I consider stupidity and ignorance the sovereign good."

"It's true," replied Alcæus, "that our beautiful Sapho has reason to complain as she does; in fact, she may not have said enough. Frankly, if it weren't for the fact that whoever writes tolerably well necessarily seeks satisfaction in herself, I assure you, she would be miserable. As for me, I've been at many courts throughout the world, and almost everywhere I've seen dreadful injustice toward those who write. Most of the great wish to be praised, but they receive what incense you offer as a tribute due them without any regard for the hand that gives it. One day I wrote a long poem for a prince who said he liked what I had written but didn't even ask to see me. But to tell you the truth, I soon consoled myself over this humiliation because having seen the way he behaved, I much prefer being the writer to being the prince. I take satisfaction from having a finer heart than he, more than if Fortune had put me as far above his head as she has put me beneath it."

"Ah, my dear Alcæus," replied Sapho, "you give me such joy when you speak as you do. Nothing gives me greater satisfaction than when I can say to myself that I have a soul nobler than those whom Fortune's fancy has put above me. Nevertheless, that doesn't mean there aren't often moments when I am sensible of all the troubles my reputation heaps upon me. I observe men and women sometimes at a loss because they get it into their heads that they can't say to me what they say to other people. I'm happy to talk with them about the beauty of the season, the latest news, everything that makes up ordinary conversation, but they return, always, to their point— they are so persuaded that I am constrained to talk to them of such things that they constrain themselves to talk about things that so distress me that, when this happens, I want to un-Sapho myself. If you could see into my heart, you would know that there is no greater insult you could offer me than to treat me like a learned lady. And that is why I beg you all to prevent this persecution by publishing instead to all the world that I am not what I am said to be; that it is Alcæus who composes the verses attributed to me, and that I am not particularly worthy of being esteemed. Maybe then I'll be left alone—neither sought after nor shunned—because I confess, I want neither to be sought after nor shunned as a woman of wit."

Just then a crowd arrived and the conversation turned to other topics, but Sapho spoke little the rest of the day, so my sister tells me, because I left just after the others joined us when I heard that two old friends who had been traveling abroad for some time had returned. Not wanting to be the last to welcome them, I was eager to depart so as to fulfill that duty. One was named Phaon,[11] and since he plays a large part in the story I am telling you, Madam, I must speak of him more particularly than of the other, Themistogene. I should tell you that they are both from Lesbos and that we

11. Phaon, the mythical boatman of Mytilene, who when old and ugly is said to have carried Aphrodite across the sea without asking payment and been rewarded with youth and beauty. Scudéry tells this story somewhat differently below, p. 32. Sappho is sometimes said to have leaped into the sea for unrequited love of Phaon, but this putative suicide is generally considered fictitious.

were raised together. When we were boys, I loved them both equally, but it turned out that when my friends returned, I found that though reunited with both, I had lost one. To explain this conundrum, Madam, you should know that when Phaon and Themistogene departed, I loved the latter somewhat better than the former because there was something more appealing in his character and even in his person. But at their return, I found quite a change: one had become less attractive and the other much more beautiful. In addition, Themistogene's wit was unchanged, whereas that of Phaon had so improved that, rest assured, there are few wits superior to his. To put it plainly, there are few men more amiable than he.

As for his person, he is incomparable. He is quite fair, but with a beauty that doesn't at all resemble that of women; he has kept all the bearing of his sex along with the beauty of theirs. He cuts a handsome and noble figure, though he is not particularly tall, with dark brown hair and beautiful, black eyes, a nicely rounded face, beautiful teeth, a well-formed nose, and a noble mien. He has lovely hands for a man, a lively air about him, and a happy countenance. He has a certain passionate *je ne sais quoi* in his eyes, but not a bit of affectation. All this serves to make him an extremely charming and worthy gentleman. Indeed, Madam, Phaon is so handsome and good-looking that the people of Lesbos have invented a bizarre tale about him. Since he is the son of a man renowned in Mytilene who had commanded fleets in various wars, the vulgar say that when Phaon was still fairly young he was playing in a skiff near one of his father's ships when Venus came to him and asked him to carry her in the skiff to an island where she wanted to go. To compensate him for the service he performed for her, she made him become as beautiful as he is. Though there was no basis for this fable, except that Phaon, unlike most men, was not as beautiful when he was a child as he later became, the people of Lesbos believe this tale as if it were true.

But Madam, if Phaon's person is admirable, his wit and character are no less so: he is courteous, kind, and affable, neither too merry nor too melancholy—he possesses everything needed to please. And besides, he is easy going and agreeable, he speaks well and to the purpose, and he has an excellent knowledge of so many beautiful things that no one knows better how to speak or act than he does. Moreover, he is naturally inclined to gallantry—there is such harmony among his person, character, and wit that you could say they were made for one another. As for Themistogene, he doesn't resemble him at all. It isn't that he is unattractive, but he has an unpleasing and aloof manner. Nor is he absolutely without wit, but what wit he has is off the mark. Themistogene is almost never right when he follows his own inclination; he chooses badly so habitually that you are almost assured of always choosing well yourself if you simply choose what he doesn't. Nevertheless, he busied himself loving beautiful things and seeking out accomplished persons, although he hadn't any idea how to get to know them.

These two men, both exactly as I have described them, had made a long voyage together without having become fast friends or traveling in the same circles. The moment they arrived in a city, their tastes separated them—what pleased one didn't please the other at all. They were together in the streets, but almost never anywhere else. As was their custom, having arrived in Mytilene, they went their separate ways, though neither one had father or mother where he might find a place to stay. I had to search for them individually, but couldn't find them because at the same time they were both looking for me. I didn't see them until the next day. But I recognized immediately the difference between Themistogene and Phaon and did it justice by changing just as they had changed. I loved Phaon more than Themistogene, whom I no longer held in the same esteem I once had at an earlier age, when one doesn't always know why one does what one does.

Since I wasn't the first person they encountered in Mytilene, I found that they had already learned of Sapho's great reputation, but not from people who knew how to praise her as she deserved to be praised. They had simply been told that she had a great wit, that she was learned, and that she wrote excellent poetry. What was amazing was that even though people had told Phaon and Themistogene exactly the same thing, it produced quite different results. Themistogene, who was always curious to know all the beautiful people, was strangely impatient to make his way to Sapho's, whereas Phaon, who had met Damophile the previous evening at a gathering where she had gone after the concert, had no curiosity whatsoever to meet Sapho. In fact, far from desiring to meet her, when I spoke of her and offered to introduce him, he fended off the visit as if he wished to avoid it rather than desired it.

It got to the point that Themistogene harassed me continually to make me take him to Sapho's, but I didn't want to because I didn't think him worthy of her acquaintance, and I harassed Phaon continually to make him go, but to no avail because he fancied that it was impossible for a woman to be learned without being ridiculous or, at any rate, unseemly and tiresome. On top of all that, Phaon didn't have much experience with love and was of the mistaken opinion, of which he has since been disabused, that it was preferable to love a beautiful fool than a woman of wit. One day at my house I was pressing him to go to Sapho's and he was refusing in an opinionated way, and I began to quarrel with him, angry that he gave no credence to what I told him. "Really," I said, "what reason can you give for not wanting to meet Sapho?"

"First," he told me, "people tell me Damophile is the copy of Sapho, and if that is the case, it is impossible that the original could ever please me because I find her ridiculous, so unseemly that I would flee from province to province not to meet the woman she imitates." "O most unjust friend," I said, "if you only knew the wrong you do the admirable Sapho, you would be horrified at your own injustice. You would see that Damophile doesn't resemble Sapho in the least, and you would repent of the injury you do me in accusing me of not knowing true merit." "I don't accuse you," he replied, "but you know, to each his own. For my part, I tell you, I only want women to amuse me; I want them beautiful, charming, capable of good conversation, not learned, because I dread terribly these talkers with their big words for little things, who are always at the top of Mount Parnassus and who only speak to men in the language of the gods.

"If you want me to reveal to you my secret, I confess that when I was in Sicily I found myself in love with a beautiful fool, and I don't want to take a chance loving a beautiful wit who will, perhaps, put me in despair. That's why I beg you, don't torment me further, because if Sapho is as I imagine her, I'll despise her, and if she is all you say she is, she will please me too much for my own good." "But is it possible," I said to him, "that you could love stupidity?" He replied, laughing, "I confess I didn't hate the beautiful fool." "I well understand," I said, "that one may love beauty wherever one finds it; I even understand that one can love, in a passing way, a very beautiful woman without wit; but I don't understand at all how you could have any real attachment for a woman lacking intelligence, however beautiful she may be. You can't know the subtle pleasures of passion if you have loved only a beautiful fool." "I can't say whether I know all the delights of love," replied Phaon, "but at least I don't know its torments." "O my dear friend," I told him, "you are a novice at love! You can't be happy in love if you haven't been miserable in love. In fact," I added, "you must suffer piteously to feel joy; you must have desired some good desperately before you can possess it with pleasure. You must have loved a woman of wit to know the sweets of love. In my own case," I added, "when I first meet a very beautiful woman, I have this fantasy: I imagine her wit equal to her beauty so that when I don't find her so, I am so surprised and put off that I can never fall in love. I prefer a beautiful portrait that can't speak foolishness to a beautiful woman who can do and say a thousand inanities." At that point, Themistogene arrived, his feelings diametrically opposed to those of Phaon; he had come to entreat me yet again to take him to Sapho's, and he kept telling me that he desired earnestly to meet her, adding that he expected to fall in love if she were as he imagined her. "If that is the case," I said to evade his importuning, "I mustn't take you there because you'll be too unhappy—you don't want to become a lover of someone who already has so many others."

So without having been able to persuade Phaon myself, and without Themistogene having been able to persuade me, we parted. But oddly enough, having gone to Sapho's after dinner, she told me that Nicanor and Phylire, who had met Phaon, had spoken so well of him that, even though she did not ordinarily seek new acquaintances, she could not help but desire his. "It's true, Madam," I answered her, "that Phaon is a person of great merit." "Since he is your particular friend," she responded, "I shall believe that he will not fail to visit Cydnon, so I shall be able to meet him there." "He will be ashamed not to have met you at home," I said, "rather than meeting you elsewhere, once he knows you." "Aha! Democedes," she said to me. "I don't want your friend to be afraid of me. I'll tell you what I think, if you wish: I think since he hasn't come to see me that you have given him a bad opinion of me."

You can imagine, Madam, how what Sapho said embarrassed me, knowing Phaon's feelings as I did. Nevertheless, I could never resolve to criticize my friend, so instead I engaged myself to bring him to Sapho. I decided to make something serious of this visit, to entreat Phaon to make the visit in the name of our friendship if not because Sapho merited it. In fact, the moment I left Sapho's, I went in search of him to try to persuade him to do as I wished. But it wasn't easy. Since he knew that I wished it, and since he didn't want to anger me if he remained obstinate, he gave in, saying I should realize that his doing so was a great sign of his friendship for me. So it was decided that I would bring him to Sapho's the next day. But what troubled me was that I dared not bring him there without also bringing Themistogene, who would otherwise be angry. So to take an agreeable man, I was constrained to take a bore.

Since I had informed Sapho of our visit, she had told her dear friends, so Amithone, Erinne, Athys, and Cydnon were with her when Phaon, Themistogene, and I arrived. Sapho is one of those people who, at first acquaintance, is the most amiable and obliging of persons when she pleases. She received us admirably and in so gracious a manner that I could see Phaon was surprised. He had not expected to find a learned young woman so open, natural, and amiable. As for Themistogene, he was just as surprised as Phaon, but in quite a different way. Since the two of them had already made up their minds as to Sapho's learning and were convinced they ought to speak to her in an elevated style, they began a very serious conversation. It wasn't that I hadn't told Phaon that one ought not to do that; it was that he didn't believe me. So thinking that he ought at the very least to commend her as if she were extraordinary, and in lofty, striking language, he began to praise her with exaggerated eloquence. But Sapho stopped him short and turning to me said, "Truly, Democedes, I reproach you." "Me, Madam?" I replied with astonishment. "Yes, you" she continued, "I reproach you because, since Phaon doesn't know me, it would be unjust of me to reproach him. So it's certainly you whom I blame for these praises he heaps on me. Had you advised him that I don't like it at all when people praise me in the way he has, I believe he is too much the gentleman not to oblige me by ceasing to flatter me in a way bound not to please me." "I assure you," I replied, "that I did not fail to inform him that such praises did not accord with your modesty." "Then he must not know me as I am," continued Sapho. "But Phaon," she added, turning toward him, "since I don't care to owe anything to Fame, I ask you as a particular favor to judge me for yourself, to take the trouble and the time to know me, because in my opinion, you will do me an injustice if you judge me according to report." "I don't know, Madam," said Phaon, smiling, "if there is as much modesty as you think in what you say because to declare that you deserve more praise than Fame accords you would be to agree that you deserve more praise than anyone has ever merited." "Truly," added Themistogene, thinking he was about to say something remarkable, "is there anything more beautiful than to hear it said that a young lady can make verses better than Homer made, or that she is more learned than the seven sages of Greece?" "Whatever the case may be," said Sapho, "I don't care to hear myself spoken of in such terms, and the greatest injury I can suffer from my friends is that they suspect me of being at ease when I am praised in that way. Since I am not at all learned, I don't want people saying that I am, and if I were, I would dislike it all the more. Certainly I can't deny that I have written some verse, but poetry is the result of a natural inclination, like music. There is no more reason to commend me for writing verse than for singing."

With that, Sapho turned the conversation easily to other topics and took studied care to talk of nothing whatsoever that even hinted at learning; on the contrary, the whole afternoon was spent in a sort of merry war among friends talking of the myriad trifles that had taken place in their circle, and Sapho made everything so easy to understand that Phaon and Themistogene took almost as much pleasure in hearing about them as did those who had been there and as I did who already knew of them. When Alcæus and Nicanor arrived, Sapho reproached the former for something he had done a day or so before at her house, and which he did almost always when the occasion presented itself. For the fact was, Madam, Alcæus was under the delusion that women absolutely had to be beautiful, and he couldn't bear those who weren't. He would get up and leave if by chance he encountered an ugly woman. And so it happened that he had arrived at Sapho's to find an unattractive woman there, and so, following his humor, he left again immediately, and so abruptly, that the lady, who was a woman of wit, perceived that he was avoiding her. Thus Sapho easily and gracefully turned the conversation and reproached Alcæus for his affectation and blamed him for a fault she perceived in many fashionable young people who did virtually the same thing. "The truth is, Madam," said he, understanding very well that she was waging war, "on the day for which you reproach me, I left you only because I wanted to visit the beautiful Athys; I protest—it was not for the reason you say." "Be fair, Alcæus," replied Athys, "don't excuse yourself saying you visited me; you didn't visit me that day." "Then I must have been at Amithone's," he countered. "Absolutely not," retorted the beautiful Amithone. "Erinne, Cydnon, and I saw you from the windows of my room, walking for over two hours with one of your friends who is one of the most ugliest men in the world, and certainly uglier than the woman you fled."

"Truly, it is strange you should be so inconsistent," continued Sapho. "Tell me why your eyes can bear an ugly man but can't endure an ugly woman? There isn't one gallant who affects female beauty who doesn't spend most of his life with incredibly ugly men and often even has a close friend who is not good-looking. It is an injury to our sex: when a woman isn't beautiful, they can't endure her and avoid her like the plague. You'd think women were put on earth with the same fate as colors—simply to please the eye. I must say, this is an injustice; if you love what is beautiful and hate what is ugly, have only beautiful friends just as you have only beautiful mistresses, and flee ugly men as assiduously as you flee ugly women. But if, on the contrary, you can accustom your eyes to the ugliness of your own sex because they have other admirable qualities, then accustom your eyes as well to women of little beauty but of much charm and wit whose beauty is in their souls. For truly, were you obliged to be the lover of every woman you see, you would be right to be as overnice as you are. But since your heart is filled with love for one of the world's most beautiful women, I fail to see the reason for your delicacy. Why can't you spend fifteen minutes talking to a woman who isn't beautiful? Why must you leave abruptly simply because an unattractive woman arrives on the scene? It seems that all young men commit this sort of injustice—even those who are ugly, incredibly ugly, can't endure a woman's ugliness. In fact, they want the fairest eyes in the world to look favorably upon them while they look upon beautiful women with the ugliest eyes in the world. I know one man who can't keep from looking in every mirror he meets as if he were the handsomest man living and sees his own ugliness with pleasure, but does not have the patience for that of others."

"What you have said is so thoughtful and well said," added Phaon, "that I suspect Alcæus, for all his wit, will be hard put to answer you." "I confess," answered Alcæus, "that I prefer to admit I am wrong rather than to try to justify myself because I would have to say a great many things against the ladies." "What you say is so wicked," said Amithone, "that you deserve to be punished—since you flee women when they aren't beautiful, beautiful women should assiduously avoid meeting you." "Providing only that one fair one should not shun me," he replied looking at Athys, "I will console myself at not seeing the rest." "Were I fair," answered Erinne, "I know I wouldn't be among those who would console you." "And since I'm not at all fair," added Athys, blushing, "I'll have to console myself at not being among those who console Alcæus." "In my opinion," said Nicanor, looking at the beautiful young girl with whom Alcæus was in love, "you know very well what part you would play in this little adventure. There isn't anyone in Mytilene who has ever seen Alcæus flee any gathering where you were present." "That is certainly because he is not so sensitive as to be unable to bear women like me who are neither beautiful nor ugly," she replied. "What you say about yourself is so unjust," exclaimed Alcæus, "that I don't see how the fair Sapho, who so loves being just to the deserving, can bear it." "It is not up to me to praise Athys's beauty in your presence," she replied. "Since your eyes are so tender they can't bear ugliness in women, I am sure they are also sensitive enough to know real beauty when they see it and to know how to praise it better than anyone else."

"I would like to know if Phaon and Themistogene are as impressionable as Alcæus," continued Sapho. "I know Nicanor and Democedes have women friends who are not at all beautiful." "Although I am powerfully moved by beauty," answered Phaon, "I would think it a great outrage to women if I considered beauty their sex's only advantage. I assure you, far from sharing Alcæus's views, I suspect that anyone incapable of having a woman friend who isn't beautiful is incapable of really loving a woman at all—as long as she isn't really horrible, that is. Our eyes become accustomed easily to all things; there are women who possess such unexpected beauty of mind and such winning grace of temperament that they can't help but please and be both charming and much loved." Then Themistogene said, "As for me, since I love beauty of mind more than a fair countenance, I would much prefer a woman who knows a thousand beautiful, important things, even if she were ugly, than a beauty who knows nothing." "As far as I can tell," replied Sapho, laughing, "I could never be the beloved of Alcæus or Themistogene, because I am neither beautiful, as Alcæus would have his love, nor learned, as Themistogene would have his. I must make Nicanor, Phaon, and Democedes my friends." "And if in seeking friends," replied Cydnon, "you find a lover, will you not be surprised?" "Certainly I will, since I have yet to find one and since I am not really trying to find one," answered Sapho.

As Nicanor, Phaon, and I were about to respond, Cynegire entered the room. Her arrival interrupted our conversation and prompted us to depart. Sapho's house was on a lovely square where we began to stroll. We had hardly begun to walk there when Phaon began speaking to me in a whisper because he didn't want Nicanor to know the opinion he had formed of Sapho. "My dear friend," he said, "how wrong I was, how much my own enemy, not to want to meet the admirable Sapho." "So, did you find her so very learned?" I asked. "Did she resemble Damophile? Must one speak to her of important matters as you imagined you would?" "I was so charmed to meet her—I can't imagine there is anyone in the world as amiable as she," he said. "And when I think, seeing Sapho so gentle, so gracious, so charming, that she also writes poetry all the world admires, and when I think that this same young girl who knows so much of lofty matters, amuses herself with the most insignificant things, I have such admiration for her that I begin to fear falling in love if I continue seeing her. But I don't think I can stop myself." "I told you that the moment you met her, you would change your mind." "But tell me," he said, "I want to know if she is always as charming as she was today? Have you really never seen in her the arrogance that seems unavoidable in the extraordinarily gifted? Tell me, dear friend, what I want to know. Does she always speak with so little affectation and so agreeably as she did today?" "All I can tell you," I replied, "is that sometimes she is as much better than you saw her today as you found her today better than you had expected." "No, Democedes," he answered, "what you say is impossible. The beautiful Sapho could not appear more amiable than she appeared to me today."

After that, Nicanor began to talk with Phaon, and Themistogene approached us and spoke to me with a certain coldness: "I tell you, I was surprised this afternoon." "What do you mean?" I said, taken aback. "You weren't satisfied meeting Sapho?" "Very little," he retorted. "So little, in fact, that were I not persuaded that she wished to hide her learning because there were so many women present, I would be completely disabused of the high opinion I had conceived of her. I didn't hear her say a thing today that any other woman with no learning at all might not say." I answered coldly, "If she spoke like a woman, at least you must admit that she spoke like a woman who speaks very well indeed." "I admit that she spoke no barbarisms," he said, "but to tell you the truth, I had expected something completely different from what I heard." "You thought she would lecture about philosophy, make irrefutable arguments, resolve difficult questions, explicate obscure passages from Hesiod or Homer?" I asked him. "I thought at least that only beautiful, important things would come out of her mouth, things that would let her knowledge be known," he said. "I tell you frankly, I believe there must be days when she shows her learning because it isn't possible for her to have the reputation she has throughout Greece if she never says anything but the bagatelles I heard her say today."

You can imagine, Madam, how amazed I was at the different opinions of Phaon and Themistogene. Since the latter spoke rather loudly, Phaon overheard something of what he was saying and since he had become one of Sapho's most zealous admirers, he joined our conversation and asked me what Themistogene had been saying. "He's been telling me," I said smiling, "that he didn't find that Sapho deserved all the praise people give her and that he had imagined she would say a thousand fine things that she didn't say." "As far as I can tell," replied Phaon coldly, "the beautiful Sapho cannot win the esteem of both Themistogene and myself, because I esteem her infinitely for the bagatelles for which he reproaches her, and I would hardly have esteemed her at all if she had discoursed on high matters as he thinks she should have. And so it goes, she can't please us both."

"I agree," Themistogene replied brusquely. "The difficulty is to know if it wouldn't be more advantageous for Sapho to gratify me than to please you." "If you wish Nicanor and Democedes to judge between us, I consent," replied Phaon. Nicanor spoke up, "Since I am completely on your side, Phaon, I can't serve as judge." "And since I utterly oppose Themistogene," I added, "it would be easier for me to be his accuser than his judge." "Now do you think I'm wrong to esteem Sapho more for speaking as she does, knowing what she knows, than I would esteem her if she went about touting her learning continually as you expect her to do," Phaon said to Themistogene, "spending entire days speaking of matters no one who frequents her house understands, and which, by the way, you probably understand hardly better than I do? I know very well that when I do understand them, I can't listen for long. Not only can I not bear a woman who plays the learned lady, I can hardly endure men of learning who pride themselves on what they know.

"But to tell you the truth," he added, turning to me, "Themistogene's opinion doesn't surprise me. It's been at least two years since we have been of the same opinion, so it was easy to foresee that as soon as I began to admire Sapho, he would not admire her and would prefer Damophile, whom I place below all other women, as I would put Sapho above all the women I have ever known. For truly, to write as she writes, to speak as she speaks, are two such admirable qualities that she deserves the esteem of the entire world." "But I ask you," responded Themistogene, irked in a way that made us laugh, "what did she say that was so beautiful or important?" "She spoke elegantly and graciously," replied Phaon, "with modesty and in a natural way, and so judiciously that she merited my admiration." "Well, it wasn't the same with me," said Themistogene, "because I admire the out of the ordinary." "I once knew a man in Athens," said Phaon, "who thought as Themistogene does. He couldn't tell the difference between what was admirable and what was merely astonishing." "I don't know if I am as you say," replied Themistogene proudly, "but I know very well that I don't see any difference between Sapho and all the other women of Mytilene. If she never says anything but the sorts of things I heard her say today and inspires only the feelings I had after hearing her speak, then I swear that if I don't hear anything more elevated than what she said today, I will believe that someone else has written the verse published under her name."

Hearing him, Phaon began to laugh in so insulting a manner that Themistogene got really angry and spoke bitterly to him. Phaon responded in kind, and they quarreled in earnest. Nicanor and I would not have been able to separate them if Alcæus and a couple of others hadn't happened along.

Since their quarrel could not be resolved straight away and it was not until the next day that the two enemies were reconciled, it made quite a stir in Mytilene. But it served Phaon well, for I told my sister what had happened, and she told Sapho. So from the very first day she met Phaon, she knew she was obliged to him. Even the reconciliation of these two enemies was remarkable because Phaon didn't want to be reconciled unless Themistogene would admit that he was wrong to judge Sapho's merit so lightly and hold his own opinion rather than that of everyone else on earth. Knowing what had happened, the admirable Sapho could not but feel grateful to Phaon and received him graciously when he returned to see her. In fact, hardly had she seen him enter her room than she went to greet him most obligingly and complimented him so particularly and with such gallantry that I must tell you all about it.

As soon as she approached him, she spoke first, looking at him with a smile: "You have so praised me because I never speak of lofty things that I dare not show the obligation I owe you for fear that, against my custom, some lofty words may escape me that might win me the esteem of Themisto-gene and might lose me yours." "What you say is so witty and charming," he replied, "that truly, I repent of having been reconciled with Themistogene.

Any man who doesn't admire you deserves to have every rational person in the world declare unending war on him." "When you know me well," returned Sapho, "you will see that I am not so jealous of my reputation. As long as no one says I am lacking virtue or goodness, I am not concerned about what people say about me."

When Sapho had shown Phaon to a seat, the conversation became very lively because not only were her particular friends there, but Phylire, Nicanor, Alcæus, and I were there as well. What is more, the quarrel between Phaon and Themistogene turned the conversation in a direction that pleased Sapho enormously. Having discussed Themistogene's error in believing that one could not be learned without continually parading one's learning, Phylire declared that although gross ignorance was a major fault, she thought nevertheless that women were better off ignorant than learned. "Imagine," she continued, "how we would suffer if there were two or three hundred Damophiles in Mytilene." "But try to imagine the opposite," said Phaon impetuously, "what felicity there would be if there were even five or six Saphos in the world? If Athens, Delphos, Thebes, and Argos, as well as Mytilene, could boast of having one of their own?" "Have mercy, please, Phaon," she said, blushing. "Don't diminish the obligation I owe you with unwanted praise—remember, I don't wish at all to be thought learned. I am convinced that if I have knowledge that other women don't possess, at least I don't know anything but what all ladies ought to know." "Truly, Madam," replied Cydnon, laughing, "you ask of them a great deal, because to speak frankly, you know so much, that I don't know how you manage to hide it, nor how you might teach it to us." "I assure you," said Sapho, "I know so little that if all women wished to use the time they now spend doing nothing, they would know a thousand times more than I."

"What the beautiful Sapho says is so well said, though not absolutely true with regard to her," said Phaon, "that I can't refrain from praising her. There is room for reproaching almost all women for wasting the most precious thing in the world, for wasting the many hours they could spend more agreeably than they do." "In my case," said Phylire, "I don't know how ladies could find the time to learn anything even if they wanted to, because I barely have time to go to the temple. I have a friend who takes so long to dress each day that she never goes out until the sun sets." "Until I took a trip to the country with her, I always believed," continued Amithone, "that to have the time to do all she does, Sapho must not sleep at all. But I was disabused of that notion—she simply uses her time so well that she has leisure to do a thousand things I don't. She finds time for enough sleep to look fresh and rested, for her eyes to look serene, and to dress as charmingly as anyone."

"She finds the time," I added, "to read, to write, to muse, to walk, to order her affairs, and to enjoy her friends, and all that without ever seeming pressed or anxious." "I wish she would teach me her secret," said the beautiful Athys, "because if I knew it, I think I would resolve to learn more than I do." "But before obliging her to give up such a secret," replied Erinne, " I think everyone here should consider well whether women generally should know more than they do."

"As for that question," replied Sapho, "I think it is easy to resolve; for I confess that (since today I am not as angry as I was a few days ago), although I continue to be the declared enemy of women who play the learned lady, nevertheless, I condemn the opposite extreme and am often shocked to see so many women of quality so grossly ignorant that, in my view, they dishonor our sex. Really," she added, "the reason it is so difficult for women to be knowledgeable in a seemly manner comes not from what a woman knows, but from what others don't know: it is doubtless being an exception that makes it hard to be different from others without exposing oneself to censure. Truly, I know nothing more insulting to our sex than to say we need know nothing. If that were true," added Sapho, "then women should also be forbidden to speak and should not be taught to write. Because if women ought to write and speak, then they should learn all those things that enlarge the mind, form judgment, and teach them to speak and write well.

"Seriously," she continued, "is there anything more bizarre than how we ordinarily educate women? We purport to want them to be neither flirts nor charmers, yet we encourage them to learn precisely what pertains to coquetry, but without allowing them any knowledge that would protect their virtue or occupy their minds. In effect, all the admonitions made to women in their childhood—you're not neat enough, you're not dressing well enough, you're not working hard enough at your dancing and singing lessons—don't they prove what I've been saying? How bizarre is it that a woman can dance respectably for only five or six years of her life, but we spend ten or twelve teaching her how to dance, something that she can do for only five or six? Yet this same person must exercise good judgment till her dying day and speak until her last breath, but we teach women nothing to help them speak agreeably or act appropriately.

"Just look how some women spend their lives—you would think they were forbidden reason and good sense, that they were put on earth merely to sleep, to be pregnant, to be beautiful—to do nothing and to speak only foolishness. I am sure there is not one of us here who doesn't know someone who fits that description. In my case, I know a woman who sleeps more than twelve hours a day, who employs two or three people to dress her, or rather undress her, since she spends half the time taking off what she has just put on. Then she employs another two or three to prepare her various meals. The rest of her time she spends receiving people to whom she has no idea what to say or going out to visit others who have no idea how to make conversation. Tell me, is this a life well spent?"

"It's true," replied Alcæus, laughing, "that there are many ladies who act like that." "I am not a party to this implied critique," declared Cydnon, "for since I pass practically my entire life in Sapho's company—you can't reproach me." "Ah, Cydnon," said Amithone, "what a satisfying and convincing excuse you have given me for explaining my ignorance." "And I have as much right to it as you," added the fair Athys, "you mustn't forbid me from using it." "If I knew what you knew," replied Erinne, "I wouldn't need an excuse." "As far as I'm concerned," added Phylire, "I can't defend myself because I don't see Sapho often enough to boast that I spend the better part of my time well. I must confess that I sometimes spend entire days when I seem not to have a free moment, yet I can't say I've done anything worthwhile."

"In my view," said Sapho, "the reason women have so little time, generally speaking, is doubtless because nothing is more time consuming than idleness; add to that that they make a great business of every trifle: a misplaced curl takes longer to arrange than doing something both useful and pleasing. You mustn't think," she added, "that I don't want a woman to be neat, to know how to dance and sing—on the contrary, I want her to have all these amusing accomplishments. But to tell the truth, I want her to take as much care in adorning her mind as her body. She should take a middle road between the extremes of knowledge and ignorance, a road that prevents her from acting indecorously whether from excessive conceit or wearisome stupidity." "I assure you," replied Amithone, "that road is hard to find." "If anyone can teach the way," added Phaon, "it is perhaps only Sapho." "In my case," continued Phylire, "I would be most obliged if she would say precisely what a woman ought to know."

"Without doubt it is difficult," answered Sapho, "to give a general rule for what you ask because there is such a diversity of minds—any universal law would be unjust. Yet this is essential: although I want women to know more than they ordinarily do, I don't want them ever to act or talk in a learned, pedantic fashion. I want it said of a person of my sex that she knows many things but boasts of none, that she has an enlightened mind, that she reads great works with sensitivity, that she speaks well and writes correctly, that she knows the world; but I don't want it said that she is a learned lady, because the woman I describe and the learned lady are completely different and don't resemble one another in the least. It isn't that a lady who is not called learned may not know many things, more things perhaps than she who is branded with that terrible name, but the woman I describe knows how to use her mind, she knows how to hide her wit cleverly, not display it tastelessly." "What you say is so clearly laid out," said Nicanor, "that the difference is easy to understand." "But as far as I can see," said Phylire, "you are saying that there are things one shouldn't know, or at any rate, shouldn't let on that one knows." "Absolutely true," replied Sapho, "there are certain kinds of knowledge women ought not to pursue and others they may, but they ought not to admit what they know—though they can certainly allow the world to speculate!" "But what good is it to know what you dare not show that you know?" replied Phylire. "It enables women to understand what those more learned than they have to say and to speak to the point without sounding like a book talking, but rather as if they know things naturally, without effort," replied Sapho. "And there are so many delightful things to know that need not be secret: a woman may know languages, she may confess to having read Homer, Hesiod, and the excellent works of the illustrious Aristaeus[12] without seeming a pedant; she can even offer her opinion in a modest way, without being aggressive, so that without transgressing what is appropriate for her sex, she can let it be known that she is a woman of wit, knowledge, and judgment.

"One can, indeed one must, know all that is necessary to write correctly because, in my view, it is intolerable for women to wish to speak well but write badly. The privilege they imagine themselves to have in this regard is shameful to the entire sex—if they understood it, they would be morti-fied." "It's true," said Nicanor, "there is so little syntax and their spelling is so bizarre that most ladies seem to write in order not to be understood." "Nevertheless," Sapho added laughing, "these same ladies who shamelessly commit gross errors in their writing and who lose all their wit the moment they begin to write, will spend entire days mocking some poor foreigner who mistakes one word for another. It is much stranger that a woman of wit makes a multitude of errors in writing her own native language than that a Scythian can't speak Greek." "Alas," said Phylire, laughing, "I hear myself in what you say." "You speak so correctly," I replied, "that I can't believe it is possible that you don't write well also." "I wish to believe that Phylire writes as well as she speaks," said Sapho, "but after all, it is true that there are women who speak well but write badly, and it's their own fault." "But I want to know how that happens," said the beautiful Athys. "That happens,"

---

12. Aristeas of Proconnesus, writer of an epic called the *Arimaspeia*, is referred to by Longinus in *On the Sublime*, X, in his discussion of Sappho.

replied Sapho, "because most women don't like to read, or because they don't apply themselves when they read. Nor do they reflect at all on what they have read so that, although they may have read over and over again the very words they write, they write them all backwards and mix up letters and create such confusion that one can't make heads or tails of what they write unless one is accustomed to their idiosyncrasies." "What you say is so true," said Erinne. "Yesterday I visited one of my friends who had just returned from the country, and I had to take back to her all the letters she had written me so that she could read them to me."

"Judge, then," continued Sapho, "whether I am wrong in wishing that women loved to read and that they read with diligence. Nevertheless, there are women who would seem to have wit naturally, without ever reading much. The strangest thing though is that women who have wit and intelligence would rather be horribly bored when they are alone than to accustom themselves to reading, to find exactly the sort of company they would like by choosing an amusing book, or a serious one, as suits their mood. There is no doubt that reading broadens the mind and forms the judgment more quickly and better than conversation alone. Conversation only gives us a speaker's first thoughts, which are often chaotic and which she may condemn fifteen minutes later. But reading gives us the perfected effort of the minds of those who write the books we read, so even if we read merely for our own pleasure, something remains to adorn and illuminate the mind of the reader and keep her from the gross ignorance that can so shock others who are incapable of such errors." "As for me," said Alcæus, "I know one of these obstinate, ignorant natures who, though she knows nothing, never gives anyone else a chance to talk. She was talking to a foreign visitor who was at her house telling of his travels, and she let it be known that she believed the Caspian Sea was bigger than the Aegean, the Black Sea bigger than the Caspian, and that the Aegean Sea was smaller than all other seas." "What I want principally to teach women," continued Sapho, "is not to say too much about what they know well, and not to speak ever of what they know nothing at all about. And to speak reasonably, I would have them be neither too learned nor too ignorant, but manage better those advantages with which Nature has endowed them. As I have already said, I would have them take as much care to adorn their minds as their persons."

"But I ask you again," said Phylire, "how do we find the time to read and to be educated?" "I demand only the time ladies waste doing nothing, or doing useless things," replied Sapho. "That would be plenty of time to learn enough, even to learn so much that you might need to conceal your learning. Don't imagine that I want this woman I have introduced to you to be an incessant reader who never talks; on the contrary, I want her to read only to learn to speak well; were it impossible both to read and converse, I would advise the latter to a lady. But since they are not at all incompatible and since there are hundreds of agreeable things a woman can learn without transgressing the modesty appropriate to her sex, providing she use them well, I wish with all my heart that women were not so lazy and that I myself had profited from the advice I offer others."

"Ah, Madam," cried Phaon, "you take modesty too far! You ought to be content that people dare not say to you what they think of you without wishing to say of yourself what no one thinks, not even you." "It's true," added Nicanor, "that the beautiful Sapho is very unjust to her own merit." "She is so just to that of others," continued Athys, "that it is strange that she is not so just to her own." "She has something even better," replied Cydnon. "Others do her justice even if she denies it to herself, and though she hides what she can, nevertheless her merit is known throughout Greece." "You endow Fame with wings too weak," continued Phaon, smiling, "because I assure you that the name of Sapho is known the world over."

"Mercy," interrupted this admirable young woman, blushing, "never speak of me in my presence—I can't stand that people think I take pleasure in such extraordinary praise. For truly, speaking sincerely and from the heart, I know that I don't deserve it." "If that were true," replied Athys, "you would be unfortunate in knowing so much and yet remaining ignorant of your own merit." "Seriously," answered Sapho, prettily discomfited, "if you don't give up this habit of praising me, I think I won't see you anymore." "But Madam," we all cried at the same time, Phaon, Nicanor, Alcæus, and I, "don't threaten us with such unhappiness." After that, Sapho continued talking with her usual modesty, saying many agreeable things and knowing so well how to charm the company that we didn't part until evening. Leaving Sapho's, we saw Themistogene walking with Damophile and the next day we learned from one of his friends that he considered her to be far above Sapho. We could hardly be more astonished at his delusion and promised ourselves to avoid him as well as Damophile.

From that day I began to perceive by all the signs that Phaon would fall in love with Sapho if he hadn't already. I also knew from my sister that Sapho esteemed him greatly and that he pleased her more than all the other men she saw. Alcæus, who was Prince Tisander's spy, soon perceived Phaon's budding love and Sapho's inclination and said something to the beautiful Athys, whom he loved. Nicanor, who was Sapho's admirer, also had a slight suspicion, and Amithone and Erinne noticed it just as the others did. As for Sapho, she didn't have to wait for Phaon to tell her he was in love with her to know he was—she was so discerning in these matters, so perceptive, and so sensitive, that she knew precisely what people felt for her—she sometimes recognized their feelings even before they themselves did. However passionate were the feelings of friendship expressed for this charming person, she never took them for love, and however weak such passion was in the hearts of those who could not feel strongly because of their mild temperaments, she never took their feelings for friendship. She knew perfectly how people felt about her. It was impossible to hide one's feelings from Sapho and folly to try, because she knew so well how to distinguish the fond looks of friendship from those of love that she was never mistaken. Not only did she know the nature of everyone's affection for her, but she also understood how those who frequented her house felt about one another. So perfect was her knowledge of the hearts of those she knew, and she knew how to manage them with such skill, that she made rivals live in peace and she was able to increase or diminish the affection felt for her as she deemed best. The latter wasn't easy to do since she was so charming that it wasn't easy to love her less, but she so managed it that her admirers rarely said more than she wanted to hear.

Sapho was as I have represented her and thus soon knew that Phaon was in love with her, but she knew without being offended, and she sensed in her own heart such sweet stirrings that she recognized immediately that if she was to defend herself from Phaon, she had better start straight away. She resolved to conquer her own feelings, but she could not resolve to do what she could to keep Phaon from loving her. Instead, she contented herself by resolving never to answer his affection with her own. Nevertheless, since Cydnon was entirely in her confidence, they had a conversation about Phaon's love that I must recount to you so that you will know better Sapho's greatness of soul.

One evening when my sister was with her, the two of them were leaning on a balcony that opened onto the sea and Cydnon could see by moonlight several ships heading for Mytilene. Smiling, she began to speak: "I hope these ships I see are not those of Prince Thrasibule bringing Tisander back to us, because the prince is so worthy that for his peace of mind I hope he does not return to this place where he will be even more unhappy than he was when he left." "I don't see that much has changed since he left," replied Sapho. "My esteem for him is the same as it has always been, and my heart still finds it impossible to love him." "If that were all," answered Cydnon, "he would be only as unhappy as he was before and no more, but I know very well that something has changed." "But what has happened that makes you speak as you do?" asked Sapho. "Since you want me to tell you, I will," replied

Cydnon, laughing. "Phaon has arrived in Mytilene." "You are so unkind," responded Sapho blushing. "I should never be surprised by your cruelty— I never know how to defend myself and I always find myself trapped." "I promise you," replied Cydnon, "that there is no malice in what I just said; it is so apparent that Phaon is in love with you that it isn't possible to be around him for even an hour without noticing it. Really, when he is in your presence, one would have to be blind not to see that he loves you, and when he is not with you, one would have to be deaf not to know by his words that he is in love with you. He speaks of you continually, and so ardently, that there is no doubt about his feelings."

"At least no one sees me responding with the same ardor," replied Sapho. "You know so well how to govern all your actions," answered Cydnon, "that one hardly knows what you think. But I know you better than the others, and I am certain that you do not hate Phaon. If Destiny has determined that you should love anyone, you will love Phaon." "As far as I can tell, Cydnon," she answered, smiling, "you pretend to have stolen my art of reading others' feelings simply by conjecture and of divining the future from the present. But in my opinion you deceive yourself in presuming so. It is true that Phaon imagined I was a learned lady when he met me, and saw me figured in Damophile when he saw her, and he was agreeably surprised to find that I didn't resemble her. And if you want me to speak frankly, I know very well that if he doesn't love me already, he has at least some inclination to love me. But no matter. I have no intention of returning his love. Right conduct not only forbids illicit passion, it forbids even the most innocent love, and it must be followed so as not to expose oneself to scandal. But I believe strongly that it is possible to love innocently."

"I believe it is not impossible," replied Cydnon, "but truly, seeing into the hearts of most men, it is a little dangerous to become involved with them." "It is so dangerous," added Sapho, "that I must say that since I have begun to frequent the world, I haven't met even two men I believe capable of an attachment of the sort I imagine. To speak to you as to myself, although decorum would have women never love anyone, a rule rightly established because of the painful consequences love so often brings when lodged in coarse minds and in hearts full of vulgar, brutal, worldly feelings, I nevertheless say positively that it is unjust. I believe, furthermore, that without straying from true feeling and unassailable virtue, you may distinguish among those you meet and share an innocent affection with a person of your own choosing. The gods never do anything in vain; they did not endow our souls with a disposition to love more powerful in worthy hearts than in others for no reason. But, Cydnon, the difficulty is in governing that affection, in choosing well its object, and in conducting yourself so discreetly that you are above reproach. But of this I am sure: I believe there is nothing sweeter than to be loved by the person you love. Of course I condemn love's excesses, but I don't condemn the passion that causes them—and besides, to tell the truth, love's excesses come about from the temperaments of those in love, not from love itself. I confess that whoever has never known that inexpressible something that redoubles the delights of love and gives a certain sweetness to suffering cannot know how far joy can reach. Women who take pleasure in being loved without loving satisfy only their own vanity. I know there are a thousand pure and innocent delights in mutual love. The agreeable exchange of thoughts, of secret thoughts between two people in love, is an indescribable delight. Judging love by our friendship, I assure you, my dear Cydnon, that I take greater joy in talking to you unreservedly about what I think than in the most magnificent festivities."

"But so you experience fully that pleasure," replied Cydnon, laughing, "I insist that you tell me your innermost thoughts. Confess sincerely that if you believe you have found in Phaon all you could desire to prompt such affection as you imagine, you will be hard put to defend yourself against his love. Take your confidence as far as you can, and tell me exactly the nature of your affection and how you imagine it." "Ah Cydnon," she said, "you ask a great deal; nevertheless, since I can never refuse you anything, I shall tell you what you want to know. To start with the last question, I tell you I don't feel at all like those who talk of love as something that can't be innocent unless you intend to marry, because I assure you that my delicacy of mind and imagination, and the idea I have of this passion, is such that I don't find marital love pure or noble enough. If I discovered in my heart merely the desire to marry, I should blush as if I had committed a crime. I would reproach myself and consider such a thing unworthy of me and be more ashamed than other women feel when involved in an illicit affair." "You want to be loved without hope?" replied Cydnon. "I would have him hope to be loved, but I would not have him hope for more than that," said Sapho. "In my view, it is the greatest folly to pledge to love someone unless you intend to love until death. To love otherwise is to expose oneself to passing quickly from love to indifference and from indifference, to hatred and scorn."

"But tell me more precisely how you expect to be loved and how you expect to love." said Cydnon. "I expect to be loved ardently; I expect that I alone should be loved, and I expect to be loved with respect," replied Sapho. "I would have this love be tender and sensitive and make of the smallest things the greatest pleasures. I want a love with the solidity of friendship founded on esteem and inclination. What's more, I want my lover to be faithful and sincere and to take no one into his confidence. I wish him to keep his feelings so locked in his heart that I may glory in being alone in knowing them. I want him to tell me all his secrets and to share all my sorrows; I want my conversation and the sight of me to be his entire felicity and my absence to wound him keenly. I want him never to say anything that might make me suspect his love of weakness, but to say always what will convince me of his ardent passion. Finally, my dear Cydnon, I want a lover without wanting a husband. I want a lover who will content himself with possession of my heart, who will love me until death, because if I don't find a love such as I describe, I don't want love at all."

"But having told me how you wish to be loved," answered Cydnon, "you must tell me how you intend to love." "In telling you the one," replied Sapho, "I have told you the other, because in regards to an innocent love, to speak frankly, there should be no other difference in feeling than what custom has dictated: that the lover be the more yielding, the more solicitous and the more submissive; as for tenderness and trust, they must doubtless be equal. If there is any difference, it should be that the lover must always give proofs of his love and the beloved must content herself with allowing him to guess at hers." "If Phaon is ever fortunate enough to give you such proofs of love and act so that you allow him to divine yours, he will without a doubt be the most envied of men," replied Cydnon. "I very much fear," responded Sapho, "that if he were to deserve such envy, I would deserve pity, for my heart is such that once in love, I would love so tenderly, so strongly, that it would be hard to repay my love with interest. Nevertheless, I am persuaded that to be happy in love, you must believe that you are loved as much as you love: otherwise, you are ashamed of your own weakness and of the disdain and lack of passion in the other. That's why, Cydnon, though I am certain one can love innocently and that Phaon is amiable and has some inclination to love me, I can't help but be resolved to do all I can not to love him."

At the very moment Sapho was saying these things to my sister, Madam, Phaon was talking with me very confidentially—we were then inseparable— and that evening we were walking on a terrace at the end of which was a balustrade that overlooked the sea one crossed to go to Sicily. After we had strolled for some time, he leaned against it and fell into a reverie so profound that I knew he no longer remembered I was there. I've already told you how I had noticed many things that made me know he was in love with Sapho, although I said nothing to him, and I knew full well that he was thinking more of her than of me. But to tease him mercilessly, I joined him at the balustrade and said, "Since you are looking out across the sea toward Sicily, I imagine you must be dreaming of that beautiful fool you loved there." "Cruel friend," he said to me, "don't make fun of my unhappiness; content yourself with having caused it without insulting the wretch whose feelings have long since changed." "What," I said, "you no longer believe it is better to love a witless beauty than a beauty with wit?" "No, Democedes," he said, "I no longer believe it at all; in fact, I am so horrified at the thought that I was capable of loving a fool that I am persuaded that I was a fool myself and that what wit I possess has come to me only since I left Sicily. But my dear friend," he added, "before I reveal to you my heart's secret, you must tell me exactly the nature of your affection for Sapho, because if you are my rival, you cannot be my confidant." "I am without a doubt Sapho's admirer," I replied, "but I have never dared to be her lover." "I am bolder than you," he answered, "because my passion for the admirable Sapho is so strong that I fear I may lose my mind."

"When I wished to take you to meet her," I continued, smiling, "you did not believe it possible that you might fall in love with a learned lady." "But Democedes," he said, "I believed she wasn't learned, that she couldn't possibly know, that she didn't know, the art of charming hearts, but alas, how wrong I was, and how right you were to tell me that to be happy in love, you must first have been miserable! For it's true, in the state I am in, I take greater pleasure when I do nothing more than meet Sapho's eyes than I ever did being loved by my fair fool. I had no trouble winning her esteem, but she often expressed her admiration so inappropriately that now I am amazed I didn't scorn her. She looked upon me favorably, and she looked at me with very beautiful eyes, but they said so little and they understood mine so poorly, that I can't imagine how I found them beautiful. The truth is, Democedes, I am very far from loving the fair fool any longer because now I love the beautiful Sapho. But alas, how difficult it is to tell her I love her and that I wish to be loved."

"But since you possess everything worthy of her esteem," I replied, "why should you not win her affection?" "For more than a week I have looked into her eyes," he told me, "to try to divine my destiny and to know if I am sufficiently in her favor that I might reveal my love to her. But to tell the truth, I can't tell what to think. There are moments when her eyes seem to say something—I don't know what—that is not to my disadvantage, but at others, I think the opposite, that they say nothing good for me. At one moment I believe she perceives my love, but at many others, I think she doesn't want to recognize it or that she simply doesn't perceive it at all. But whatever I say, there isn't one look of hers that doesn't increase my passion. I have never yet been able to meet her eyes without feeling an extraordinary emotion in my heart, which disturbs me, but never fails to inspire in me such indescribable sweetness and delight that I am unable to express it. I can do nothing but look at her when I am near her and all I can remember when we are apart is that she looked at me. Don't be surprised then, dear Democedes, at my reverie; I dream even as I speak, that I am speaking to Sapho.

"My soul is so preoccupied with this admirable young woman that I can think of nothing but her. I do nothing but imagine the pleasure it would be to be loved by someone like her, to be able to claim that I had provoked some weakness in a mind so great as that of the marvelous Sapho, and that I had inspired love in a heart as tender as hers. I imagine all we would say to one another were we in love; I have long conversations with her even when I am alone; I am even bold enough to think that she might write verses that portray my passion. I imagine a thousand pleasures I will perhaps never enjoy and which never fail to give birth to a hundred thousand different delights that stir my heart and trouble it strangely. Without a doubt, I find the beautiful Sapho civil, sweet, and obliging to me, but for all that, she reveals nothing and I have never been able to make her show me anything she has written."

"This admirable young woman is so modest," I replied, "that you shouldn't be surprised that she refuses you because you haven't known her long enough to be so privileged. But you have this advantage: until now she has never even been suspected of love even though everyone knows she has a passionate soul."

After that, Madam, we retired without even noticing that the moon was in an eclipse, but as we retired, we met Themistogene with five or six erudite astrologers whom he was taking to Damophile's to debate the eclipse before her. We learned later that they spent most of the night at her house, speaking about the earth's interposing itself between the moon and the sun and many other similar things. The fair and gallant company that regularly gathered at Sapho's and was there as usual amused itself talking of this adventure. Cynegire, at whose house Sapho lived, knew well her wisdom and discretion, so Sapho had people to her room even when Cynegire didn't care to see anyone. Amithone, Erinne, Athys, Cydnon, Nicanor, Phaon, Alcæus, and I were all with her and we made amusing conversation about the follies taking place at Damophile's. Ordinarily, Sapho didn't like us to ridicule others in her presence and didn't care for that sort of mockery, but it was she who first made fun of Damophile in order to make it known how far she was from such behavior. Sapho painted a diverting portrait of a learned, convoluted conversation that amused the whole company extremely, and Cydnon said,

"At least we can take some comfort from Damophile's foolish conversation: it makes ours the more amusing because of this agreeable portrait Sapho has just drawn."

"I wish she would be so good as to describe all the other sorts of fantastical conversations to be found in the world," continued Phaon. "It's true," added Athys, "there are conversations amusing to recount if Sapho wanted to bother noticing such impertinence." "That's too much work," replied Sapho, "it would be quicker and much more fun if each of us were to complain of the most boring conversation he or she has endured." "I'm ready," said Erinne. "I accept the challenge because yesterday I made a family visit that so oppressed me that I thought I would die of boredom. Imagine: I found myself in the midst of ten or twelve women who spoke of nothing but their trivial domestic cares and the faults of their slaves and the virtues and vices of their children, and there was one woman among them who went on for more than an hour repeating syllable by syllable the first prattling of her three-year-old son. Judge for yourself if I hadn't a miserable time of it." "I promise you," replied Nicanor, "that I was no better off than you; I found myself engaged with a bevy of ladies—you can easily guess who—who spent the entire day talking only of their clothes, good or bad, lying continually about how much they cost: some claimed theirs cost more than they really did out of vanity, others claimed theirs cost much less than they did in order to appear clever. So I spent the whole day talking of things so low and foolish that I am still suffering from it."

"In my case," replied the beautiful Athys, "two weeks ago I found myself with several ladies who, though they possessed some wit, importuned me strangely. To tell you the truth, these ladies are professional flirts,[13] each of whom was involved in at least one affair, affairs that occupied them so completely that they could think of nothing but stratagems for stealing away someone else's admirer. Even if you are not involved in their intrigues, you find yourself so caught up with them that you either embarrass yourself or embarrass them. When I was with them, I heard them talking continually without understanding a thing they said. There was one on my right who was saying to the person next to her that she knew from a good source that so and so had broken up with so and so, that a certain *she* was back together with a certain *he*. Then the woman on my left spoke with feeling to a lady near her saying the most incredibly foolish things you've ever heard. 'Really,' she said, upset, 'she ought not to brag about stealing my admirer—she only

---

13. The French is *femmes galantes de profession. Galant(e)*, as noted above, has a range of meanings from gallant to flirtatious to courteous and polite.

succeeded because I had already rejected him; but if I should wish to, I could call him back and do it so well she wouldn't have a chance.' Elsewhere I heard someone talking about a dinner party given for her and saying affectedly and emphatically how awful it had been, as if she believed she could diminish the beauty of the woman who had given the party for her by saying her lover wasn't grand enough. I promise you, never in my life have I been as impatient as I was that day."

"As for me," replied Cydnon, "if I had been in your place, I would have found some way to amuse myself at the expense of the bores, but even I couldn't find a way to escape being bored two or three days ago when I was with a man and a woman who talk about only two things: the genealogies of every family in Mytilene and how much their houses are worth. For except in very particular circumstances, what possible amusement can there be in hearing all day long that Xenocrates is the son of Tryphon, Clidemes is descended from Xenophanes, Xenophanes is the descendent of Tyrtaeus, and on and on? What amusement can there be in hearing about some house in which you have no interest whatsoever, where you've never been and never will go in your life—that it was built by so and so, bought by a certain someone, exchanged by someone else, and at present is owned by someone you don't even know?"

"Doubtless that's disagreeable," Alcæus replied, "but not so disagreeable as finding oneself with people who've been involved in some irksome affair and can talk of nothing else. What happened to me not long ago was that I found myself with a sea captain who claimed that Pittacus ought to compensate him for a ship he had lost. He kept me three hours not only telling me all the reasons he claimed he should be compensated, but what had been said to him and what he had responded. To make me understand the loss he suffered, he began telling me in detail how much the ship had cost, and who built it; then he named all the parts of the boat one after the other— which I certainly didn't need to know—so I would understand that it was one of the best, and the most expensive, and what an injustice they would be committing if they didn't compensate him."

"It's true," said Amithone, "one feels persecuted by people like that. But truly, what gives me a headache are these serious, solemn conversations in which no enjoyment is permitted—they overwhelm you. People speak in a monotone, they never laugh—it's as if you were in church."

"Such conversations are doubtless tiresome," continued Phaon, "but there is another sort, quite the opposite, that annoys me strangely. One day I was in Syracuse with five or six women and two or three men who got it into their heads that to make good conversation, you must laugh continually.

Whenever these people are together they do nothing but laugh at whatever is said, even if it isn't very amusing. They make such a racket that often they end up not being able to hear one another speak, and so they laugh simply because the others are laughing, for no other reason. They laugh so whole-heartedly you would think they knew what they were laughing about. But what is strange is that their laughter is sometimes contagious and you can't keep from catching the disease—one day I found myself with these people who are eternally laughing and they made me laugh so hard I laughed almost to tears without knowing why I was laughing. To tell the truth, fifteen minutes later I was so ashamed that I went from joy to melancholy in an instant."

"Although it is certainly foolish to laugh for no reason," replied Sapho, "I wouldn't be as embarrassed to find myself in that sort of company as I would be to find myself with people whose entire conversation is nothing but long, pathetic speeches that bore one terribly. I know a woman who knows every tragedy that has ever taken place and who spends entire days bemoaning life's misfortunes and recounting dreadful things in a sad, faint voice as if she were paid to bewail the whole world's misery."

"I know yet another house where the conversation is impossible," continued Erinne, "because they talk of nothing but neighborhood gossip so that people from the court who end up there by chance can't understand a thing. In my case, one day I heard twenty people named whom I didn't know, and a hundred obscure little intrigues repeated which I could care less about, and news of which should never have left the street where they happened. And what's more, they were so unexciting in themselves that I was bored to tears."

"It is agony to find oneself in a large company where each one has a secret, particularly if you don't, and you have nothing better to do than to listen to the murmur of others whispering together" said Nicanor. "If they were real secrets," replied Sapho, "I could bear it, but often what is said with such mystery is nothing but nonsense." "I know people," added Alcæus, "who in my view are tiresome although also somehow amusing: they imagine they always have important news to tell and never speak except about battles, or a chief city under siege, or a major revolution in the world. You would think, listening to them, that the gods transform the face of the universe to furnish them with conversation because they never say a word except about such significant, important things. They won't hear anything else with the result that, unless you are prepared to discuss political principles and know your history precisely, no matter what it is, you can't talk with them about it. But people who care nothing about what's going on in the world and want to know nothing but their own particular affairs are still more troublesome. You see them always busy, as if they had a million things to do, when in fact they have nothing better to do than meddle in others' business so they can go from house to house retailing what they know like public spies who tell one person news of another whenever the occasion presents itself and get nothing for it—they don't want to know things to know them; they only want to know so they can pass them on to others."

"As for me," said Cydnon, "I am embarrassed to hear you all talking like this. If it isn't good to talk about science and learning, like Damophile; and if it's boring to hear about a family's little worries; if it isn't seemly to talk much about clothes and imprudent to talk about intrigue and flirtations; if it's dull to talk only of genealogies and uncouth to talk about property sold or exchanged; if it is even forbidden to speak of one's own affairs and if serious conversation is not amusing; if it is foolish to laugh too often and without reason and if sad and amazing tales don't please; if neighborhood gossip bores those who aren't involved and conversations about trivial things whispered in your ear are annoying; if people who talk of nothing but important issues are in the wrong and if those who seek continually to know people's private affairs aren't right either, what ought we to talk about? What makes for good, elegant conversation?"

"It should be about all those things we have censured," replied Sapho amiably, with a smile, "but formed by good judgment. Although everyone we have spoken about has behaved indecorously, I vigorously maintain that we can talk of nothing else but what they talk about, and that we can converse of such things agreeably even if they haven't." "I understand very well the truth of what Sapho says," replied Phaon, "even if at first it might not seem so. I am fully persuaded that all sorts of things can come up appropriately in conversation—I except nothing." "Don't imagine," added Sapho, "that there are things that can never be spoken—there are certain encounters where it is perfectly appropriate to speak of things that would be ridiculous on some other occasion."

"As for me," said Amithone, "I declare that I want there to be rules for conversation as there are for so many other things." "The principal rule," replied Sapho, "is never to say anything that shocks good judgment." "But again, I want to know what you think conversation should be?" added Nicanor.

"In general," said Sapho, "I think conversation should be about everyday life rather than higher things, but I believe, nevertheless, that anything may come up in conversation. Conversation should be free and appropriate to the time, place, and company. The great secret is always to speak worthily of trifling things and simply of grand things, to speak delightfully of *galanterie*[14] and to speak without affectation or undue gravity. And though conversation should always be both natural and reasonable, I wouldn't hesitate to say that there are occasions when even the various learned sciences may enter the conversation gracefully and when agreeable foolishness can also find a place as long as it is charming and clever. Be assured I'm not lying, you can speak well and reasonably, yet there is nothing you can't say in conversation as long as you use wit and judgment, as long as you consider well where you are and to whom you speak and who *you* are yourself. Although judgment is absolutely necessary to ensure that you don't say anything that isn't apropos, conversation ought to appear so free and easy that it seems as if you are not holding back your thoughts, as if you say whatever comes to mind without seeming to have any plan to speak of one thing rather than another. Nothing is more ridiculous than people who have certain subjects about which they say marvelous things, but outside those, talk nothing but nonsense. Thus I want us never to say only what we ought, but always to speak of what we do in fact know. If we behave as I have suggested, women will be neither unseemly pedants nor impossibly ignorant and everyone will say simply what he or she ought to say to make good conversation.

"What makes conversation pleasant and amusing is a certain witty *politesse* that banishes bitter mockery completely and all that might offend modesty, even slightly. I want us to be so practiced in the art of conversation that we may recount a love affair to the most censorious of women and make a trifle agreeable to the solemn and serious; that we can speak appropriately of learning and science to the ignorant if forced to and tune our wits to whatever is being spoken about and whoever is present. But in addition to all I have just said, I want there to be a certain *joie de vivre*[15] that reigns, but that has nothing at all in common with those fools who laugh eternally and make much of nothing, a *joie de vivre* that inspires in the hearts of the whole company a disposition to be amused by everything and bored by nothing. I want people to talk of both great and small things as long as they speak well; there should be no constraint, and yet people should talk only of what is appropriate."

"Without troubling you to speak further about conversation and its laws, one can only admire yours, and do as you do, to merit the admiration of all the world," added Phaon. "No one will disagree with me when I say that

---

14. See note 9 above.

15. Literally "joy in living"; the expression means zest for life, to take pleasure in or relish, enjoyment.

you have never been heard to say anything but what is agreeable, charming, and appropriate and that no one, whoever it may be, knows as well as you the art of pleasing, charming, and amusing." "I very much wish all you said were true," she replied, blushing, "but to show you that I am not as you say I am, and that I am often wrong, I tell you frankly that I have just said too much. Instead of saying what I think about the art of conversation, I should be content to say of all of you what you have just said about me." After that, everyone took a turn protesting Sapho's modesty. We praised her so generously that we feared we might make her angry. What followed was such a delightful and enjoyable conversation that it lasted almost until evening when our company finally separated.

Phaon fell even further in love that day than he had been before and lingered another half an hour at Sapho's to talk. He found himself so driven by his passion that he resolved not to leave without giving her some sign, so that when we had left, he asked her pardon for troubling her longer. "But Madam," he said, "when I see you only in company, I don't see you enough. I am certainly a party to all the beautiful things you say; I hear them and admire them with more pleasure than anyone; but above all, I take even more pleasure when I am alone listening to you. Three or four words heard only by me would content me more, would transport me—if you would say them—more than all the beautiful things you have said today, however much they have charmed me."

"If you were in love with me," she replied, smiling, "what you have just said would be both agreeable and gallantly put, but since I only have friends and don't wish for a lover at all, I must reproach you for not having profited from what I dared to say today concerning the art of conversation. For you are malapropos—what would be quite charming if it were said to someone you love is not at all so when you say it merely to a friend."

"But Madam," he added, "are you sure that what I have just said would be very charming if it were said to the one I love?" "Since you know that I am sincere," she replied, "you must believe what I have said." "Believe, then, Madam," he replied, gazing at her, "that what I have just said is the most charming thing I have ever said, because far from saying it to a mere friend, I say it to the person with whom I am desperately in love, but whom I love so respectfully it ought not to offend."

"If it were permitted to declare love without offending propriety," replied Sapho, smiling, "I think I would not be offended by the declaration you have just made so gallantly; but as that is not the case, Phaon, I have no choice except to be angry or not to believe you." "Oh, Madam," cried Phaon, "I don't hesitate between these two choices—I would rather be badly treated than not believed." "Since you have never seen me angry," she replied gallantly, "you don't know what you're asking; that is why, since I know what is good for you better than you do, I will not be angry, but I won't believe you at all." "Mercy, Madam," he said to her, "be angry and believe me, if it's true that you can't believe I love you without being angry. I tell you yet again, I would rather see you angry than disbelieving." "Since we have no control over belief," she replied, "we can't believe as we will; therefore, when I said that I had a choice either to believe you or to be angry, I think I spoke improperly and it would be better to tell you that, since it is impossible for me to believe you, it is impossible for me to be angry." "But Madam," he said, "why won't you believe I love you? Are you not beautiful enough and charming enough to have made me fall in love? Haven't I enough intelligence to know your worth? Is my soul so hard, my heart so incapable of tender passion? Have my eyes never met yours and said what my lips have just spoken? Does the admirable Sapho find the unhappy Phaon so unworthy of bearing her chains that she prefers to believe him unfeeling than to permit him to wear them? Madam, whatever you say to me, I will never believe that someone who perceives so much doesn't know that I adore you."

"I assure you," replied Sapho, gallantly, "that far from knowing it, I am persuaded you do not know it yourself. That is why, in order to give you all the help I can, I give you three months to consider carefully your feelings without saying anything to me, and if after that you still believe you love me, I will judge whether I should believe you or be angry. In the meantime, let us live, I beg you, as we have been used to living."

Sapho expressed herself with such discretion and grace that Phaon couldn't help but think that she did believe he loved her and considered himself happy to have said so much without being treated too badly. And since Sapho did not want him to make her angry, she sent him away. She had chosen her words so carefully that if her beautiful eyes had not a little betrayed her heart's secret, Phaon would have garnered nothing from them. But since she in fact felt a passionate inclination for him, some of her looks assured Phaon that his passion did not displease her, so he left quite satisfied and very much in love.

It was not the same for Sapho. My sister told me that she was very distressed. It wasn't that she didn't feel all she might feel for Phaon, but that she knew her tender heart and feared being in love. She feared it all the more because she sensed in her soul so favorable a disposition toward this lover that she realized her reason was weaker than her inclination. She knew how much she ought to fear her feelings when she noticed that everything

Alcæus said to her in praise of Tisander irritated her more than it had before; she also realized that when Phaon wasn't there, she was less amused by her friends than she had been before she had made his acquaintance. When in a humor to write poetry, she couldn't keep herself from thinking of Phaon, though she didn't yet write for him. He so occupied her memory, her heart, and her imagination, that she often said his name to someone else so that Cydnon mockingly attacked her by asking what progress she was making in Phaon's heart and he in hers. At first Sapho responded in kind by laughing as much as Cydnon; then she responded more seriously; next she stopped responding at all; and in the end she responded with chagrin so that Cydnon stopped teasing her for sometime. But after a month's silence on this subject, she, who had not wanted to respond to my sister any longer when she spoke of Phaon, was the first to speak, though it's true that their conversation was the result of an adventure I'm going to tell you about.

You should know that a certain painter named Leon had arrived in Mytilene and that all Sapho's friends pressed her to let him paint her so that they might have her portrait. She agreed in a very particular way: it was settled that all her women friends would have a portrait of her, and her men friends as well, so that her lovers could only profit from the occasion by trying hard to pass merely as friends. The whole affair took place in so delightful a way that she couldn't get out of it. One day Nicanor, Phaon, Alcæus, and I were at her house when Amithone, Erinne, Athys, and Cydnon were there too, and we were pestering Cynegire about making Sapho give us all her portrait, each of us declaring our right to one. Nicanor and Phaon, although they were Sapho's suitors, spoke as if they were only her friends, and Alcæus, as the confidant of Tisander for whom he principally wanted the portrait, affected only friendship, so I was the only one who actually said what I thought. You could tell easily that Nicanor was angry that he could not have Sapho's portrait without Phaon's having one as well, and Phaon was not at all pleased that Nicanor would have a portrait that he believed only he deserved. You could also tell that Alcæus would have preferred neither of them to have one because he said, laughing, that if Sapho listened to him, she would give her portrait only to him. "In fact," he said, "since I am a great wit and everyone knows my heart was engaged long before I had the honor of laying eyes on you, you can give me your portrait without fear of any dangerous consequence. And speaking as the great wit I pretend to be on this occasion, I tell you that propriety permits you to give it to me since I am the lover of a beautiful lady everyone knows: the beautiful Sapho can give me her portrait without a second thought. But as for Nicanor and

Phaon, I say that since no one knows their secrets, it is to be feared perhaps that though Sapho may think she is giving her portrait only to her friends, she may well be giving it to her lovers."

As soon as Alcæus had spoken, Phaon and Nicanor looked at one another as if wondering what to answer. They needn't have bothered because I spoke up for myself, since everyone seemed to be speaking self-interestedly, and replied to Alcæus: "I can't speak for Nicanor or Phaon, but I declare boldly that since I am simply Cydnon's brother, I may ask for the charming Sapho's picture." "And I declare," added Phaon, "that Alcæus doesn't deserve to have it however worthy he is, because since he is in love, Sapho's portrait will be placed beneath another if he is fortunate enough to have one of his mistress." "Since he will perhaps never have one," replied Athys, blushing, "I don't think that is a good reason why Sapho should refuse him, for in my opinion, he could never have a mistress he could put above her." "However that may be," said Phaon, "I think the beautiful Sapho should only give her picture to friends who are not at all in love, but Alcæus is in love." "But if that is the case," added Nicanor, "who will assure the beautiful Sapho that you are worthy of her portrait since you have just arrived in Mytilene and you stayed so long in Sicily that you may well have a mistress there? My situation is quite different because I haven't left Lesbos at all in a very long time, and I regularly visit no one but the beautiful Sapho, and I'm not involved in any sort of affair that would make me unworthy of her portrait."

"Since I have returned to Mytilene," replied Phaon, "with no pressing reason for doing so, it is to be believed that I wasn't in love while in Sicily as you have suggested. But without seeking further to justify myself, I consent to the admirable Sapho refusing me her picture if she believes that I was in love in Sicily." "As for me," said Amithone, "if you take my word, only I should have Sapho's portrait." "If you followed my advice," said Erinne, "you would send it all over the world." "As long as I get it," replied Athys, "she can do as she pleases." "Provided my brother gets one," replied Cydnon, "I agree that she can refuse Alcæus, Nicanor, and Phaon." "Truly," said Sapho, "I think to do the right thing I shouldn't give my portrait to anyone." "No, no," Cynegire said to her, "you shall not decide. So as not to disappoint anyone, you will give your portrait to all your friends without exception, because if you except someone, you will perhaps do that person more favor than were you to give it."

Although Cynegire's words ought to have pleased the entire company, Nicanor and Phaon continued to argue for some time. But in the end, in order to have Sapho's portrait, they had to make peace since the one couldn't have it without the other having it as well. Since Sapho knew what Phaon had told her, she determined that she shouldn't let him win too easily and that it was fitting she should make things particularly difficult for him. She took up Nicanor's point and said to Phaon that perhaps he had twenty portraits that he would put above hers and there ensued between them a completely charming conversation. Though he seemed to have no other reason to protest that he wasn't in love in Sicily than to obtain her portrait, nevertheless, he made a thousand protestations of love that she well understood though she didn't admit it. She embarrassed him cruelly in fact, and he found himself thwarted when he wanted to respond. "You believe you've said enough," she said to him, "when you have sworn that you weren't at all in love in Sicily, but that isn't enough: you must also swear that you haven't been in love in Mytilene." "But Madam," he said to her, struggling to avoid embarrassment, "since I see only you, I think I need say nothing more than what I have said, for you must know my life since coming here as well as I do." "I have such amiable friends," she replied, smiling, "that even without going elsewhere it would not be impossible for you to have fallen in love here in this very room." "Don't deny your portrait to Phaon for my sake," replied Amithone, laughing, "because I declare that he isn't at all in love with me." "I can say the same," added Erinne.

"I can even say more than that," continued Athys, "because I can say he loves neither Cydnon nor me." "Were that so," said Alcæus, "still it is not enough to oblige Sapho to give her portrait to Phaon because he may be in love with her. So if she wants to give her portrait to her friends, and doesn't want to give it to her lovers, he must swear that he doesn't love her at all, if he wants her picture." "As for that," replied Sapho, "I don't require it because I am sure he harbors nothing in his heart for me that would prevent my giving him my portrait." "Since that is so," said Cynegire, without giving Phaon time to answer, "let the painter begin his work tomorrow." And so Leon began to sketch the portrait of Sapho the next day. And by this means, Sapho's men friends and lovers, rivals and women friends were all rewarded. And Phaon took some pleasure in knowing Sapho knew of his love, but that she didn't let that stop her from allowing him to have her picture. But these agreeable thoughts were troubled by another that followed a moment later—he couldn't think without pain that Nicanor was as favored as he. Nevertheless, since he didn't know if his rival had revealed his passion for Sapho, he presumed to hope not. He knew perfectly well that Alcæus was Prince Tisander's confidant, but everyone had assured him that he had nothing to fear from that quarter, so the portrait that Tisander would doubtless have hardly worried him.

On her side, given the violent inclination she felt for Phaon, Sapho wasn't sorry that chance had given her an innocent way to give him her picture. He acted so courteously with her that she had no choice but to be easy about obliging him: he had stayed within the terms she had laid out, had never since spoken of his passion, but nevertheless, he found many ways of letting her know it, and he knew very well the art of speaking of love without speaking of it—no one knew how so well as he. Though he did nothing but what he could turn to his advantage when he was with Sapho, he appeared to behave without any affectation. If chance put him next to her, he let her know so clearly the joy he felt that she judged his love rightly from the satisfaction he expressed. If on the contrary his misfortune separated them, he showed his wretchedness so cleverly that Sapho could accurately judge his love by his sorrow, which she couldn't help but notice was great. If he spoke to her without being overheard, he spoke with an air so clever, so gallant, so altogether passionate, even though he never spoke openly of his passion, that he couldn't help but benefit. If he looked at her, his eyes revealed all the tenderness of his love, and I noticed hundreds of times, by a delightful rosiness that appeared on Sapho's countenance, that she found Phaon's looks told her all too much. Even though she wished not to respond, her beautiful eyes sometimes spoke despite herself, and not sternly. In fact, while the painting was being done, and while we watched the painter work, the admirable Sapho was so deep in reverie that she would fix her eyes on Phaon's face without seeing it. But what was strange was that she later told my sister that when she looked at Phaon without seeing him, he was all the while the object of the very reverie that made her blind. Nevertheless, since her thoughts of him were not to his disadvantage, her eyes looked dreamy and loving, but completely without affectation, so much so that Nicanor could not suffer his rival to be looked upon so favorably. He told her she didn't look enough at the painter for him to be able to get a good likeness and that if she continued to daydream as she had been, he would paint her looking too melancholy.

Nicanor had hardly said these words when Sapho began to blush because she knew quite well what sentiment prompted him to speak. Yet she knew so well how to respond to him suitably that she persuaded the entire group that it was impossible to be painted without being caught in such reveries, which came, according to her, from the difficulty of remaining still. As for Phaon, he was so irritated by Nicanor that he disagreed with him time and again throughout the rest of the day: if Nicanor said that he believed the painter had succeeded happily in catching Sapho's eyes, Phaon would say that he did not agree and that it seemed to him he had caught better the line of her lips. If Nicanor found the portrait too pale, Phaon would say the contrary, that it was too lively. If the painter had attended to the divided opinions of these two rivals, he would have made a very bad portrait of their mistress. But what was most amusing about Phaon's contradictory humor was that after the rough sketch was done, Nicanor said that it didn't do justice to Sapho because she was a thousand times more beautiful than her portrait, and Phaon dared not contradict him because he couldn't without seeming to say that the portrait was more beautiful than its subject. He didn't contradict Nicanor, but you could see from his eyes that it vexed him not to and he even wished to praise the painter whom Nicanor blamed. Phaon wanted to oppose Nicanor, so he said it was no surprise that it was impossible to make a portrait that resembled the admirable Sapho since she had a fire in her eyes that was inimitable: he was convinced that Leon had accomplished what no other painter could. Since the entire company knew what motivated the two of them to disagree, we took some pleasure in their bickering, and since their differences were not really bitter because they both respected Sapho too much to quarrel in her presence, we were admirably entertained. Sapho herself was not much aggrieved to receive a new sign of Phaon's love in his obstinate determination to contradict Nicanor.

At the end of the conversation, we had yet another amusement: we wanted to know from the painter the precise day he expected to finish the portrait and when he would begin those of the other ladies who wished to give their pictures to Sapho as she had given hers to them. He said he could begin neither the next day, nor the day after, because he was busy doing a large portrait of Damophile on which he had much work yet to do. "But why is there more work to do on hers than on mine?" Sapho asked him. "Because Madam," he said, "she wants me to represent her at a large table at which there are many books, pencils, a lyre, mathematical instruments, and many other sorts of things that are signs of her learning. I think she even wants to be dressed as a Muse, so it won't be easy or quick to sketch her portrait." "Enough, Leon," cried Sapho laughing. "Dress me as they dress the shepherdess Oenone[16] so that my portrait doesn't resemble Damophile's in the least." And so the painter, who had sketched her clothed as a nymph, promised her he would clothe her as a shepherdess to make her happy, and then Sapho made innocent fun of the portrait of Damophile, which passed the day agreeably.

16. Oenone, a nymph of Mount Ida in Greece, loved Paris, son of Priam, who exposed him at birth after the oracle said Paris would cause the fall of Troy. Raised among the shepherds, Paris deserted Oenone following the Judgment of Paris in which he awarded the golden apple inscribed "For the fairest" to Aphrodite in return for the most beautiful woman in the world, Helen of Troy.

But Madam, to shorten my narrative as much as I can, you should know that the portrait, once done, was one of the most beautiful in the world. The shepherdess's costume so suited Sapho's face and expression that nothing could have been more charming than this picture. So the copies that she was to give to her friends having been made, and the portraits of Amithone, Athys, Erinne, and Cydnon having been done, Sapho gave hers to her women friends and they gave theirs to her. But as for Nicanor, Phaon, Alcæus, and I, who were her men friends, we could only thank her for this present that was so precious to us. But we thanked her in different ways, for Nicanor, who dared not speak to her of his passion, could only thank her as a friend and dared not speak as her lover, but Phaon thanked her with such passionate words, though he never pronounced the word love, that Sapho couldn't hear his compliments as mere friendship. As for Alcæus, who wished always to serve Prince Tisander well, he said in a low voice that he was not alone in thanking her for her precious generosity and that one day she would be thanked by a person who valued it even more than he. So I was the only one who showed my gratitude with friendly feeling and an ordinary acknowledgement.

Phaon, being always the most assiduous in his visits, stayed last at her house on the day he thanked her for her picture. Looking at the original of the portrait which was still lying on the table, he began to speak of Damophile's extravagance in wanting to have herself painted with all the trappings of learning and of what Sapho had said when she asked the painter to clothe her as the shepherdess Oenone. "Madam," he said, "at least you are assured you will never suffer her fate even though you wear her costume, because if you ever love someone, it would not be possible for your lover to abandon you." "When the goddesses begin to hold a new contest every day over who is most beautiful, that will be when I am of a humor to love a shepherd as did Oenone," replied Sapho smiling, "so he will never be their judge and his constancy will not be put to the test as was that of Oenone's shepherd." "Ah, Madam," he cried, "had that happy shepherd Phaon's heart, he would not be susceptible to the promises of the fairest of the three goddesses when she showed him the same beauty that made Paris unfaithful. To me, Madam, you are the only beauty in all the world. In fact, nothing is delightful to me but you; you possess my heart so completely that you defend its gate from all other ladies on earth. I even think you drive out my friends. The power of my feeling for you makes me insensible to everyone else."

"Stop," said Sapho interrupting him, "think carefully about what you are saying because if you are to me more than a friend, you must return my portrait to me so I won't be faulted for having given it to a lover." "No, no, Madam," he said, "it is not possible for me to return your picture—I would lose my life before I would let it be torn from my hands. I waited until I had it to tell you that I suffer so from never telling you what I think, that I can no longer obey you. Even if you become angry and banish me, and treat me terribly, I must tell you that I love you every time I can say so privately—I beg you not to hate me. I cannot live without loving you, and I cannot love you without speaking; I cannot say I love you without begging you to be just to the greatness and loyalty of my passion and to prefer it to the worth and merit of my rivals. I can tell, Madam, that you are about to say many angry things to me," he added, "but I am resolved to endure it all with profound respect, but nevertheless not to obey you when you forbid me to tell you I love you."

"This is something new," replied Sapho, "to profess your disobedience before even having received the command you expect to disobey." "Whatever happens, Madam, things have arrived at such a point that I can no longer live as I have lived. You absolutely must permit me to love you or command me to die." "Since I don't pretend to any right to govern either your love or your hate," she replied, "I have nothing either to forbid or command. And since you are too much a gentleman to desire death, I will give you no commandment that would oblige you to seek it. But I will tell you that when I am persuaded that I can suffer you to love me without offending propriety, I must in fairness tell you that I will be the most difficult person in the world to please. I seek so many different things in the person by whom I wish to be loved that it will be difficult to find them in one person alone. That is why it would be better not to be engaged in an affection that won't last, however passionate it is at present, because all men have in their hearts a natural propensity toward inconstancy so that, were I a thousand times more charming than I am, it would be imprudent of me to believe I might find one wholly faithful man. If I were to wish for a lover, I would wish for one over whom neither time nor absence had any power. The lover I wish for is not to be found in this world; that is why I advise you to content yourself with being counted as my friend because if I suffered you to love me, you would perhaps be very unhappy or you wouldn't remain my lover for long."

"Ah, Madam," said Phaon, "I will love you all my life no matter what you do; what remains to be known is only if you will allow me to tell you I love you and if I may hope to be loved?" "Since there is nothing wrong with being curious," replied Sapho, "I would not be sorry to know how you would love. That is why, without promising anything, I agree only to your speaking of the feelings your passion inspires in you because, until this hour,

I have known only men with vulgar notions of this passion that I conceive of in a purer and more delicate fashion." "All I can tell you, Madam," he said, "is that there is no feeling you could not inspire in me since you are the absolute mistress of my heart, my mind, and my will. Yes, Madam, you have only to make known to me the manner in which you wish to be loved and you will find in me blind obedience to all your wishes. Feeling as I do, I maintain that perfect love is to want all that one's beloved wants."

Without amusing myself by recounting the entire conversation to you, Madam, I will make a long story short: without according anything to Phaon, Sapho did not leave him in despair, and Phaon, without having obtained anything from Sapho, left her with his heart filled with hope. Though her lips had said nothing really favorable to him, they had said nothing really angry either, and yet her eyes had spoken to him so sweetly that he could not think himself unhappy in the circumstance in which he found himself. Nevertheless, he would have been even happier had he been able to hear a conversation that Sapho had the next day with my sister because, as I have already said, this person who had sworn to my sister that she did not appreciate the war Cydnon waged against her over Phaon, spoke first and spoke to her with such trust that she opened her entire heart to her. "Ah, Cydnon," she said, "I wish ill to Democedes for having introduced me to Phaon! It would seem that he is determined to love me, and I may not have the will to refuse his affection. I sense already that my reason only weakly defends my heart and that my heart is so little my own that if Phaon's is not more his, I am most unfortunate. Really, I don't know what I am thinking to admit my weakness to you. Sometimes I think I do it so that you would condemn me and I would repent, but at others I think the contrary, that I do it so that you will encourage me. Nevertheless, I am not in despair at feeling all I feel in my soul: it is not that I don't find some sweetness in my anxiety, but that my reason, not yet entirely possessed, sees the peril to which I am exposed in having engaged myself to suffer Phaon's affection. Truly, it is almost impossible that he should love me as I wish to be loved and for me not to love him more than I would wish."

"It is true," responded Cydnon, "that if you wish to be loved but never to marry, it will be difficult for Phaon to obey you." "But he must face that," Sapho replied, "if he wishes me to love him: he must content himself with the hope of being loved without expecting anything more."

Such were Sapho's feelings, Madam. Nevertheless, although she had a very great inclination for Phaon, she fought against it for somewhat longer by not suffering him to say to her that he loved her and by not permitting him to hope to be loved. Yet she behaved so courteously with him that there finally came a point when she no longer kept secret from him what she had written or was writing. One day, he and I, finding ourselves alone with her, pressed her to have the goodness to show us all the verse she had written, and finally she agreed to show us some. But since her modesty would not suffer her to read her verse aloud to us, she offered it to us and went into her study to write two or three pressing letters she had to answer from some of her relations. But Madam, I regret not being in a position to show you what we saw, not only because of the pleasure you would have in seeing the most beautiful things in the world, but even more because you would better understand the bizarre and surprising effect of our delightful reading on Phaon's heart. But since I do not have these admirable verses, I must try some other way to make you understand. Imagine then, Madam, that after Sapho had placed in our hands several magnificent copybooks in which the verse she wished to show us was written and had gone into her study, Phaon took it upon himself to open one straight away and to read an elegy that Sapho had written for my sister some time ago during her absence. But Madam, he found there such touching sentiments, so tender and passionate, that his heart melted reading them and he stopped over and over to admire them. Finally, having forced himself to read other verses, he read a song that she had written at my sister's return in which there were in few words all the transports of joy that the most ardent love can cause in a loving heart when reunited with a loved one after being apart.

Then Phaon read another little piece that Sapho had done to express the joy one feels at encountering unexpectedly a person one loves. This joy was depicted with such power that one could see what she described. She represented admirably the sweet looks and beating heart that such a pleasant surprise provokes, from the expressive face to her agitated spirits to all the motions of a passionate soul. But Madam, after Phaon had finished reading these verses aloud, he read them again to himself and then looked at them attentively without saying anything and without turning to read the others. To satisfy my curiosity, I recalled him from his reverie, which I thought was caused simply by admiration, and forced him to read some verses that Sapho had written about jealousy in the friendship between Athys and Amithone. Madam, this jealousy had the true character of love; all the violence this tyrannical passion could inspire in the heart was expressed there so marvelously—it was impossible to express it any better. I did no more than sing Sapho's praises continually as Phaon read her verse, but he read it with a melancholy attention that began to surprise me. Nevertheless, so as not to lose time asking him the cause of his melancholy, I began to read certain verses that Sapho had written during a week's journey she had made alone with my sister to her very pleasant house in the country. In these verses, she represented the happiness of two people in love and proved thereby that they had need of no one but themselves to live happily. Then she described their tender affection, their sincerity with one another, their pleasures, their walks, their conversations about the sweetness of friendship, and a thousand other such things. Madam, all the delights the most delicate love could invent were described in these verses, though they may have exaggerated the sweetness of friendship. Never in my life have I read anything so beautiful, so charming, and so passionate.

However beautiful these verses, I didn't finish reading them because Phaon, who had listened to them with extraordinary attention, interrupted me brusquely with these words: "Ah, Democedes," he said, "Sapho is the most admirable person in the world, but I am the most unhappy lover on earth and you are the least perceptive man of all men." "As for the first thing you have said," I replied, "I agree; but I don't understand at all the second or the third: why are you the most unhappy lover on earth and why am I the least perceptive man of all men?" "I am the most unhappy lover on earth," he replied, "because without a doubt, Sapho loves someone, and you are the least perceptive of men because you assured me that she loved no one." "Tell me further, on what grounds do you base your opinion that she is in love?" "I base it," he replied, "on what I have just read, Democedes, for it is absolutely impossible to write of things so tenderly and passionately without having felt them." As Phaon said this, his spirit strangely agitated, Sapho returned to us thinking she would receive a thousand praises from Phaon. But Madam, had I not praised her, she would not have been praised as she deserved because Phaon's spirit was so agitated by this jealousy without an object that had taken root in his heart that he could barely speak. After I had given him some time to recover while I praised Sapho, the very jealousy that had caused his silence made him break it with a view toward trying to discover in the eyes of this admirable young woman if his suspicions were well founded.

"What I have just seen, Madam," he said to her, "is so surprising that you must not find it strange that I cannot declare my admiration." "Since you have known me long enough to know that I don't care for people to praise me in my presence, you will do me a great favor if you say nothing more about what you have just read." "Ah, Madam," he said impetuously, "I must say one more thing to you: I ask you boldly, what do you do with all the tenderness that fills your heart, because there are things so touching in what I have read that at the least your heart must be open to passion." "I owe it to the merit of my women friends," Sapho answered, blushing, "for the friendship I feel for them is so tender that if I had as much wit as I do friendship, I would write even more tenderly than I have." Phaon watched Sapho attentively and didn't fail to notice her blush, but he did not guess that her blush was favorable to him and that Sapho had only changed color because she reproached herself in secret for her too tender feelings for him. On the contrary, he interpreted her blush in quite another manner and was certain that Sapho had a passion in her soul for one of his rivals, and this belief so afflicted his spirit that instead of continuing to make merry war against her in order to try to discover her true feelings, as had been his plan, he suddenly became quiet. If people hadn't arrived just then, his silence would have doubtless seemed strange to the beautiful Sapho, but since Nicanor, Phylire, and some other ladies came in, Sapho hastily hid the verses that she had shown us and didn't notice Phaon's silence. But realizing how troubled his spirit was, he made a sign to me that we should leave, and while Sapho greeted the ladies, we left without saying good-bye to her and went for a walk along the seashore.

We hadn't been there long, Madam, when Phaon began to complain to me: "How could you be the brother of Sapho's best friend and not know whom she loves? For it is certainly true," he added, "it is undeniably the case, that she is in love or that she has been in love, because you cannot know how to convey so delicately the tender passions she expresses without having experienced them. Truly," he continued, "there are certain strange, tender, and passionate feelings in what Sapho showed us that friendship alone could not have taught her—she must be in love, or she must have been in love."

"I have known Sapho from the cradle, known everyone who has ever seen her and everyone whom she sees now," I said to him, "and what's more, I am the brother of the young woman who knows all the secrets of her heart. Though Sapho has been loved by almost everyone who has ever met her, I protest that she has never yet been in love. But at the same time, I am certain she has a great capacity for love, and if this passion were once to possess her heart, she would love with more tenderness, more constancy, than anyone has ever loved."

"Ah, Democedes," he said to me, "either you deceive me or you deceive yourself; Sapho loves someone, she must, to have written what I saw today."

"But had you seen a poem Sapho wrote for a victory Pittacus won," I said, seeking to calm his mind, "you would see that she writes as well of war as she does of love, and you would take from that some good for yourself and for her because, since she writes admirably of war without ever having fought a battle, so she may also speak admirably of love without having been in love."

"Democedes, it's not the same thing. Simply reading Homer could teach her how to speak of war, but Love alone could teach her how to speak of love." "I don't understand your reasoning," I replied, "but I know that Homer speaks of love as well as war and Sapho could have learned how to speak of love from him."

"Democedes," he said with a strange melancholy, "what you say so astonishes me that there are moments when I almost wish to believe that you had taught Sapho to write as tenderly as she does, because if you understood with any sensibility, you would say what I say, and maintain strongly what I maintain, that you cannot write well of love without having been in love. If you compare the sentiments of love in Homer to those in Sapho's verse, you would find a great difference: the great Homer represented the friendship of Patroclus and Achilles better than the love of Achilles and Briseis. And if Sapho had only spoken of the grand feelings love inspires and only of what violent passions make one say, I would say like you that she could not have understood them and written of them without being in love. But Democedes, that is not the case. The feelings that persuade me Sapho knows love or has known love are certain delicate, tender, and passionate feelings that one cannot guess or even believe are in others' hearts if one does not have them in one's own.

"In fact, my own experience proves what I am saying," he added, "because when I returned to Mytilene, I tell you frankly that I knew love only in a way so gross that I would not have recognized the beauty of Sapho's verse: the fair fool I loved in Sicily had only inspired in me feelings in proportion to her mind. So Democedes, it is the love I have for Sapho that has taught me to know what, undeniably, she has in her heart. There is nothing more to know except who—who is this happy one who was able to be so loved by the admirable Sapho, or who is he still, to have inspired in her feelings so tender? That is why, my dear Democedes," he added, "if it isn't you who taught Sapho to love, help me to discover whom she loves so that I can do one of two things, either be cured or be rid of my rival."

"Seriously," I said to him once more, "I do not believe Sapho has been in love because she loves neither Prince Tisander nor Nicanor, and what's more, these two lovers who have observed her closely have never suspected her of love. That is why I do not think you are right to trouble your mind with this bizarre, ill-founded jealousy."

"I don't know how, Democedes, you can think what you say you do because I have seen with my own eyes, and heard with my own ears, a thousand things that make me know Sapho knows love or has known love. I could not believe it more strongly than I do. That is why, if it is true that you don't love this fair one and you have no hidden interest in saying what you say,

I beseech you to use all your ingenuity to discover what I wish to know. Cydnon loves you so tenderly, and you are so clever," he added, flattering me, "that, if you wish, you will learn quickly who the happy one is who reigns in Sapho's heart and inspires such tender feelings. Oh, gods," he said, "how worthy of envy would I be if the admirable Sapho thought of me as I see she thinks of another! What terrifies me," he added without giving me a chance to say anything, "is that there should be a man to have had the glory of having inspired love in this marvelous young woman, but not the joy of having their intercourse discovered—how could one hide such passionate felicity?" After that he said a hundred more things that made me see equally well his love and his jealousy so that I promised him that I would try to find out what he wished to know as if I had been as persuaded of Sapho's love of another as he was. Nevertheless, I was sure that I knew very well that Sapho had never been in love and was not now in love and that what enabled her to write so tenderly was her naturally passionate soul. To satisfy my friend, however, I didn't hesitate to question my sister as if I suspected otherwise, but in vain, because she did not tell me that Sapho had begun to love Phaon, and she could say without lying that Sapho had loved no one before having met Phaon. So, when I said to Phaon that I could discover nothing, he was strangely troubled and has told me since that there were days when he believed Sapho loved me and that the friendship that she claimed to have for my sister was merely to hide what she felt for me. Nevertheless, since he saw nothing else that confirmed him in this belief, he dared not avow it, but still he could not restrain himself so far that I did not perceive that his soul was on the rack.

This bizarre jealousy tormented him so cruelly that everyone, not just I, noticed that something was troubling him. Sapho herself asked him the reason for his changed humor, but he didn't dare tell her and he didn't dare talk to me any more because of the suspicions his fantasy had raised, so he led a melancholy life. What's more, every day was a fresh torment since it wasn't possible to avoid often hearing Sapho's verses recited and he couldn't hear them without strange feelings. He watched not only all the men who frequented Sapho's house, but even those who hardly ever went there. Jealousy has never tormented anyone more than it did Phaon, though he had no cause for jealousy and Sapho loved only him of all her lovers. Finally, not knowing what to do or think to dispel his suspicions, chagrined at the uselessness of his anxiety, and sensing he could no longer hide his fears, he resolved to spend some time in the country to try to cure himself of both his jealousy and his love, and he resolved to do so without even letting me know, so his departure was quite a surprise. Sapho complained as well that he had departed without saying good-bye to her, and so did his other women friends who kept on asking me the reason.

Meanwhile, by chance, business called me to the country and I left two days after Phaon. Hardly had I left Mytilene when Prince Thrasibule landed there to leave Prince Tisander, whom the invincible Cyrus, then still calling himself Artamène, had wounded in several places. The two of them had fallen into the sea and engaged in combat so formidable and extraordinary that Prince Thrasibule, then called the famous Pirate, wished to save the life of his implacable enemy as if he had been a cherished friend. But to go on, Madam, Prince Tisander returned to Mytilene with his heart sicker from the wounds inflicted by Sapho's beautiful eyes than from those inflicted by the illustrious Artamène, who honored that admirable young woman with several visits that so pleased her that she spoke of nothing but him for some time.

Prince Thrasibule having departed with Artamène, I returned to Mytilene, and Phaon, knowing of the return of his rival Tisander, returned as well. But he returned driven by his jealousy and imagining that perhaps Sapho loved Prince Tisander even though no one said so. When he returned, everyone scolded him for his hurried departure, but he was so little able to bear their mockery that they felt constrained to stop. Sapho saw how melancholy he was, so she hardly spoke to him. Persuaded that his sadness was the result of his love for her, the admirable Sapho pitied him and wished to speak of it to him no more. Meanwhile, Alcæus never ceased speaking on behalf of Prince Tisander, day in and day out, but no matter what he said, Sapho said nothing in Tisander's favor. Things could not have been otherwise because in truth Sapho already loved Phaon tenderly, or at least was much disposed to love him. Nevertheless, Tisander's merit and nobility obliged her to receive him well: she refused him her heart most courteously, but she did not refuse him her esteem. And Sapho had a quarrel to pick with Alcæus because she knew he had passed on the portrait she had given him to Prince Tisander, but he knew so well how to excuse himself that she pardoned him in her heart even though she continued to tell him she would never forgive him.

Sapho had enemies, women who told Tisander when they saw him that she had given her picture to so many people only so that she could give it to Phaon without impropriety. People spoke of this new admirer of Sapho's so highly that jealousy was joined with love to torment Tisander. But what made his jealousy even greater was that the prince found Phaon so admirable that he couldn't help but think that Phaon was loved, so that he was hardly less jealous than Phaon. Nor was Nicanor exempt—he was jealous of both the man who was loved and the one who was not. He feared that Tisander's nobility and condition would finally carry the day and Sapho would make the prince happy, but he feared even more that Phaon's extraordinary merit would make him miserable.

In the meantime, this beloved lover who made his rivals so unhappy was even more unhappy himself because he often read Sapho's tender, passionate verses and his anxiety and jealousy redoubled by the minute. He couldn't read them without applying all that was most loving in them to this imagined lover who made him so jealous: he envied his happiness and imagined what must be his joy in reading of such tender feelings. "Alas," he would sometimes say, "what happiness would be mine if, in reading such passionate expressions, I might hope to be the beloved of a person who knows so well how to love and whose tender heart gives to her beloved a thousand delights that no one else knows and that the greatest beauties in the world do not know how to give? After all, eyes are soon accustomed to beauty and what one has seen day after day no longer possesses the charm of the new. But the tenderness of a loving, passionate heart is an inexhaustible source of new delights that are born from moment to moment and that make love grow with time even though time ordinarily diminishes love. But all Sapho's tenderness is for another, which makes me unfortunate and makes one of my rivals a happy man. The beautiful, touching things that she writes, which would give me so much joy were I her beloved, torment me horribly because I am not he." Being in such distress, not knowing what to do, and no longer trusting in me, Phaon thought that if he did all in his power to see everything Sapho had written, he could perhaps discover what he wished to know and find out at last who it was who, he imagined, had inspired such tender feelings in the woman he loved.

From that moment on he did nothing but ask everyone for Sapho's verses and press her when they were alone to show them to him. What's more, when he was at her house, he looked carefully on her table to see if he could find a forgotten copybook. Finally, pretending that he was curious to see such beautiful verses, he resolved to try to bribe one of her women to steal them if she could from her mistress's study, but no matter what he did, he could not succeed. Nevertheless, Madam, chance let him see what he would perhaps never have seen otherwise had an accident not happened that disordered and afflicted his mind. You should know then, Madam, that as soon as Prince Tisander was healed, he came to see Sapho, and he was accompanied by such a crowd that the visit didn't afford him the chance to make his usual pleas to the fair Sapho. The visit passed in talk of indifferent things: Cynegire, with whom Sapho lived, had redecorated her house since the prince's departure and so they talked of all that she had done and principally of Sapho's study, which had been painted. The prince demanded to see it and the fair one, not daring to refuse him, opened the door and the entire company entered. So Phaon, entering like the others, noticed that Sapho had blushed on seeing the copybooks on her table and hurried to slip them immediately into a half-opened drawer that she could not shut completely because of her haste and because Tisander had led her toward the windows on the pretext of the beautiful view, but really to speak with her for a moment alone. Phaon, his mind filled as always by his bizarre jealousy, had a strange desire to see the copybooks that Sapho had hidden so diligently and that had made her blush. So without wasting any time, while Tisander spoke with Sapho and the others looked at the paintings in her study, he softly pulled out the drawer, took the copybooks Sapho had put inside, and shut the drawer as it had been before.

Not being able to stand being there any longer, he went back into the other room to see if he should keep or return what he had taken. But he had hardly opened the copybooks when he saw there was verse written in them, verse written in Sapho's hand, and judging that he would not have time to read them there uninterruptedly, and judging by the first word he saw that they merited the curiosity he had to see them, he left Sapho's and began to walk alone in a garden open to everyone at the edge of the sea. He had hardly entered when he opened the copybooks without delay and read the verses that I am going to show you, for I had them just as he did, without the name of him for whom they were written, as you will see by the copy I am going to show you.

At these words, Democedes gave a copybook to the Queen of Pontus who read aloud the following verses:

> Great is my pain, extreme my delight:
> I dream away the day and sleep not at night;
> I know it not if love this be,
> But very like love it seems to me.
> One object only fills my mind,
> In no other object can I pleasure find.
> If to love is to have a wounded soul,
> I feel all I should feel, in part or whole.
> Certain rays shoot through my being,
> I find the sun's brilliance less pleasing;
> My own flame cannot be seen as yet,
> But its heat even so me sore besets.
> When I see ***** my soul is replete,

If I see him not, my heart feels pain,
Still I pay no heed to my defeat,
My vanquisher perhaps, and not in vain.
All he says seems to me filled with charm,
All he doesn't say is nothing to me,
My heart, have you lain down your arms?
I know nothing, but I believe it to be.

After the Queen of Pontus had read these verses, she returned them to Democedes and exhorted him to tell her immediately what effect they had on the mind and spirit of Phaon.

I later learned from Phaon himself, Democedes replied, continuing his story, that these verses troubled his heart so that he could not reread them for at least a quarter of an hour even though he wished to desperately. For though he thought that Sapho was in love, or had been in love, he had not believed it so strongly that he wasn't extremely surprised to see it written in her own hand. But finally, having reread the verses and found them even more loving the second time than the first, he was transported by fury and thought he would tear up the copybook and throw it into the sea. As he was ready to do it, the idea came to mind not to, but to search carefully for what name among Sapho's acquaintances would fit the meter of the verses where the lover's name ought to be. Despite his despair, he judged that if Sapho had given her lover any other name but the lover's own name, she would have written it in her poem; therefore, he concluded reasonably that the name that was not filled in, but that would fit the meter, was the name of him for whom they were written. So he looked again at the four lines with the blank,

When I see ***** my soul is replete,
If I see him not, my heart feels pain,
Still I pay no heed to my defeat,
My vanquisher perhaps, and not in vain.

He began to look at what name would fit into the line, but he found to his embarrassment that Tisander was too long by a syllable, Nicanor as well, and mine was even longer than Tisander's. Phaon found that Alcæus was of the length needed to complete the line, but his love for the beautiful Athys was so well known by everyone, and everyone knew that he was Tisander's confidant, that this discovery made no impression on him. He went on searching out the names of all the persons of quality who visited Sapho without finding any that would fill out the line because they were all too long. He even considered the names of those who did not visit her without ever dreaming that his name was the missing name. Because he knew that Sapho had written the verses that first made him jealous before knowing him, it never occurred to him to think, had he only known, that these verses that so distressed him ought to have given him much joy. In fact, he was so far from such a feeling that he didn't even think to see if his own name would fit, and at that moment, happily, I arrived.

What was wonderful, Madam, was that Phaon had treated me somewhat coldly since the onset of his bizarre jealousy and had never quite believed me completely when I swore to him I had no private intercourse with Sapho. Assured that I had none by the fact that my name would not fit the blank left in the line and feeling himself overcome by his sorrow, he greeted me with his accustomed openness and took me fully into his confidence as if I had played no part in his jealousy. In fact, he no sooner saw me than he came up and embraced me and said, as if we had both been in the wrong, "We must forget the past, my dear Democedes, and renew our friendship because finally, today, I know plainly that I was wrong to believe it was you who taught Sapho to know all the delights of love. But I will prove to you that you were wrong to believe she has not known love." "Is it possible," I said to him, "that you have such clear proof that I could not doubt it?" "You will see soon enough," he said to me, "when you read the verses I give you that I stole from her without her knowing. You know her style, her hand, and perhaps you will guess easily the name of him for whom they were written. Because my spirit is strangely troubled, I am not in a state to guess the name myself." After that I began to read Sapho's verses, but in reading them I saw immediately that Phaon's name fit perfectly into the uncompleted line. I remembered so many things that had made me believe Sapho did not hate Phaon that I no longer doubted that the lines were written for him. I believed it all the more because I could find no other man of quality among Sapho's acquaintance, past or present, whose name would fit, except Alcæus for whom the verses could not have been written. So I comforted him, saying, "I admit I don't find it difficult to discover the missing name; I am sure that the beautiful Sapho intended the following:

> When I see Phaon my soul is replete,
> If I see him not, my heart feels pain,
> Still I pay no heed to my defeat,
> My vanquisher perhaps, and not in vain.

"Ah, Democedes," he cried, "my name fits the line, but the line doesn't fit me. I don't know how you managed to think of trying to see if my name was the right length—as for me, I didn't remember my own name. But this fortuitous fit does not console me because all these beautiful, tender, loving, and passionate things written by the fair Sapho were written before I knew her, so we must believe that the verses I have shown you were made for him who had the good fortune to have taught her all the tenderness of love by making her love him." "For my part," I replied, "I don't know if I am wrong, but it seems to me that the characters written in this copybook do not look as if they have been here long. I am the most mistaken of men if these verses are not made for you, and instead of being the most unhappy lover in the world, you are not the happiest lover on earth."

"What?" he said. "Do you believe that Sapho could love me without my perceiving it? That a man who watches her at all times and observes her every word and move and who does everything in his power to divine her thoughts wouldn't know that she loved him? Ah, Democedes, that isn't possible—it is only too true that these verses were not made for me."

As he said this, we heard the sound of many people talking, and turning, we saw Prince Tisander bearing down upon us, leading Sapho with some of her women friends as well as Nicanor, Alcæus, and several others. I returned the copybook I was holding to Phaon who hastily put it in his pocket. But since Sapho had noticed that Phaon had left her house abruptly, she made war against him by teasing him charmingly for preferring solitude to such amiable company, and he found himself drawn into the promenade the entire company was going to take. Phaon and I followed her even though we really did not want to because he had his sorrow and I had some business to attend to. Finally, we reached the end of a path in the garden that gave onto the sea where we found a boat that we all boarded and that was so crowded we couldn't easily change places. By chance, Phaon found himself very near Tisander and Sapho, so it was easy for him to tell that the poem had not been written for this prince because Sapho didn't respond to a single glance of Tisander's and she acted with a courtesy so cool and unwavering that it was easy to see that love did not unite their hearts. Nevertheless, he was so preoccupied by what was going on in his mind that he took no part in the general conversation. What I had said to him kept coming to mind; he was slightly flattered, but a moment later when he came to think that the loving things Sapho had written were written before he knew her, his jealousy returned. So, passing from hope to fear, he kept his own counsel and conversed with no one and fell into so deep a reverie that he leaned over the boat rail and looked intently at the roiling sea foam that always adorns the prow of vessels and ships as they sail swiftly. Phaon was too dear to Sapho for her not to perceive his melancholy; she took notice and alerted the others. Among them was Tisander, who knew that Phaon was in love with Sapho and that Sapho did not hate Phaon and who observed him with careful attention to try to guess why he was so melancholy. He wished, if possible, to determine if his sadness came about because he was in Sapho's disfavor or if it were simply because he was so much in love. So as Tisander watched him almost as closely as he watched Sapho, without realizing what he was doing and still in his reverie, Phaon took something from his pocket and unfortunately also pulled out the copybook with Sapho's verses. Having fallen almost without making a sound, it slid the length of the boat and landed almost at the feet of Tisander who, having seen it fall, leaned over and picked it up without anyone noticing.

Once he had the verses, Madam, he was almost as preoccupied as Phaon, for believing Phaon was his rival, he feared finding out exactly what he didn't want to know. In the meantime, Cydnon saw clearly that Phaon's preoccupation worried Sapho and began to speak to him and ask the cause, which, as you might imagine, he didn't want to reveal. Since he had nothing but Sapho's verses on his mind, he put his hand in his pocket to make sure they were still there, which he was sure was the case—lovers have a habit of often doing futile things that they wouldn't if their minds weren't preoccupied. Having put his hand in his pocket to be sure that he still had Sapho's copybook, Phaon was surprised by the strange discovery that he no longer had it; nevertheless, he dared neither let his surprise show nor say what he had lost, for if he had, Sapho would have known of the theft he had committed. And so he found himself strangely confused: he didn't know for sure whether he had lost it in the garden or on the boat or even if it had fallen into the sea, but he dared make no lament about his loss out of regard for Sapho, for though he was still filled with jealousy, he was also filled with respect, and the reputation of this admirable young girl was as important to him as was his own peace of mind. What's more, what I had just said to him sometimes put an agreeable doubt in his mind and made him still more cautious, so he contented himself with looking calmly about him without saying what he was looking for. But since he searched very carefully, though he tried to do it unobtrusively, Tisander knew very well that his rival had lost what was dear to his heart and that what he had found would perhaps bring an all too painful resolution of his doubts.

Having finished our maritime excursion, we escorted the ladies home and even accompanied Prince Tisander to his house. The moment he arrived there he went instantly into his study and opened the copybook he had found and read the verses you have read, Madam, which had so distressed his rival. It wasn't hard for him to guess what name should go in the uncompleted line marked with tiny stars, for the moment he read it, he had no doubt that Phaon's name belonged there. He believed that Sapho had given the verses to his rival with her own hand and that they were joined so firmly in their affections that nothing could part them. You may judge, Madam, how this thought vexed him; he has said since that he has never suffered as much and that he spent a sleepless night.

Nor was Phaon at ease. He said such touching things regarding the loss of Sapho's verses and declared so forcefully his fear that this accident would work against him that I realized he was as much in love as could be, for despite his jealousy, he was concerned for Sapho's reputation. But she was even more upset than he. For only think, Madam: this admirable young girl had felt such anxiety when she stuffed her copybook hastily into the drawer where Phaon found it, and she repented so thoroughly of having put her verses where they might be seen, that the moment she returned home she went into her study with the intention of burning them and never again writing such poetry. She was quite surprised and upset when she found they were no longer where she had left them; she didn't trust her memory, but searched high and low in all the places they could possibly be. But finally, doubting no longer that these verses had been stolen, she felt a pain greater than she had ever known. Nevertheless, in this strange confusion of mind, she could find no sweeter hope than that it was Phaon who had taken her poem, even though she was discomfited to think he had seen it. Since she knew nothing of his bizarre jealousy, she imagined that he would know he was its subject, but though she desired it, she couldn't bring herself to hope it was Phaon who had her verses because she had seen how sad he was and therefore didn't suspect him. In addition, she remembered that he had left her house only a moment after Tisander had come into her study, so she didn't think he had had a chance to commit this theft. So, not knowing whom to suspect, she found herself strangely troubled.

For his part, Tisander, being as much a man of honor as could be and seeing by these verses that Sapho loved Phaon and that, what's more, Phaon was worthy of Sapho, and not doubting that his rival had received these verses from his mistress's hands and that they were completely joined in their affections, resolved to conquer his passion. He carried the respect he had for Sapho as far as it could go: though Alcæus was still his confidant, he did not show this marvelous young girl's poem to him. It's true that it took him three days to decide what to do and during that time he did not see Sapho at all.

For her part, Sapho carefully avoided company for fear of hearing talk that might displease her about her poem. It wasn't that she hadn't resolved, if anyone spoke to her about her verses, to say that they were written to no one in particular, but merely out of curiosity to see if it were possible for a woman to speak of love without impropriety, but deep in her heart, since she knew there was a real cause, she was in a strange state of confusion.

Phaon dared not try to see her because he knew full well he could not avoid giving her only too many signs of his guilt, distress, and jealousy. So for three days no one saw Prince Tisander, Sapho, or Phaon, and Nicanor was so hard pressed to find out why two of his rivals and his mistress all remained alone at the same time that he was hardly less troubled than they. But in the end, Tisander made a great effort to conquer his feelings and asked to see Sapho alone on important business. Sapho dared not refuse him, given who he was, and so agreed, but she awaited him strangely troubled by the fear that he came to see her to speak of her verses. It wasn't that she didn't know perfectly well that it was impossible that Tisander had taken them from her study because he had been in her sight the entire time, but she feared someone else had given them to him. The hour having arrived for this meeting, Tisander was at Sapho's without anyone attending him, but instead of greeting her as he ordinarily did, he addressed her with sober and distant courtesy, though with a great deal of respect, which made her understand that he had something unpleasant to say to her. Since there was no one in the room but one of her women, Tisander was immediately at liberty to speak to her, so without losing any time, he said, "I come, Madam, to render to you the greatest mark of love anyone has ever given: returning to you verses Phaon has lost and that you have given him. Anyone else would have avenged himself for your cruelty by showing them to the world. But the respect in which I hold you is so great that, however severe you have been to me, I still fear displeasing you and wish at the least to preserve your esteem, though I cannot win your affection." So saying, Tisander returned to Sapho the copybook with the verses written for his rival, but he handed it to her open so she could see that he had written Phaon's name in the place where it ought to be.

You may judge, Madam, that Sapho did not receive this copybook without blushing; nevertheless, after having collected herself, she undertook at once to do two things: first, to succeed at disengaging Tisander's affections, and second, to persuade him that these verses were not written for Phaon in particular, nor for anyone else. But though she said everything that might be said at such a delicate moment with skill and sensitivity, she only succeeded in half of what she hoped to accomplish. She managed to disengage Tisander from his love, but she couldn't make him believe that the verses were not written for Phaon. She could not even succeed in persuading him that she had not given them to Phaon with her own hand, even though she told the truth when she assured him that Phaon had stolen them. "No, no, Madam," Tisander said to her, "you will not persuade me, for she who has once given her heart may certainly give her poetry." "One may sometimes give one's whole heart," replied Sapho, "without giving anything else. This circumstance that you count as nothing is for me considerable—there is no comparison between having written the poem for Phaon and having given it to him with my own hand. Assuming that I have a strong inclination for him, it would not be strange to admit to myself that which I feel despite myself. Though it were a weakness, it would be no shock to modesty because it would be known only to me. But my lord, in accusing me of having given these verses to Phaon, you tender me so great an insult, and what you think of me is so indefensible, that I am surprised that you haven't shown them to the whole world. Because truly, I would be unworthy of your discretion if I had been so indiscreet as to have given these verses to Phaon. Nonetheless, I won't fail to thank you for having returned them to me and to beseech you to tell me exactly how you came to have them because, since I have no private intercourse with Phaon, I can only know from you."

"Oh, Madam, what you say is outrageous!" replied Tisander. "My actions little merit yours! Nevertheless, since Phaon perhaps dares not tell you how he came to lose these verses that he ought to have guarded so carefully, I will tell you that I saw them fall from his pocket the evening we made our maritime excursion, and I picked them up without knowing that I would find there my death sentence." "Phaon was so sad that evening," she replied, "that it seems to me you ought to be convinced that I did not give him this poem and that he didn't in fact believe that it was written for him because, truly, Sapho's heart is not so easily won that he who wins it should not draw some satisfaction, and ought even to feel some joy, from having won it." "However that may be," said Tisander, "I am certain that Phaon is as loved as I am hated, and if I didn't have more respect for you than any mistreated lover has ever had, being who I am in Mytilene, I would find a way to send Phaon back to Sicily. But I would banish him from this island in vain since I cannot banish him from your heart and because I do not wish to be your tyrant after having so long been your slave. So skillfully have you convinced me in the past that loving me was not within your power," he added, "that I wish you to know frankly that what you have done is against your own interest. But Madam, in acknowledgment of my respect for you, you ought to be sincere and admit to me openly the true state of your soul, just as I have admitted the true state of mine; after that, I will leave you in peace and try to find peace myself."

"My lord," replied Sapho, blushing, "if I were able to give you all my affection, as I give you all my esteem, I would certainly do so in recognition of your generosity. But to speak sincerely, there has always been in my heart so powerful an obstacle to your goal of winning my love that I have never been able to surmount it however hard I have tried. More than that, my lord, don't ask me; since I cannot love you, it hardly concerns you whether I love Phaon or not." "I don't ask you because I am uncertain," he replied, "I have no doubt whatsoever; I ask you so that I may at least have the opportunity to praise you once more in my life." "Enough, my lord," replied Sapho, "don't insist on wanting something both unjust and useless; be content when I tell you that I cannot love you, but that I do not feel for Phaon the same impossibility of feeling some affection." "That is enough, Madam," he said, rising, "to make me the most unhappy of men; nevertheless, since I am resolved to respect you always, I will do all in my power to loosen the bonds that bind me to you without severing them violently. In leaving, let me say I hope you will one day know that if you have given your heart to the most worthy of your lovers,[17] you have not given it to the most loyal or the most in love." After that, Madam, Tisander departed, but with such sadness in his looks that Sapho's heart was somewhat touched, even though she was indifferent to him. But since there were things that touched it even more palpably, she thought more of Phaon than of Tisander. Soon thereafter my sister paid her a visit that made her think anew about them both.

You should know, Madam, that having seen Phaon in such despair, and being very curious myself to know if these verses that wreaked so much havoc were indeed composed for Phaon as I believed they were, I sought out Cydnon, who was not only a dear sister to me, but also a very faithful friend. After making her promise to keep all I said to her a secret, I told her of my friend's jealousy and about the episode of the verses and exhorted her to tell me if they had been written for Phaon. "If they were written for someone," she replied, "they were certainly written for him, but I know nothing about it, Democedes. Sapho has not shown me the poem you have told me about." "Nevertheless," I said to her, "poor Phaon, who believes it was written for someone else, is overcome by such unbearable jealousy and such violent grief that I believe he will die if you do not help me comfort him." "In truth, my brother," she responded, "it will not be easy because, though Sapho has never kept anything secret from me, she has said nothing to me of this incident and I don't see how I can bring it up if she doesn't speak of it to me. It's true," she added, "that I have only seen her for a moment since

17. The French is *honnête homme*; for the range of meanings, see note 1.

our evening sail, so the most I can do is to promise you I will see Sapho and do what I can for Phaon if she gives me any chance of doing so."

After that, I exaggerated to her as much as I could this lover's jealousy so that she would take pity on his unhappiness, but the more I talked, the more I could see she wanted to laugh. Since she knew Sapho's true feelings for Phaon, she found it amusing to think that he was himself the beloved rival that was causing him such pain, and she could barely refrain from laughing. "But cruel sister," I said to her then, "I do not describe my friend's suffering to entertain you; he deserves pity, not laughter." "If I believed he was to be pitied," she replied, "I would not respond as I do, but since I don't see that Phaon has any rivals he ought to fear, I can't help but be amused by his misery. Nothing is more amusing, when one's heart is free, than what even the wisest people do when they are caught up in something of this sort. That is why you must forgive the enjoyment I naturally feel in response to such things, an enjoyment that I am helpless to overcome. But believe me, I will do all I can for Phaon."

As soon as I had gone, Cydnon went to see Sapho and arrived there not fifteen minutes after Tisander had left, so her mind was too full of all that had happened to be able to keep it secret from my sister. She ushered her into her study and gave orders that they were not to be disturbed and then begged her pardon for having kept secret for three days an adventure that had befallen her. "Really my dear Cydnon," Sapho said after having told her what had happened, "it was so cruel—nothing so vexing and painful has ever happened to me in my life. What could be more intolerable than that Tisander has seen such verses? Could there be anything more terrible than to think that Phaon himself has read them? I don't think I can see him—I haven't seen anyone for three days so as to avoid meeting him. Of course, there have been moments when I wished it were he who had found the verses, but I wished it when I thought he didn't have them. But it isn't that way today—I don't know but that I wish a hundred other people had read them rather than Phaon and that he didn't have them in his power: how can I dare see him after this? Should I not fear that, confident in the passion he knows I feel for him, he will speak to me with less respect? Should I not admit as well that he will consider me an easy conquest that brings no glory to him?"

"If you have anything to fear," replied Cydnon, "it has nothing to do with what you have said. To prove my devotion to you," she added, "I must betray a secret my brother confided in me and report that Phaon is the most unhappy and most jealous of men." "He isn't in love with me then," Sapho replied brusquely, blushing. "He is more in love with you than anyone has ever been," replied Cydnon, "but he is so jealous, and jealous for such bizarre reasons, that I don't know how you will be able to cure him." "This is a mystery so baffling I don't understand it at all," responded Sapho. "When I have explained it," Cydnon replied, "you will understand it better, but you will be no less amazed: the day that you showed your poetry to Phaon and Democedes, Phaon found in it such passion that he concluded that you must once have been in love, or that you were still in love, since it was impossible for you to be able to write of feelings so tender without having been in love. With this bizarre fantasy in his head, he has since suffered incredible torment and has done almost nothing but seek his supposed rival whom he believes inspired in you all the tenderness to be found in your verse." "Stop, Cydnon," interrupted Sapho, "tell me sincerely if what you say isn't some sort of joke?" "Not at all," Cydnon answered. "What I am saying is absolutely true—it could not be more true. In effect, the unfortunate Phaon is so preoccupied with this fantasy that after having stolen the verses we've been talking about, instead of applying them to himself and rejoicing in his good fortune, he has done nothing but search through the names of everyone he knows to see which one fits the blank in the line—I tell you, this is so amusing that if it weren't that I see you are upset, I would laugh with all my heart. Seriously, though, I beg you to find a way to cure poor Phaon of his jealousy—my brother tells me he is so miserable that he deserves to be comforted."

"But as far as I can tell," responded Sapho, "Democedes has seen these terrible verses that have caused me so much trouble; after saying a hundred times that, were I to want a lover, I would not want him to have a confidant, I find myself exposed to as many witnesses to my weakness as there are men in Mytilene. It isn't that I doubt Democedes' discretion," she added obligingly, "but after all, Cydnon, admit it, he guesses the truth better than Phaon." "He didn't say so to me," she replied, "but I assured him that these verses were intended for no one unless they were intended for Phaon. Since Democedes is his particular friend, I believed in that way to enlist his discretion and prevent him from inquiring of others what I promised to explain to him." "But Cydnon, what can you possibly tell him that would not be unfavorable to me?" Sapho replied sharply. "Because to tell him that I love Phaon would be terrible; to swear that I don't love him would make him think I love someone else; to insist that I love no one, given the folly Phaon has in his head, would simply increase his jealousy without excusing me. Nevertheless, I would like to find some way to prevent his jealousy, preserve his affections, hide mine from Democedes, and let Phaon alone guess mine."

"For my part," replied Cydnon, "given how my brother spoke of Phaon,

I think it will be difficult to cure him of his jealousy if you do not show him all the tenderness you feel for him." "Ah, Cydnon," replied Sapho, "I would rather he were eternally jealous than show him all my weakness." "You are not worried about preserving his heart," responded Cydnon, "for you know better than I that lasting jealousy destroys love." "Phaon's jealousy is so baseless that I don't believe it will last," Sapho replied. "On the contrary," my sister answered, "it is precisely because it has no foundation that it will be difficult to dispel. If, for example, Phaon were positively jealous of Nicanor, you would simply have to treat him badly and refuse to see him to end Phaon's jealousy, but there is no way of curing him except by letting him think you love him alone and that the verses he read belong to him, since he is jealous because you write with such tender and passionate feeling that he imagines you must love someone else." "Just as I was able to guess his passion for me before he told me of it," she responded, "he should be able to guess the tenderness I feel for him, because if he doesn't, he will never know it."

"But don't you need to say something definite to him," Cydnon said then, "about these verses in which the name is missing?" "Isn't it enough," said Sapho, "that he sees that none of the names of the men who could be in love with me fit, except his, to make him understand that the verses were either written for no one in particular or were written for him?" "Were his imagination not preoccupied," replied Cydnon, "what you say would no doubt be enough; but given his feelings, if guarding Phaon's affection is dear to you, you need to do something more and at least allow my brother to console him in his grief and offer him some hope." "As long as he has no suspicion that I have given my consent," replied Sapho, "Democedes can tell him whatever he wishes to persuade him that I have never been in love. After all, misery for misery, I could endure more readily Phaon believing I love him than his believing I would even tolerate the love of someone else."

After that, Sapho told Cydnon everything Tisander had said to her: "So you see that Phaon's rival is much better informed of my affection for him than he is himself. Truly Cydnon," she added, "this is a strange adventure. Tisander knows that I love Phaon and he is so sure of it that he has given me up, while Phaon, on the contrary, is ready to leave me because he believes that I don't love him at all and that I love someone else. Being his own rival, you might say, he does himself more harm than all his rivals could possibly do, and he leaves me in the most embarrassing of circumstances for someone like me. Women must never say they are in love, but only suffer themselves to be loved. That is why, Cydnon, we must leave the resolution of this situation to Fortune." "Take care that you don't repent these words," she replied." "If I repent my words," answered Sapho, "I will only do what I have done a hundred times already since I met Phaon. Honestly, I have repented having asked Democedes to introduce us, repented the hour I first spoke to him, and repented having loved him and having written the verses that have caused this latest confusion. And to tell you all, I sense that no matter what you say, I will repent all of this my whole life. For if I keep Phaon by measures unworthy of me, I will repent of it eternally, but if I lose him because of an overly scrupulous strictness, I will repent it until death."

That was Sapho's state of mind, Madam, when my sister spoke with her. Knowing full well that Sapho would give her consent to all she could do to cure Phaon's jealousy that did not engage Sapho too far, my sister did not press her further. After having seen her, she told me that Phaon was wrong, that I ought to advise him to see Sapho as soon as he could, and that I might assure him he had no rivals to fear. What was amazing about this encounter, Madam, was that Sapho's mind was so preoccupied and troubled by contradictory feelings that she didn't think to be angry at Phaon for his audacity in stealing the verses from her study. Meanwhile, Cydnon dealt with me so well, and I dealt with Phaon so cleverly that, although he didn't believe positively all I told him, it did not keep him from going to Sapho's determined to tell her all that was in his soul.

Nevertheless, he arrived having changed his mind yet again. Great ones can do nothing secretly: all Mytilene was talking about Tisander having resolved not to see Sapho anymore, and since Phaon imagined that the prince would only leave Sapho because he had discovered that she loved someone else, his jealousy redoubled and upset his initial plan. It wasn't that he believed Tisander was the reason for his jealousy; it was that he didn't know that he, Phaon, had released the prince from loving Sapho, so he drew conclusions from the change in this lover that made him very unhappy. But in the end, having spent two days in uncertainty, he suddenly decided to go to Sapho's to reveal to her all the greatness of his love and all the violence of his jealousy.

The next day he went so early to her house that there was no one about. To tell you what they felt, Madam, to see one another again will not be easy: Sapho was covered in confusion at her own weakness and pitied Phaon; her lover felt such diverse feelings that one doesn't know how to describe them. He told me that he felt both his love and his jealousy redouble, but that nevertheless he also sensed his hope renewed. After having greeted one another nervously, Phaon asked Sapho's pardon for not having seen her for so long. "But Madam," he added, "maybe, having asked your pardon for not having visited you, I should also ask your pardon for coming to visit you again. Although I am resolved to say nothing that isn't worthy of the love and respect I have for you, because I came here resolved to say so many different things, I know I shall say something that will displease you and make me unhappy."

"So little has passed between us since we met," Sapho replied, "that I can't imagine you could have so much to tell me." "I ask you, Madam," he replied, "if I am wrong in being the most jealous of men? I beg you to speak to me sincerely: I beseech you to have compassion for my weakness, to examine well the passion that caused it, and to wish, if it is possible, not to drive me to despair."

"What you tell me," replied Sapho, "shows a mind greatly disordered; therefore, pity makes me want to do what good sense would not, if I obeyed only strict justice and propriety. So even though I have hardly suffered you to speak to me of your love, I wish to hear about your misery and I permit you to speak to me of your jealousy. Speak, therefore, Phaon," she continued. "Tell me who makes you jealous."

"I have no idea, Madam, but I know very well that there are moments when I believe I have every imaginable cause—Madam, you write of such feelings that you must have felt them. You have written verses that I had the audacity to steal from you, that have cost me a thousand sighs, and that will, perhaps, cost me my life if you do not have the goodness to tell me what will heal me."

"But what must I say to heal you?" asked Sapho. "You must persuade me that you have never been in love and that if you ever love anyone, it will be the unfortunate Phaon," he replied. "But since, Madam, that isn't possible, I don't ask it; instead I ask truly the state of your soul, whatever it may be, and I ask you the name of the one for whom you wrote the verses I took from your study."

"To respond generally to all you have asked me," she answered, "I tell you that I write tenderly because by nature I have a tender soul; then I assure you that if I must make anyone jealous, it ought not be you. I tell you, as much for my own honor as for your peace of mind, that I had never been in love up to the day you arrived in Mytilene, and I can also tell you that I have done nothing since that ought to give you cause for jealousy. But to prove to you that I am telling you the truth, I consent for you to observe all my actions, all my words, my every glance, and if, after having observed me in this way, you find that you ought to be jealous, then be jealous to a fury and be persuaded that in permitting you to be jealous, I do for you what I have never done for anyone."

"Since you cannot permit me to be jealous," he replied, "without permitting me to be in love, I must thank you for this permission, Madam, as if it were the greatest favor in the world. Yet I would be all the more obliged to you," he added, "if you would tell me clearly that you wish I were in love, than for you to assure me you would suffer me to be jealous. Tell me, then, Madam, I beseech you, if I might be permitted to hope that one day you might feel for me some part of that tenderness you know so admirably how to express. Would it be too presumptuous to imagine that you might one day ascribe to me the verses that have made me so cruelly jealous? But Madam, to make such a glorious assurance believable, you must be sincere: you must tell me what you haven't said; you must reveal your heart to me, as I have revealed mine, and not make a secret of all that passed in your soul before I knew you. Because were you to have loved someone before I had the honor of knowing you, I would have no reason to complain. It isn't that I don't wish, with a strange passion, to have the honor of being the first to have a little touched your heart: I do; but if that is not possible, I will not fail to count myself extremely happy to be the successor to a happy rival. Speak, divine Sapho, and tell me if I should be jealous, if I should be happy or miserable; in other words, should I live or die?"

Phaon said all these things with an air so respectful, and there was in his tone of voice something so persuasive, and he looked at Sapho in so submissive and passionate a manner, that finally the beautiful young woman did not have the heart to mistreat the lover whom she wished after all to keep. She spoke to him with such skill, that without telling him immediately that she loved him, she renewed his hope, increased his passion, and restored joy to his soul. In the end, Madam, these two told one another everything, even though when their conversation began they hardly knew what to say to one another and had in their hearts a thousand feelings they believed they might never share. They exchanged their most secret thoughts with such sincerity that one could say that everything that was in Sapho's mind passed into Phaon's and all that was in Phaon's mind passed into hers. They even agreed about the conditions of their love: Phaon promised Sapho solemnly that he wished never to desire anything from her but possession of her heart, and she promised Phaon to receive only him into hers. Then they told one another of all that had happened to them in their lives, and since then, Madam, this admirable union between them has so long endured—its equal has never been seen. In fact, Phaon's love grew with his happiness and Sapho's affection became even more intense as she came to know the grandeur of her lover's love for her. Never have there been two hearts so united, never has love joined together such purity and passion. They shared all their thoughts, they understood one another without words, they saw in each other's eyes the motion of their hearts and feelings so tender that the more they knew one another, the more they were in love. But their peace was not so great that their affection became lukewarm and languishing, because they loved one another as much as it was possible to love and complained sometimes by turns of not being loved enough. They had enough little quarrels to always have something new to wish for, but these quarrels were never really serious enough to trouble their tranquility.

From the day that Phaon and Sapho were united in their love, however, Nicanor was very unhappy, and Tisander counted himself as fortunate as he was prudent for having been able to disengage himself from his former passion. If truth be told, he soon cured himself with another since Pittacus had decided he should be married to the beautiful Alcionide and he had gone to Cnidos[18] where she was and had fallen as much in love with her as he had been with Sapho. And though he was no longer in love with the admirable Sapho, he still felt great esteem for her. But Sapho's brother, Charaxus, who didn't like it at all that she had refused Tisander's affections, found it intolerable that she would entertain those of Phaon and so took himself off on a long voyage without even saying good-bye.

As for Nicanor, although he loved Sapho as tenderly as ever and hated Phaon strangely, he was not carried away to any violence toward either of them. Sapho's demeanor was such that everyone showed her the respect due her and those who were most at odds were brought together. If she didn't maintain complete peace between the two rivals, she at least prevented them from all-out war. What contributed still more to this peace was that Phaon, being certain he was the preferred of all her suitors, was jealous of none, or if on occasion he felt twinges of jealousy, it was when his old fantasy returned to mind and he imagined that Sapho must have loved someone else before him to have written of such tender feelings as he had read in her verse. But to tell the truth, he was quite fortunate in not being capable of jealousy toward those who loved Sapho because she gave her love so generously to so many that Alcæus himself, though in love with the fair Athys, felt he shared a place in her heart. With the exception of Themistogene, who couldn't love anyone who didn't resemble Damophile, there wasn't a man of wit who didn't feel love for Sapho. As for me, since I was Phaon's particular friend and, what's more, was always careful to defend myself, I wasn't head over heels in love, but I felt such affection and attachment for her that I loved no one else.

Meanwhile this universal admiration for Sapho didn't fail to irritate all the ladies who pretended to great beauty but no longer had admirers when

18. Cnidos was a Greek city in Asia Minor claiming descent from Sparta and sacred to Aphrodite, goddess of love.

Sapho, who they didn't believe was as beautiful as they were, was nearby. It was extraordinary how this admirable young woman maintained her empire in the hearts of all her suitors without being unfaithful to Phaon in any way. She acted with such discretion that no one said anything to her she didn't want to hear and she had, therefore, no cause for complaint and thus no need to banish her suitors from her presence. There were certainly days when Phaon protested respectfully that there were too many people at Sapho's, but the moment she spoke to him, she made him understand that prudence required that he be hidden in the crowd. For if she had banished some, she would have had to banish him as well, or she would have had to make their intercourse public, which would have diminished her reputation somewhat. So Phaon had to endure all Sapho's lovers who, in their turn, dared only appear as friends.

As for me, I was surprised hundreds of times at the power Sapho had over her slaves since there wasn't a one who didn't know that she loved Phaon, and Phaon alone. Nevertheless, not one gave up hope even though she gave no hope to anyone, and although they all hated Phaon, they dared not, nor could they, offend him. Since they could only be jealous of Phaon, they got along well enough and came to have a sort of trust in one another. Thus Sapho, the lovers and her chosen lover and the ill-treated ladies were always together without any disagreement to trouble their society. What was even more admirable is that even in the midst of such a crowd, Sapho didn't fail to find ways to give a thousand signs of her affection to Phaon and to sacrifice all his rivals to him without anyone perceiving it. Thus, without doing anything against the laws of strict propriety and without being a co-quette, Sapho had the glory of an infinite number of suitors. Her faithful lovers were not severe in their judgment, though they were driven almost to savagery by that effort, and she and Phaon enjoyed all the delights of a pure and innocent love. They were not the sort of people who, once assured of being in love, renounce romance[19] as if they were married. Phaon was as attentive and assiduous as if he had still to conquer the heart he possessed, and Sapho was as correct, as unfailingly sociable and serene as if his conquest of her were not already complete and certain. Moreover, joy, festivities, and pleasure followed them wherever they went, and although they were certain of one another's esteem, they exercised every care imaginable to preserve it. This was the life Phaon and Sapho led, Madam, while they were happy.

But since love's empire is even more subject to great revolutions than others, the tranquil and profound peace in Sapho's heart could not endure

19. See note 9; the French is *galanterie.*

forever, though it seemed as if it ought to since no lover knew better the art of expressing love than Phaon. What's more, he saw no one in Mytilene but Sapho: he scarcely saw his mistress's friends, although he was always with them, because the marvelous Sapho was always in his mind's eye so that she could not doubt, whenever he found himself with her, that she was the only one in his thoughts. Nothing was more agreeable than this clever distinction he drew in the midst of such a large company: he knew so well how to oblige Sapho in that way that he never in his life missed an opportunity when the occasion presented itself. When he was around her, he seemed so happy and content, so sensitive to the little attentions he received from her, that Sapho, whose soul was as tender as could be, believed her lover left nothing to be desired.

She was infinitely charmed with the delicacy of his mind, which was all she could ever have desired. He had sometimes a certain sweet, melancholy gaiety, if one can call it that, which prompted him to say the most delightful things, but to repeat them would rob them of their charm. Since he was naturally curious, they were always engaged in some friendly debate that made their intercourse all the more agreeable. Sometimes he wished to know why she had blushed or why she was daydreaming—he carried his curiosity so far that one day they had a tender lovers' dispute because Phaon asked Sapho why she had been kinder to him that day than another. He took it to heart when she wouldn't say why, almost as if she had treated him badly. Perceiving this inquisitive curiosity that she did not wish to satisfy, she said to him, "But you ask me sometimes about such small things, with such great insistence that I must ask you in my turn, what is the cause of this inquisitiveness that prompts our little quarrels? Because if you doubted your place in my heart, I wouldn't find it strange that you would want me to tell you, or that you would be curious about essential and important matters, but your humor is to want to know everything large and small."

"Yes, Madam," he said, "I am curious about everything that concerns you, and if I could, I would oblige you to make an accounting to me of your every thought and glance. Madam, you have put such infinitely narrow limits on my desires that the possession of your heart is the only thing to which you have permitted me to aspire. How do you think I can be confident I possess it if I do not know what you are feeling? Don't find it strange, therefore, if I can't bear for you to refuse me what I ask of you because, after all, in teaching me why you have sometimes blushed, or why you don't look at me, or why you do, you put me truly in possession of the heart you have promised me and you give me inexpressible joy. For in truth, I put more store in one of these trifling, hidden feelings that you reveal to me so obligingly than many things that appear as great favors to those who aren't capable of feeling all the delicacy of love. So don't refuse to satisfy my curiosity, even when it makes me ask you about trifles that don't seem reasonable to you, Madam, because" he added, smiling, "Love is a child who knows how to take his pleasure in his own way, who has innocent whims that, when satisfied, give great happiness and when not, lead to great discontent. As far as my excessive curiosity is concerned, which is an effect of the greatness of my love, I hope you will oblige my weakness and rather than distressing me by saying nothing, you will tell me all I ask."

From what I have just said, Madam, it seems to me you may judge that Phaon's love was tender, gallant, and ingenious. He loved the person in the world who knew best how to love, with the most spirit and wit; they exchanged a thousand innocent pleasures every day, pleasures unknown to those who share only a vulgar love. Nevertheless, there were days when Phaon thought about Sapho's desire not to marry and about her remarkable virtue, and he became somewhat melancholy. But she discovered quickly the cause of his melancholy and knew so well how to dispel it that he was forced to admit that he was the happiest lover on earth. Meanwhile, as I have already told you, Nicanor still loved Sapho and Alcæus was also only just short of loving her as well, so that jealousy took root in the heart of the beautiful Athys as well as in that of Nicanor, jealousy that in the end disturbed the bliss of these oh so happy lovers.

To make you understand the cause of this change, I must tell you about a small party that Sapho gave at her country house some hundred stades[20] from Mytilene in what is without a doubt one of the most agreeable places on our island. You should know, Madam, that everything one could desire in a country house could be found there: it was not far from the sea and had perhaps the most beautiful springs one could ever hope to see; it also had woods and meadows, gardens and grottos, and it was beautifully designed and built. Not a summer passed but Sapho and Cynegire made two or three excursions, and Sapho was visited there by all her women friends. Since we were then in the agreeable season sometimes called the year's childhood, when the first green of fields and trees makes the countryside so beautiful, Sapho was there with Cynegire and invited all her dearest friends to come spend an entire day. Although she didn't ask either her men friends or her lovers, a few came: Nicanor, Alcæus, Phaon, and I accompanied Amithone, Athys, Erinne, and Cydnon. Chance had it that the same day we were there, Phylire and two of her friends and two of Sapho's admirers came by in the

---

20. A Greek unit of measure approximately 180 meters (195 yards) in length.

afternoon without knowing we were there—the company was delightful that day. I won't stop to tell you all the details of this little party, Madam; I will tell you only that although Sapho and all her women friends were dressed only in white and adorned simply with flowers, they were nevertheless so charming that you couldn't find a prettier sight.

When we arrived at Sapho's, we found that she awaited us, attended by two girls, in a thick little grove in the center of which was an admirable spring whose rushing waters streamed from a rock in the middle of a rustic pool bordered with grass. The spring was at the foot of a large tree with branches so thick and spreading so wide that it shaded not only the fountain, but several other grassy seats that surrounded it. Sapho was there, dressed as I have already told you, and received us with an air so graceful and charming that never in my life have I seen the like. She had in her countenance all the freshness of spring: her eyes shone like a sunrise in a cloudless sky, and the joy she showed at seeing us so lit up her face that, surrounded by play, love, and laughter, we couldn't have had a happier sign of the day to come than seeing the way in which she welcomed us. There was no one in our group to whom she didn't say something obliging and who didn't think that she had said more to him or her than to anyone else. But since I always observed her closely, I didn't delude myself like the others, for in the midst of this tumultuous joy that she showed at seeing us at her house, I saw something particular for Phaon in her beautiful eyes when he paid her his compliments, so that I could tell easily that he held a special place in her heart.

Meanwhile, since the whole charming band wanted to stop for a time in this beautiful spot, the carriages that brought us were left behind the grove at Sapho's house and we stayed in the shade conversing to the agreeable murmur of the spring and the delightful rustle of leaves stirred by a fresh breeze. This first conversation was often interrupted as we passed from one topic to another: first, all the ladies from Mytilene praised Sapho's beauty and, knowing that she walked all the time while in the country, marveled that she wasn't sunburned. For her part, Sapho said many flattering things to them that have become the custom among the young and beautiful women of the world. Then she asked for news of Mytilene, and we in our turn asked what she had been doing with her solitude. Cydnon reproached her for not having written, Erinne for not having thought of her, Athys for having left without saying good-bye, and we all together said that she loved her solitude too much and that her absence pained us too much for us to suffer it any longer.

"To prove to me what you say," replied Sapho agreeably, "you must tell me everything you have done in the week since I came here, because if you can show me that you were in fact all bored without me, I think I will return with you. But to tell the truth, I believe that you haven't failed to entertain yourselves."

"For myself," said Nicanor, "I haven't been out at all except to Pittacus's where I had to go two or three times on important business for one of my friends. Though I was in her neighborhood, the beautiful Athys knows very well that I didn't even see her." "It's true," she said, "that Nicanor has been quite solitary since you left, but not me," she added maliciously, "I have seen lots of people and gone for promenades often enough, but that hasn't prevented me from being bored and wishing for you a hundred times. In fact, Phaon, who was with me on two of my walks, well knows that I spoke to him in just such terms and even reproached him about not being sad enough at your absence." "I admit that you reproached me just yesterday, but you did so unjustly since the joy that appeared in my eyes came from my knowing I would come here today," replied Phaon. "You have extricated yourself cleverly from the pretty pass in which the beautiful Athys has put you, perhaps without thinking about it," replied Alcæus, "but I don't know if you will be able to escape so easily from the predicament in which I am going to put you when I say that the day after Sapho left, we made five or six visits together where I was extremely bored, but where you conversed as if you were highly entertained."

"Sapho has taught me so well that one must never be uncivil," he answered, "that I could never decide to call on people and then have nothing to say—I'd rather not go at all. Cydnon saw me two days later and can tell you that she found me melancholy enough." "It is true," added Amithone, "but I don't know if it was on account of Sapho's absence: you played cards the day before and lost a lot." "Since the beautiful Sapho knows I haven't a worldly soul, I don't fear being suspected of feeling more pain at losing at cards than I feel at losing sight of her." "However that may be," Sapho said half smiling and blushing, "you have hardly had the leisure to be bored: you have taken walks, made visits, gambled, and no doubt paid court at Pittacus's—as your good friend I should rejoice that you have passed your time so pleasantly, but I shouldn't thank you for thinking too much of me." "But Madam," he said, "don't judge me without hearing me out." "I will hear you out another time," she replied, "because today we should follow your example and think only of entertaining ourselves." Sapho said this so lightheartedly that Phaon was no longer troubled. He was certain that she had been a little piqued at first by the attack launched at him to make her believe that he hadn't been bored during her absence, since she had had letters from him every day that she was in the country and so knew he had lived as he did more out of prudence than from some failure at love.

So Sapho was as cheerful throughout the rest of the day as she would have been had this all not been said in her presence. But later, when the beautiful band had rested for some time and when I had also given an account to Sapho of what I had done in her absence, she led us through this delightful grove to the gate of a large garden. There we found a wide path that traversed it and that led us to the staircase leading up to the house where Cynegire received us. I won't relate fully the tasteful furnishings, the gracious meal, or the agreeable scent one breathed inside that house because I don't wish to dwell on small things, but I will tell you that an hour after we rose from the table and had removed to a delightful chamber next to the room where we dined, Phylire and her companions, whom I have already mentioned, arrived. As our company grew, so did Sapho's joy, and she did the honors of her house so well that Phaon was charmed to see her, and being unable to master his passion, he expressed it so openly that Sapho made a sign to him more than once to keep the passion of his heart a little more under control. He praised her so hyperbolically, he sought her out so intently, and he looked at her with such love that one might easily have thought, seeing his joy at seeing her, that when she was out of his sight he would be in despair.

A little while later Phylire arrived, and after she had introduced everyone she had brought to Sapho, this admirable young woman said to the assembled company that she wanted to take them to a place even more delightful than where they were, where they would pass the midday until the hour appointed for a walk. Cynegire and Sapho then led us by way of a wide, covered allée into a wood that appeared so wild and uninhabited that we might as well have been in a desert. What was most delightful was a large grotto in the thickest part of the forest that Nature had begun, but Art and Sapho's helping hand had completed. It was one of the most beautiful spots in the world—large, cool, deep, but nevertheless, reasonably bright. The rock was variegated, and what had been added imitated Nature so well that Art seemed to have no part in it. In addition, the seats at the edge of the cave were of a rustic material that appeared to have been made by chance and were surprisingly comfortable because through a special technique, moss grew there making them less hard and even more beautiful. There was also a quiet little spring whose fresh coolness made the cave all the more delightful.

But Madam, besides what I have just said, there were many little openings that led to a second cavern that you couldn't reach from the first—its entrance was opposite the first one and formed an echo chamber so you could hear what people said to one another. This delightful place was just as I have described it, and Cynegire and Sapho led us there. We had hardly arrived when suddenly we heard the most admirably harmonious music emanating from the second grotto where we were not seated. It wafted into the first and filled it so agreeably that there has never been such a captivating surprise. At first we all thought it was Sapho who had arranged this entertainment, but she herself was so surprised that we quickly realized it wasn't she. Everyone looked around and Sapho looked at us, and she had hardly glanced at Phaon when she knew that this was a gallant attention he had arranged for her.[21] He didn't want to admit it openly, so throughout the day everyone acted as if it had appeared by magic, and it furnished us with an enjoyable topic of conversation.

Since Cynegire was the most curious among us, she rose and left the grotto with one of the ladies Phylire had brought in order to go into the other cave to discover from the musicians themselves who had arranged for them to be there. Then she walked on with her companion onto a solitary path not far away. In the meantime, this charming diversion Phaon had arranged so graciously made each of us praise him, even though he said over and over that he didn't deserve to be praised and that he wasn't gallant enough to have done such a thing.

"In truth, Phaon," my sister said to him, smiling, "if we were to believe you, you would be found out because those whose souls are truly chivalrous know it and are not at all pleased if people think they aren't. And they are right not to wish to be denied a quality prized before all others, however worthy they may be." "You must be gallantly inclined to speak as you do," replied Alcæus, smiling. "In my opinion you need reason as well as gallantry," she answered, "because if things aren't done in the way I mean them to be, I hardly find them agreeable." "As for me," continued Amithone, "I want to know exactly what sort of gallantry this is of which Cydnon means to speak." "In my case," interrupted Phaon, "I would prefer that we discuss the sort of gallantry she has said nothing about because, I tell you, I see so many inferior suitors everywhere, who nevertheless succeed in making enough progress in the hearts of some ladies that if one isn't careful, true lovers will find no more conquests to make. That is why I would like for us to begin here to censure false gallantry so that when we return to Mytilene we can instill our maxims in the spirit of the entire city." "We should also establish rules for the beauties whom they court," continued Phylire, "because it will serve no purpose to criticize the one if we don't teach the other."

"Since I am the declared enemy of false suitors and naturally like a courtly air in all things, I would be thrilled to have such a conversation if we weren't here," replied Sapho. "But to tell the truth," she smiled and added,

---

21. The French reads *galanterie.*

"I don't want it to be said in Mytilene that we got together to make laws governing love." "As for me," replied Phaon, "I well know that today, I will speak of nothing else." "And in my own case," I added, " I don't think I can find a thing to say about any other subject." "It is in fact so agreeable a topic," added Nicanor, "that it would be hard to change it for a better." "And it is so needed," said Alcæus, "that I don't know of what we would speak if we don't speak of it." "And since we exchanged all the news we knew before dinner," replied Phaon, "and have praised the beauty of our surroundings and spoken of almost everything . . . . So there is nothing for it," he said to Sapho, "either you must submit to being praised or suffer us to speak of courtship as it pleases us." " I assure you," she replied, "I would rather you speak of courtship than praise me." "So let's speak of it for the rest of the day," replied Phaon, "because my soul is so disposed today that it seems to me I will have almost as much wit as you do on your least admirable day." "Should you never have more than you have today," she replied, "you couldn't be more charming than you are right now."

"But tell us, I beseech you," said the beautiful Athys to Sapho, "what have you done, and what do you do, to be the most captivating person in the world? I don't mean, in speaking so, to accuse you of coquetry," she continued wickedly, " but I mean to praise you in effect by saying there isn't a thing you do or a word you say that doesn't captivate." "Though I haven't sufficient vanity to believe what you say about me," replied Sapho, "I do recognize it well enough in others. I can discern that sort of gallantry without love that sometimes gives to even the most serious things one does or says an inexplicable charm. However, the refined air I mean doesn't consist of great wit or judgment or learning; it is so singular, so difficult to come by if one doesn't have it that one can't find it or seek it out. For in the end," she added, "I know a man whom you all know as well, who is handsome, intelligent, splendid in his attendants, household, and dress, always correct, and who speaks wisely and to the point, and who does all he can to have a gallant air, but who is, nevertheless, the least courtly of men." "But what is it then," asked Amithone, "this courtly manner that is so pleasing?"

"A *je ne sais quoi*[22] born of a hundred different things—finally I am convinced that Nature must endow the mind and person of those who would be gallant with a certain receptive disposition; considerable experience of the world and the court also helps, as does the conversation of women. For I maintain that there has never been a man of gallantry and grace who flees interaction with persons of my sex. If I dare say all I think, I would say what's

22. Literally "I don't know what," but meaning indescribable or beyond words.

more that a man must have had at least once in his life some inclination to love if he is to acquire perfectly that gallant air of which we have been speaking." "But take care that you don't go too far," added Amithone, "in saying what you say." "Amithone is right," added Alcæus, "because if it is necessary to have been in love to have this gallant air, then it follows that a woman who is distinguished by it must have loved more than others." "Not at all," replied Sapho, "because at the same time that I maintain that for a man to have this air about him his heart must have been a little engaged, I maintain that for a woman to have this very same air, it suffices for her to have been favorably disposed to it by Nature, to have seen the world and known refined people, and to aim to please generally, without loving anyone in particular."

"It seems to me that we are abusing this word, 'gallant,'" said the beautiful Athys, "because although I approve of saying 'what a gallant thought' or 'how gallantly said' and a thousand other things like that in which the mind and spirit play a role, I don't know if I think it is appropriate to say 'that costume is gallant' or 'that man is gallantly dressed.'"

"I disagree," said Phaon, "because it is that certain air that distinguishes Sapho's mind and her entire person, that makes the dress she wears today suit her so well—truly, one sees women at a ball, beautifully adorned, whose dress cannot compare with the simplicity of this gown, which takes its charm from she who wears it and she who foresaw how pleasing it is."

"As for me, I agree that anything can have such an air and I think it can last a lifetime," added Sapho, "but to tell the truth, and to speak generally, this sort of gallantry is certainly born from the other kind, and one must have loved or desired to please, to acquire it. As I have already said, many things are necessary to attain it and there are even people born with many fine qualities who don't know how to achieve it. It is a great misfortune, however, not to have that certain air because nothing is more agreeable than a charmingly natural turn of mind that knows how to add a certain pleasing *je ne sais quoi* even to what is least pleasing and that endows even the most mundane conversation with a secret charm that is both satisfying and entertaining. This *je ne sais quoi* that pervades the entire person who possesses it—mind, actions, even dress—is what we mean when we speak of persons who are refined and cultured—and what makes them amiable and loved. In fact, there is a way of saying something that gives it worth and value; it is always the case that those who possess a courtly turn of mind can often say things that others would only dare to think. But to my mind, a courtly manner of conversation consists principally in approaching things openly and naturally, in leaning rather toward gentleness and pleasure than toward the serious and abrasive, in speaking easily, using the appropriate words, without affectation. You need a mind in some sense almost ingratiating or flattering to seduce the minds of others. If I could explain what I mean well, I would make you admit that one cannot really be good company without possessing the gallant manner that I have described."

"It's true," replied Alcæus, "that without it, it is difficult to please. But you must admit nonetheless that those for whom it is absolutely necessary are those who make a profession of amorous pursuit." "Certainly a lover without gallantry is pitiful," responded Sapho, "and even more irritating," she added, "is the infinite number of young people who have just entered society and who believe that being gallant and charming consists entirely of following the most bizarre fashions, fashions invented by others on a whim, of being pushy and aggressive, of talking too much and coming and going continually to houses whose doors are always open even though they have no business there but to engage in idle chitchat that is neither witty nor gallant nor passionate." "There are also those," put in Cydnon, "who believe themselves gallant just because they are able to say they've seen all the charming women in the town, and who in fact spend their whole lives being everywhere at once simply to have the pleasure of saying 'yesterday I was with her,' 'I escorted so and so the other day,' 'I serenaded her,' 'I gave a banquet for Sapho and her circle,' 'I was with some other ladies the next day,' and on and on."

"Those you describe are certainly not very gallant," replied Sapho, "and are weak and not very bright; but I find even more alarming these sweet talkers who are eternally languishing, now for blue eyes, now black, now gray, equally ardent for them all, who think they are dishonored if a day goes by when they are at a woman's side without sighing for her. I simply can't bear that and am so convinced that they've said what they say to me a hundred thousand times before that I can't listen to them or answer them."

"I agree that these eternally sighing fawners are strange people," answered Phaon, "but we know a few rude, proud lovers who aren't particularly agreeable either, and all our company knows one such, who loves a certain very beautiful person and swears constantly, in every possible way, that he loves her as no one has ever loved before, that he would die to serve her and would kill anyone who dared displease her. He even believes that continually offering to kill someone in her service suffices to give him the right to demand great favors in return." "He is so brutal," said Erinne, "that he doesn't merit our talking about him; but I really want to know what I ought to think about these jovial gallants who never speak of love except in jest and yet speak of it all the time and, without being either flirts or lovers, go eternally from salon to salon, doling out their cheery gallantry without an

idea in their heads." "Since such types never stay in one place very long,"
continued Erinne, "they don't bother me much when I meet them; there are
even some whom I find entertaining. But those who make me angry are the
real philanderers who carry on ten or twelve intrigues at once but love no
one and have a hundred affairs going without having a one that is true."

"I swear," replied Phylire, "that these obstinate lovers who are always
moping around aren't very amusing for their men or women friends. I know
one who is always so solemn that every time I see him I think he must be
jealous and wants either to murder his rival or is thinking of poisoning him."
"There are no doubt some stubborn lovers who are as irritating as you say,"
replied Phaon, "but my dear Phylire, there are also faithful lovers who are
not so troublesome." "It is always the case," said Cydnon, "that there are few
men who are really in love, who are truly gallant, and who are as agreeable to
others as they are to those they love. Though love seems only a trifling thing,
nevertheless it is the rarest thing in the world to find a lover who loves with
good grace." At that, I said to Sapho, "It isn't right only to consider lovers—
it would be better to talk about love in general so that we may also speak a
little more particularly about women."

"Let me assure you that there are those whose attempts at gallantry are
so terrible that we do them an honor not to speak of them at all," replied
Sapho. "Nevertheless, I feel bound to declare that we owe the false gallantry
of men to women, for if they knew well how to manage the privileges of
their sex, they could teach men how to be truly gallant and would not permit them ever in their presence to forget the respect they owe them. In
fact, they would never permit the hundreds of vulgar familiarities that so
many new young blades want to introduce into society, for there is, finally, a
long way between a forced ceremony and downright incivility. If all gallant,
charming ladies understood well what they were about, their suitors would
be more respectful and courteous, and thus more agreeable. But the trouble
is that women who have taken it into their heads to be gallant and charming
imagine that they will win and keep their suitors by being indulgent. I mean
those who think neither of their reputations nor of their own love affairs but
only of stealing a lover here, attracting one there, keeping another, and en-
snaring a thousand if they could. There are even those who do worse," she
added, "those whom their greed prompts to carry on a hundred intrigues
instead of one."

"Certainly I know women who are horrified at the very thought of a virtuous woman engaging in flirtation and courtship," said Amithone, "but the
reality is they can't manage a thing and act so imprudently that they glory
in what should make them ashamed. And I am sure their suitors mock them
when they see how they act—such women can never win their esteem. As

for me, I am convinced that you must conduct yourself not only prudently, so as to give the world no cause to speak badly of you; you must even do so to preserve your own lover's esteem, for would a gentleman find it admirable for the person he loves to risk her honor for him?" "We see many who do, though," replied Erinne, "and who hardly trouble themselves about the reputation of the ladies they love." "Since they don't bother about it themselves," replied Cydnon, "I don't see why men are so wrong not to bother about it either."

"Is it possible that you have nothing good to say about love and lovers?" said Nicanor. "In truth," replied Sapho, "it is easier to say what is bad than what is good given the large number of people who meddle in what they don't understand. I am sure that if women in general knew how to manage their many advantages well, it would be possible to introduce into the world a kind of courtship so divine, so delightful, and so innocent that it would shock neither prudence nor virtue. Truly, if women would value their lovers according to their merits, and not according to their attentions and favors, the conquest of their hearts would be more difficult, men would be more accommodating, more attentive, more obedient, and more respectful than they are, and women would be less selfish, less ignoble, less deceitful, and less weak than we see them to be. So if each were in his or her rightful place, if mistresses were mistresses and servants, servants, every pleasure would come thronging back into the world: civility would rule, true gallantry would shine its brightest, and we wouldn't see what we see daily, men who speak of women in general with such obvious contempt or who boast publicly of the favors they have received. Nor would we see so many women abandon that exacting modesty so necessary to them and that is the very soul of love."

"We wouldn't see women quarreling among themselves over a lover, putting one another down, selling their hearts like diamonds for mercenary reasons," I said, "because if gallantry is sometimes permitted, then those who practice it cannot be censured for being unable to prevent themselves from loving another more than they love themselves." As we were speaking, Cynegire and her companion returned, and the conversation was interrupted because they told us how lovely it was to walk, so our entire company left the cave and entered a shady bower into which the musicians followed us, and we had the most delightful hour of dancing in the world.

Though it seemed impossible that Phaon would manage to find a way to converse with Sapho privately on a day when she was obliged to make everyone feel welcome at her home, he managed nevertheless. After the little ball, we each wandered wherever inclination took us and he offered his hand to Sapho, and by walking imperceptibly less quickly than the others, he separated the two of them from the rest of the company till they were some eight or ten steps behind. He spoke to her of his passion and was so carried away that even Sapho, who was so difficult to please in matters of the heart, was content with him that day. In fact, he said so precisely what she thought he ought to say, and he spoke so obligingly, that she decided he deserved to see a part of the joy she felt in being loved by him. She reproached him for being amused during her absence, but he responded so earnestly that she believed only chance, not choice, had engaged him in various entertainments. He seemed so happy to see her that she had no doubt that he had suffered at not seeing her. However much pleasure she found in conversing with Phaon, propriety triumphed over inclination so that after letting him see how disappointed she was not to be able to talk with him longer, she made her way back to our company.

The group so enjoyed themselves that they didn't leave until after dinner that evening. Sapho kept Cydnon with her, and the others promised to write to her. After we had left, the two of them talked for a long time, but on Sapho's side, it was a little sad because she loved with so ardent an attachment that she couldn't help but feel Phaon's absence. It was, however, a sweet sadness that occupied her spirit but didn't overwhelm it, and didn't keep her from saying a thousand beautiful things to my sister about her tender love. "Truly, my dear Cydnon," she said, "love is a strange passion. Though you want nothing more fervently than the happiness of the person you love, nevertheless, the moment after I speak with him, I would be in despair if Phaon didn't feel as much sorrow in being out of my presence as I feel when out of his. There are times when I feel so upset at not knowing exactly what he is doing and thinking when he is away from me that I am almost as sad as I would be if I thought for sure that he no longer thought of me when I was out of his sight. Nevertheless, these are the very feelings that would fill me with joy were I able to know them and find them in Phaon's heart as they are in mine."

While Sapho spoke to my sister, Madam, our entire troupe returned to Mytilene in such joyous spirits that I can hardly express them. Nicanor was the exception: he could never be merry because he had no hope of being loved by Sapho, but everyone else amused themselves greatly. You may think me mistaken, Madam, when I say Nicanor was the only exception and think I ought to except Phaon as well. But Madam, I must somehow make you know, I must make you understand, that Phaon had something in him that perhaps no other lover has ever had. For though Phaon had a tender and passionate soul, and though he loved with an unimaginable ardor, it is nevertheless the case that, except when he was jealous, his soul was not subject to sorrow. Absence, however painful to other lovers, pained him only slightly, even though he had more joy when he was near his beloved than one could ever imagine. Truly, I have seen him with Sapho so overcome by pleasure that he was almost in ecstasy, and I have seen him separated from her without suffering excessive sorrow. It wasn't that he didn't love her absolutely as much as he possibly could, or that when he saw her he didn't love her more than anyone has ever loved, but his soul was more responsive to joy than to sorrow, and from the moment he lost what gave him the greatest delight, he sought lesser delights to console himself. His soul sought out all that might please him and avoided everything that might make him sad, so he could be absent sometimes from the one he most loved without being really unhappy. But that didn't prevent him, when he saw his beloved again, from being as happy as if he had in fact been suffering all along in her absence. You could see the joy shining in his eyes and spreading across his face—I can't describe it—but it witnessed so strongly his satisfaction at seeing once more the one he adored that you could never imagine a man who so enjoyed being reunited with what he cared about not suffering great sorrow at its loss.

And you had to forgive Sapho for not understanding for so long that Phaon knew only love's delights and not its sorrows, because she saw him so transported by joy when he was near her that she easily imagined him overcome by sorrow when he was away from her. At the beginning, I believed he acted as he did out of prudence, in order to hide his love for Sapho. The evening we returned to Mytilene after leaving the admirable Sapho, I still believed that the enjoyment he showed during the journey back was designed to fool all our company. But Phaon's good humor was amazing and only increased the ill humor of Nicanor, who believed that his rival's gaiety came from Sapho having said to him such agreeable things that he couldn't hide his joy.

As for Athys, her growing jealousy put her in mind to worry Sapho. She remembered how Sapho had noted all she had said about Phaon's amusements during her absence so that, acting with as much wit as spite on this occasion, she sent a slave to Sapho two days after her return with a letter that I must tell you about. If I'm not mistaken, it went something like this:

Athys to Sapho

I haven't forgotten the promise I made to send you the news, and I would like to be able to keep it, but since there is no news in Mytilene, I am forced to report only on our return journey, which was no less amusing than our journey out to see you. Phaon and Alcæus were in the best humor in the world, and with the exception of Nicanor,

who was very melancholy, the rest of our company found the trip very
short. Phaon and Alcæus said so many delightful things that, were I to
write them down for you, I would send you one of the most delightful letters in the world. But since I am persuaded that it isn't good to
amuse you too much while you are in the country, for fear that you
will remain there longer than your friends would wish, I won't tell you
a thing. Anyway, I am rushing to finish my letter because I am going
for a walk with Phaon and Alcæus and fear they are waiting for me. I
saw them this morning at temple looking so merry that I think they
must still be in good spirits. As for me, I assure you that I will not be
until I have the pleasure of your company.

                                                              Athys

Such was Athys's letter, Madam, which doubtless contained all the malice imaginable: it hurt Alcæus; it worried Sapho because of what it said about
Phaon; and it hurt both Phaon and Alcæus by doing Nicanor a good turn.
Even so, this letter probably would not have been as successful as it was
intended to be had not chance made Amithone, Erinne, Phylire, Alcæus,
Nicanor, and Phaon each write things confirming what Athys had written,
even though each of them wrote separately. Amithone, who was on easy
terms with Sapho, took the liberty of pretending to wage war on her by
telling her, after bits of news about their set, that she just had to tell her
about something to Phaon's credit, that he had been more merry since their
return than she had ever seen him. As for Erinne, to prove her tender affection, she sent word to Sapho that she could claim to be the most melancholy
of all those who had left her except Nicanor; Phylire wrote that had Phaon's
good humor not consoled her a little in Sapho's absence, since her return
she would have been bored to tears. As for Alcæus, without saying precisely
whether Phaon were gay or sad, he cleverly set down in his letter several
amusing things Phaon had said, along with such a melancholy example of
Nicanor's remarks that, though it was an amusing satire for the entertainment
of our whole troupe, it confirmed what all the others had said.

But strangest of all, Phaon's own letter worked against him. Though he
attributed his continued joy to his feelings of love, the effect was not as
he had intended, as you will see when I have told you about Phaon's letter,
which went like this:

Phaon to the captivating Sapho
    You must have a strange power over me, and your words, when
it pleases you, must have more power than those used to cast spells,
for the delightful and obliging things you said to me at the moment

we parted created such great joy in my soul that all the harshness of your absence can't prevent me from remembering them with intense pleasure. Imagine, then, what my pleasure will be when you return. I expect that you will understand what I say as a greater token of my love than if I were in despair, for it is far more extraordinary to receive favors with such sensitivity that they can console even in absence, than to suffer absence with such anxiety that it wipes out the very memory of such favors. I don't know but that it may in fact demonstrate greater love to be more sensitive to the kindnesses of the beloved than to the pain we suffer in being parted. Nevertheless, I hope with all my heart that I will learn soon from your beautiful lips what I ought to believe, and that I may soon declare on my knees that I am the most in love of any man alive.

Phaon

So that was Phaon's letter, Madam. As for mine, it was the only one that did him neither good nor hurt, because I didn't speak of him at all. Since I found him too merry for an absent lover, and since I didn't want to say anything negative, I preferred to say nothing rather than say something to his disadvantage.

While these letters were being brought from Mytilene to where Sapho was, she and Cydnon entertained themselves with all the freedom the country and their friendship allowed. They conversed of far away things, of Phaon's feelings, and sitting on the edge of the beautiful spring of which I have told you, these two young women spoke of the pain of absence, of the sorrow it causes the soul of those capable of feeling it.

"As for me," said Cydnon, "I am so sensitive that I can never accustom myself to not seeing the one I love and I tell you that since your departure from Mytilene, I have had no settled pleasure. If I make calls, I wish you were there, if I take a walk, I regret that you aren't with me, if I hear some pleasant news, I am vexed that we didn't hear it together to amuse us both. I have done nothing, said nothing, and thought nothing in which you didn't have some part. The mere thought of your absence makes me sad."

"For my part," said Sapho, "I am much obliged, for in my opinion the most moving and certain sign of a tender affection is sorrow in absence." As she pronounced these very words, Madam, the slave carrying Athys's letter arrived and gave it to Sapho who began to read it half aloud so that Cydnon could hear, but when she came to what Athys said concerning Phaon's good humor, she blushed and felt a strange emotion in her heart. Rebuking herself, however, she continued and ordered the slave to await her response. She got up intending to go write immediately to Athys, but she had barely stood up when another slave, this one from Phaon's household, arrived, having taken a different route. He carried all the other letters about which I have already spoken, all except Nicanor's, for he had sent his by a man who arrived some fifteen minutes later. But Madam, my sister told me that there has never been anything to equal what was in Sapho's heart on this occasion, for after having read Athys's letter with the emotion I have described, she then read Amithone's with even greater anxiety, Erinne's with even greater surprise, Phylire's with even greater vexation, Alcæus's with even greater melancholy, Nicanor's with even greater confusion, and Phaon's with even greater sorrow, though she had saved it for last hoping it would bring the greatest pleasure.

This coincidence seemed to her so extraordinary that at first she thought that so many people had written to her of Phaon's gaiety only because they were in league against her, but then she remembered that the day he had visited her, many people had told her of the various amusements in which he had taken part during her absence, and she had to abandon that idea. In fact, after having reread the sundry letters, she was absolutely sure there was no conspiracy and she had no doubt that Phaon was as composed as everyone said. Imagine, Madame, the effect this thought must have had on the soul of one who could not suffer Phaon's absence without unaccustomed anguish and who had spent the whole day talking with my sister about the pain of absence, exaggerating the pleasure of knowing that the person whom you love is unhappy at not seeing you. Cydnon told me that there was such amazement on Sapho's face after reading these letters that she thought some strange accident had happened in Mytilene, because Sapho had read aloud only Athys's letter. Cydnon couldn't long ignore Sapho's surprise, for as soon as she had reread the various letters, she passed them to my sister and sighing, began to speak: "See, Cydnon, Phaon doesn't resemble you; friendship affects you more than love does him." After that, Cydnon started to read, but she wasn't as surprised by what people wrote as Sapho was because she had already noticed that Phaon could be entertained in almost any situation and was almost never bored no matter where he was. Nevertheless, since she knew that I loved Phaon dearly, she wished to excuse him. She told Sapho that she ought not to be angered by what people had written to her because, she said, "you should suspect all that Athys, Nicanor, and Alcæus write, and you should read what Phaon writes to you as something he wrote because it seemed original and new. You ought not even to be anxious about what Amithone, Erinne, and Phylire sent you because it is perfectly possible that on his return Phaon saw that everyone was observing him closely, so that for prudence's sake, he acted happier than he really was."

"Oh, Cydnon," replied Sapho, "I think myself as prudent as Phaon, but I could not appear happy an hour after he had left me—the best I could do would be to try not to appear melancholy. That's why I beg you, don't excuse him—truly, there is no excuse. I know perfectly well that Phaon is Democedes's closest friend, but Cydnon, you must take my part against him; you must feel sorry for me and blame him." "If I believed him guilty, I would condemn him," she replied. "What?" interrupted Sapho. "You believe that Phaon could be so merry as to prompt so many different people to speak of his gaiety, without giving me any cause to reproach his lack of love? Ah, Cydnon, if you believe that, you are blind. I feel so strongly his lack of feeling at my absence, that were I able, I would undertake to banish him from my heart because, my dear Cydnon, I cannot endure feeling an overwhelming melancholy at Phaon's absence while he amuses himself and others with the same free spirit as if he had never laid eyes on me."

"What I think," said Cydnon, "is that he is so happy and at ease when he is with you, that I can't believe he isn't suffering mightily when he isn't near you." "Reason and love would have it so," replied Sapho, "nevertheless, six people bear witness against him and he condemns himself in his own letter." "Appearances are so deceiving," Cydnon said to her, "that it is unreasonable to torture yourself excessively about something so uncertain." "To know better, my dear Cydnon, I beseech you to return to Mytilene," she replied. "I will ask Cynegire to give you a coach,[23] and you have only to say you were called back on important business. Meanwhile, I will stay another two weeks so as to see if Phaon continues to amuse himself as he has been doing. But my dear Cydnon, each day you must give me a faithful account of Phaon's pastimes, of his mood and his pleasures. Because if he only loves me when he sees me, I want no more of his love and I want, if I can, to deprive him of mine."

Cydnon did all she could to calm Sapho, but Sapho found it so strange that Phaon could be merry when she wasn't with him, while she was so melancholy when he was not there, that all my sister's persuasion could not make her change her mind. So she had to do what Sapho wished and return to Mytilene after having promised her a fidelity so exacting that she dared not fail in any particular. In the meantime, Sapho answered everyone who had written her without admitting openly to Phaon her unhappiness at his

---

23. The French is *chariot,* which in modern French usage means wagon or shopping cart; Scudéry probably means to invoke the familiar ancient Greek two-wheeled cart or chariot, in which driver and occupant stand. Coach seems the most appropriate rendering since they are each seated in the conveyance.

gaiety. But in truth, she could not long contain herself, so she made the letter so short that it said only this:

Sapho to Phaon

I do not doubt that joy may sometimes be a heartfelt sign of a very tender affection, but I know not if it be so in the way you understand it to be. When I return to Mytilene, I will see if I may count yours as such and whether I find it worthy of those testimonies of your affection that you have shown me.

Sapho

Although this letter was somewhat dry, Phaon did not think Sapho was vexed at him; he believed only that she had so many replies to make that she hadn't had the leisure to write at greater length, and he didn't change his behavior. After Cydnon's return he continued to behave as he had before, which is to say that he sought as best he could to console himself in Sapho's absence. Meanwhile, not a day passed but Sapho sent a slave secretly to Cydnon to have news of Phaon, so not a day passed when she didn't learn things that tormented her. Phaon's character was such that he couldn't refuse any pleasure that came his way. And the reason he was always with Sapho when she was in Mytilene was because nowhere else in the world could he find more pleasure; but that did not prevent him, when he was unable to have the pleasure of seeing the one he loved, from seizing on lesser delights. So Sapho, who had made my sister promise to send her word of everything Phaon did, knew that he took part in all the amusements to be had in Mytilene and behaved like a man who had no aversion to being there.

And Sapho found her spirit strangely vexed and could not decide to see Phaon again without letting him know she was displeased with him. Toward that end, on the day before her return to town she sent an exact chronicle of all the amusements he had had during her absence, the agreeable visits he had made listed day by day, the walks and outings in which he had taken part, the amusing conversations he had had with those he met, in short, with all the pastimes in which he had been engaged. But with this record she sent along a letter that went something like this:

Sapho to Phaon

Since it is impossible that seeing me might give you as much joy as you have had in my absence, I think I must console you for returning and, perhaps, interrupting your pleasures. You will see by the record I send you that I wished to keep an exact account of all your entertainments, but it is hard to know if it is to punish or reward you, for to tell the truth, I do not think we are of the same mind. I am persuaded that if you do not have as much sorrow at having displeased me as you have had joy in my absence, you will have from now on but a small share of my affection and esteem.

Sapho

Since Phaon was in fact very much in love with Sapho and knew that she would return the next day, he couldn't help but receive this letter with a mind greatly agitated. He hoped to make his peace with her as soon as he could see her, but so that he might see her before she reached Mytilene, he came to find me and entreated me, after having shown me the letter she had written him, to go with him in advance of her arrival. And so the next day we were awaiting her in a place along the road that was so rugged that everyone who passed over it in a coach had to get out and walk. Knowing that Cynegire was fearful and would not fail to do so, Phaon and I stationed ourselves under some willows near this difficult passage made by a torrential runoff. But after having dismounted so as to await the ladies in this place that was quite agreeable despite the ruggedness of the road, I began to tease Phaon about his character. "How is it," I asked him, "that you are so head over heels in love with Sapho, yet your soul is so insensitive to the pain of her absence? When I see you near her, you are so transported by joy that I can't believe you won't die when she is out of your sight."

"It's true," he said, "no one could have a stronger passion than I feel in my soul; the mere hope I have today of seeing Sapho at this very hour stirs my heart so passionately that, could you know how I am feeling, you would declare that I love Sapho more than anyone could possibly love. But with the exception of jealousy, not much can cause me great sorrow. In truth," he added, "if I were to fear that Sapho no longer loved me, I believe that here, in this very place, I would despair. But when I can reasonably hope to be loved, when I have news of her every day, and when I know that she will soon return, I admit that I don't know how to make myself sad without reason. I have a soul that so inclines to seek pleasure and avoid sorrow that I do what I can to lessen the hardship of her absence. And once I see Sapho again, you will see me constantly at her side and the most in love of all men."

"In loving as you do, Phaon," I told him, "it might be said that you love yourself more than you love your mistress." "The truth is," he replied, "that no one in the world would undertake more difficulties than I would for Sapho if she commanded me to do so. What's more, I believe I am capable of obeying her blindly; I am more attentive, careful, and exact than anyone else has ever been. I have more tenderness in my heart than anyone else has ever had. I make the greatest pleasures out of the smallest favors; the least favorable of her looks overwhelms me with joy. I have thousands upon thousands of tumultuous feelings I cannot express when I find myself near her: I esteem her, I admire her, I adore her with so profound a respect that I don't feel as much for our gods. I feel such perfect joy when I am able to converse with her alone that never has any other lover felt as much, not even when possessing his mistress. Judge, then, if I know not how to love and if you are right to accuse me of loving too little. It is true that my soul naturally refuses pain and seeks pleasure. What difference does it make to the person I love if I am horribly unhappy when I don't see her, if I fail in none of the duties of a true lover, and if, when I see her, I am everything I ought to be to satisfy her?"

As he said this, we saw Cynegire's coach appear up ahead so that Phaon stopped himself, mounted his horse quickly, as did I, and, transported by uncontrollable passion, went as fast as he possibly could to meet Sapho. And Madam, he arrived so eager and filled with feeling that no one could doubt that he was desperately in love. The beautiful Sapho, as irritated as she was, could not see him without repenting almost every word she had written to him. He met her in a way that made her see such joy and love in his eyes that if she hadn't had complete confidence in my sister, she would have doubted the things Cydnon had sent her and believed that Phaon had done nothing but sigh throughout her absence. But since she could not doubt what my sister had written her, she received Phaon with cool politeness, and she would have received him still more coldly had Cynegire not been there.

The first compliments having been paid, the coach Cynegire had halted began to move again and reached the dangerous spot I told you about where the ladies had to alight and proceed on foot. Since I was too much Phaon's friend not to give my arm to Cynegire so that he could talk with Sapho, I didn't fail to do so, and Phaon was thus able to talk for a time with Sapho. It was some two hundred feet till the end of this difficult stretch, and in addition something broke down in Cynegire's coach, which meant we had to sit down and wait under some willows nearby. I drew Cynegire aside on the pretext of talking with her about some great plan Pittacus was negotiating so that Phaon could talk with Sapho, but Madam, this young woman who was dying to reproach him no sooner saw him at her feet in the most passionate manner in the world than she felt her heart softening despite herself. Nevertheless, making a great effort to keep herself from giving up her anger altogether, she asked Phaon how he could abandon his ordinary amusements to meet her. But she asked him blushing so much and making it so plain that she complained only in order to be mollified, that Phaon, who understood all her expressions, didn't fail to satisfy her.

"What, Madam," he said. "How can you ask me that? Have I given you cause to say what you say to me, I, whose only true joy is what you bestow? Because, Madam, how do you imagine that a man whom you graciously allowed to believe you do not hate, how could such a man ever be unhappy? When I am away from you and not in despair, it is for no other reason than that I well know that you have not banished me from your heart. That thought is so sweet, Madam, it creates in my spirit a joy so unending that I defy Fortune to make me miserable as long as I am loved by you. Yes, Madam, I could lose all the favors Fortune bestows; I could be exiled, imprisoned, overcome by all sorts of misfortunes, but I would not think myself miserable as long as I believed myself possessed of your affection. Accuse yourself, therefore, Madam, of the innocent pleasures for which you reproach me, if they displease you. But as for me, I tell you what I believe, and I am persuaded that I am not lacking in love and respect for you, if the joy of being loved by the divine Sapho is not more powerful than the sorrow of absence could be.

"For the rest, Madam," he added with infinite tenderness and passion, "in order to judge what I feel when I do not see you, you have only to see what I feel when I see you again. See in my eyes, charming Sapho, what is in my heart. If these eyes do not tell you that I find you more beautiful than I have ever seen you, that I have greater joy in seeing you again than any person has ever had, and that I am the most in love of all men, consider them imposters for betraying the tenderness of my passion and punish me for their crime. But if, on the contrary, they say to you that I love more than anyone has ever loved, then don't amuse yourself by wishing to know precisely what I do when I don't see you, and remember only that you have never seen a lover at your feet whose passion was as strong or as tender as mine. Because finally," he continued, "what does it matter to you how I prove my love for you when you are not there, as long as I am not unfaithful, as long as when we are reunited you find in me the same ardor and passion? For my part," he added, "I hoped that you would amuse yourself in the country; I wished you beautiful days, and I hoped that the good humor of Cydnon would prevent you from being bored in your solitude."

"Ah, Phaon," cried Sapho, "you don't know how to love if you desire that your absence should not affect me! I declare to you that I will never be satisfied with you if you do not become the most unhappy of men from the moment I am out of your sight." "But Madam," he said, interrupting her, "I must then forget that you love me, because if I don't, I won't be unhappy." "On the contrary," replied Sapho, "that memory ought to make you even more unhappy, or at least I well know that the melancholy your absence causes me comes from being separated from the person by whom I believe myself loved." "Ah, Madam," replied Phaon, "your feelings and mine are quite different in this regard, for it isn't possible that you could have as much joy at being adored by me as I have glory in being loved by you, so it isn't strange that the memory of my passion doesn't console you in my absence. What's more, it isn't that the memory of your generosity to me diminishes some part of the sorrow your absence makes me feel, but again, Madam, I cannot conceive how one could be sad when certain of being loved by you."

"Doubtless there is intelligence in what you say," replied Sapho, "but hardly any love. If your eyes did not give the lie to your words, I would have reason to believe that you do not love me at all. For to be absent from the one you love without being miserable is the greatest sign of a lukewarm affection one could ever give." "But Madam," he said, "how could you believe I don't love you, or that I hardly love you? Is there some action of mine, some word, that might permit you to doubt it? Has even one of my looks suggested I don't love you?"

"Everything I see of you," she answered, "speaks to me of your undeniable passion; but all that I don't see speaks your indifference. During my absence, you made pleasure visits, you went on outings, you were good-humored, and I find your face with hardly a sign of melancholy, as if you had no reason to be sad. But what terrifies me," she added, "is that you don't fail to show tender, delicate feelings, to say such sweet and flattering things, just as if you would be in despair the moment I am out of your sight. Nevertheless, I cannot conceive how one could possess with such pleasure what one could lose without pain. There are moments when I think that seeing me gives you no joy because my absence causes you no sorrow."

"Madam," he said, looking at her with such passion that she blushed, "I defy you to believe that when I am near you I am not more in love than any man alive. Yes, divine Sapho," he added, "even if you were told that I frequented balls every day of your absence and that I entertained all the beauties in Mytilene, and even if you were assured that I was unfaithful, I am certain that the moment your eyes met mine, the joy that you saw there would convince you that I love you more than anyone has ever loved and that no other lover has ever had such reason to love as I have. First of all, you are, without exception, the most delightful person in the world. I desire you more than anyone ever has; I esteem you beyond all admiration. I love you so much because my desire drives me and because reason counsels me and gratitude demands it."[24]

"As for that last cause," replied Sapho, "don't ever say that to me. My feelings are too sensitive to endure it." "What, Madam," replied Phaon, "would you wish me not to be grateful for your goodness to me?" "I want you to acknowledge it," she answered, "but I do not wish it to be the unique cause of your affection for me. If someone were to love me only because I loved him, he would do me the greatest injury. I want to be loved for so many other reasons that even were I ungrateful from birth, still he would love me ardently. Never put gratitude among the causes of your passion if you wish to persuade me that you love me as I wish to be loved, for that is not courteous, or gallant, or passionate. Gratitude may," she added, "sometimes give birth to friendship, but it can never give birth to love. It is fine for you to tell me that gratitude gently strengthens the ties that bind you, but I do not want you, as I have already said, to count it among the causes of your passion. Next it will be that my favors preceded your affection, whereas I maintain the contrary, that your affection preceded my favors. If I owe your love to something, it is to your inclination and to my own merit, because given my character, I cannot endure being loved in any other way.

"I remember once," she added, "almost hating a perfectly amiable woman because I discovered that all the eagerness she showed to be loved by me wasn't because she loved me tenderly, but only because she hoped her name would turn up in some of my verses and that I would perhaps do her portrait. Imagine, then, Phaon, if I should find it good that you should love me for any other reason than because you found me lovable and because you couldn't help but feel affection for me." Cynegire's coach having been repaired as Sapho said this, they had to end their conversation as I had to end mine with Cynegire, with whom I had been in a deep discussion of politics in order to give Phaon time to speak of his love to Sapho and to make his peace with her. Nevertheless, the beautiful Sapho couldn't let him go without giving him some further sign of her unhappiness, for as they were about to take leave of one another, she asked him in what agreeable company he intended to spend the evening. "As for us," she added, gesturing at Cynegire, "we will see no one today." "I will spend it alone with Democedes," he replied, "and I will spend it conversing with him about the joy I feel at your return."

24. The French word is *reconnaissance*, literally acknowledgment, gratitude, or recognition, a term associated with love and courtship in the period. Phaon declares that his love is motivated by admiration, desire, and reason, and also out of gratitude and acknowledgment of Sapho's love for him.

"You would have done better to have spent the days past speaking of the sorrow you felt at my absence," she replied. After that, Sapho got into the coach where I had already put Cynegire, but in helping her get in, Phaon gave her his hand so gently and respectfully, and he made her see in his eyes such indescribable love, that it didn't take much for Sapho to repent of having accused him of not loving her enough. And in fact it is true, no one could love more ardently than Phaon even though he was not particularly sensitive to the sorrow caused by absence and, on the contrary, consoled himself easily enough at the loss of one pleasure with another.

Yet Sapho's reproaches caused him to spend the evening alone. He was so happy at having made his peace with her that he needed no other pleasures. It wasn't that she had said she would pardon him, but that they were so used to understanding one another without talking that they habitually believed their looks more than their words so that, though Sapho had reproached Phaon a great deal, he couldn't help but believe that he had seen in her eyes that he was as much in her heart as he had ever been. And the next morning he was at her house so early that no one else was there, and he succeeded in making his peace. They were together almost an hour, with all the joy that follows reconciliation after such trifling quarrels and only makes love grow. But finally their pleasure was interrupted by Alcæus, who loved Sapho almost as much as the beautiful Athys and was therefore one of the most eager to see her. It's true that his mistress arrived soon after, but you can be sure that jealousy played as great a part in her visit as friendship. She knew perfectly well that Sapho didn't love Alcæus, but that didn't prevent her from being extremely jealous. Nor was Nicanor among the last to pay his respects to Sapho, and Amithone, Erinne, and Cydnon having also arrived, the whole charming company found itself back together.

First, Athys, Amithone, and Erinne talked about their return journey, which didn't much please Phaon, and they would have talked much longer if Phylire hadn't arrived and brought a stranger of noble bearing whom she introduced to Sapho and whom I now know was the brother of the valiant prisoner Mereontes, whom the invincible Cyrus had saved from the flames after having defeated him. But Madam, he seemed so little like a foreigner that one would have thought he was from one of the most civilized cities in Greece. One would never suspect that he was Scythian,[25] though he had neither the coloring nor the hair that Greeks ordinarily have. His complexion was fair and he was almost blond, but since there is no general rule

---

25. The Scythians were a nomadic and military people of central Asia with whom the Greeks fought and later traded.

in these things, no one, as I have said, doubted that he was from one of the Greek cities. Not only did he have the air of a Greek about him, but he also spoke our language quite eloquently. Even his person was infinitely pleasing:[26] though he isn't particularly tall, he is of noble height and build and moves gracefully and easily. His features are handsome and agreeable: his eyes a little languorous and his carriage that of a man of high station. What's more, he is a brilliant wit and wise at the same time, with an air both gallant and spirited. He has a subtle conception of things and expresses them in similar fashion—this illustrious Scythian is in fact one of the most amiable and accomplished men in the world.

Since Sapho always took particular care to welcome foreigners of merit who came to visit her, she received him with that charming courtesy that was natural to her. To show him how agreeably surprised she was to see him, she complained to the assembled company that they had not let her know there was a stranger who was such a gentleman in Mytilene. "No one could have let you know," replied Phylire, "because it was only yesterday that one of my brothers returned from a very long journey and brought him to me. He was in no state to present himself to you because he wasn't feeling well, and he needed me to present him to you when he had recovered. Knowing I was coming here, he wanted me to introduce him to the admirable woman of whom he had heard so much and who was held in such esteem throughout the cities of Greece where he had traveled." "If I preferred glory to my own happiness," Sapho replied, "I should be sad to see a man who doubtless esteems me more without knowing me than he will once we are acquainted. But I care not to come by esteem dishonestly and would rather be in danger of losing some part of your esteem if only I might win some part of your friendship."

"To destroy a part of the esteem I have for you would be a very bad way of winning your friendship," the agreeable stranger replied, smiling. "But Madam, you are so sure not to, that if modesty didn't permit the occasional telling of white lies about ourselves, you would not have been able to say what you just said, for though you have hardly spoken I cannot help but believe you always speak well."

"Wait at least before praising me," answered Sapho gallantly, "until there can be some semblance of truth to the praises you offer. So, do me the honor of not saying anything flattering until you have had the time to learn whether I am worthy of the admiration of a gentleman such as yourself."

---

26. Scudéry shifts tense here from the moment of meeting in the past to an ongoing description of Clirantes in the present.

"You are bold, Madam," replied Clirantes, "to bestow so promptly this glorious appellation—honnête homme[27] or gentleman—on a Scythian." "I have such a reputation for recognizing the merit of gentlemen and ladies," she replied, "that I have a woman friend who tells me sometimes that I don't really know it so much as divine it. That's why you mustn't suspect me of judging precipitously, because it is a particular talent of mine, to be hardly ever wrong in my choice of those I find worthy of praise."

After that, the entire company joined the conversation, which proceeded delightfully. But Sapho couldn't help her surprise at Clirantes' manners and courtesy, so she asked him how it was possible that the civility of Scythians, if they were all like him, should not be as renowned as that of the Greeks. "My country, Madam, is so near Scythia that some people confuse us with the Scythians," he replied, "but if you knew it, you would be all the more surprised that I am as civilized as you appear to be in finding me somewhat more polite and courteous than most Scythians. I am not simply a Scythian; I come from Sarmatae[28] originally, which is even more removed, and the manners of the Sarmatae are extremely strange. Yet though I am from Sarmatae, I am from a country that doesn't hold to their customs—we call ourselves the new Sarmatae to distinguish ourselves from them. We have hardly any trade with them because our policy is to have no neighbors so their foreign manners and customs don't corrupt ours. We do all we can to live on what our own country produces so that we need have no commerce with other nations." "What you say seems fascinating to me—it reminds me of the Spartans who take particular care not to allow foreign customs to be introduced into their city. But when you tell me you have no neighbors, I must admit that I don't understand. It would doubtless please us all if you would take the trouble to help me understand and tell us something about the origins of your people and the customs of your country, which must be delightful if many people resemble you."

"I beg you, Madam, not to judge my country by me; to do it the justice I owe it, I wish to tell you something about it. You will know already, Madam, that the Sarmatae in general, some of whom are confused with the Scythians, as I have already told you, and others of whom are quite distinct, have always had such bizarre customs that even their sacrificial practices show the ferocity of their nature. Instead of building temples to Mars, whom they

27. See the volume editor's introduction and note 1.

28. The Sarmatae were an Asian people related to the Scythians whose women hunted and fought alongside men and who originally lived east of the river Tanais. Herodotus links them to the legendary female warriors, the Amazons.

worship, or raising statues to him, they make an enormous pyre that they set afire, and when it has burned, they plant a sword in the middle of the huge pile of ashes before which they sacrifice prisoners they have taken in war. These people were once even more cruel and savage than they are now, yet they are less ferocious and bizarre than they once were because the prince who governs them today has civilized them somewhat. But in their most savage days, Fortune brought among them some Greeks said to be descended from the Callipides who lived along the banks of the river Tanais. By teaching them their own customs, they so tamed some of the leading Sarmatae that they became horrified by their own customs so that, little by little, the Greeks acquired such authority in a rather large part of the country that the people recognized one among them as their leader.

"Things went so far that when the prince who ruled the Sarmatae wanted to oppose this faction, he found himself thwarted—there was such a sudden uprising among the people that they came to blows. But as the Greek chief was at once valiant and prudent, the prince of the Sarmatae could not vanquish him; on the contrary, he was forced to let him form a small state in the middle of his own and there was nothing he could do to stop him. Finally, Madam, this illustrious Greek, having brought together all those who voluntarily wished to be at once his disciples and his subjects, laid out the borders in which he chose for them to live. Not only did he defend this tiny country against those who would destroy it, but he so ravaged the lands surrounding their chosen home that he made a great desert all around his state so that it was not easy to make war against him.

"After some five or six glorious years the prince of the Sarmatae was forced to make peace and to endure, in the very heart of his state, another small state surrounded by desert. One of the terms of this peace was that both the subjects of the old prince of the Sarmatae and those of the new sovereign were prohibited from cultivating or building in the lands that the latter had wasted. And this provision was so rigorously enforced by our forefathers, Madam, that even now it is at least three days journey across the desert in any direction in order to reach the place where I was born. There one finds one of the most civilized countries in the world, hemmed in by another that is not at all civilized. One could say that your island is not as absolutely without neighbors as is my country even though it is on the mainland, because it is easier to get to Mytilene from Phrygia than from my country to those that surround it."

"What you tell me of your birthplace seems to me so unusual and so beautiful," replied Sapho, "and the idea of this tiny, neighborless state so pleases me that if women traveled as often as men, I think I would be curious to go there." "Your curiosity, Madam, would be satisfied even more than you imagine," answered Clirantes, "because this illustrious Greek who was our first prince enclosed his state in a desert only in order to lock in all the virtues and all the arts and sciences that he wished to inspire in his subjects and to prevent the vices of their neighbors from opposing his plan. Since he had many clever people around him, he established such good order among those who obeyed him that in no time at all their manners were entirely reformed. Since this prince died in advanced old age, he had the time to consolidate his laws and left a son old enough and prudent enough to up-hold them. He had the satisfaction of seeing all the arts and all the sciences flourish in his state, and his memory is still so dear among us that, when we want to promise something, we do it in the name of our first king."

"I beg you," said Sapho, "tell me in more detail about your particular customs." "Since they are almost all Greek," replied Clirantes, "I would bore you if I told you what you know better than I do; instead I'll tell you what is particular about ours. Therefore I won't tell you, Madam, that we think of the gods just as you do, and that with the exception of some traces of ancient Sarmatae rituals that our first king preserved for political reasons, our sacrifices are made as yours are; our city, our villages, our houses are much the same as those one sees here. But I will tell you that our state is not very big: there is only one major city, fifty towns, and two hundred villages. It is true that our city is one of the most agreeable in the world, and if foreigners were permitted to come freely or to leave once they have come, its reputation would be worldwide. But since it is one of our customs almost never to permit a foreigner who has come among us to leave the country, our reputation is closed in by the deserts that surround us. We are so happy not to envy others and to be envied by no one that we don't care that no one speaks of us."

"Why can one not leave after one visits your country?" asked Amithone. "You can only come on that condition," replied Clirantes. "There are guards at the borders wherever you arrive and you are always stopped—you don't do whatever you like there and you can't even enter if you are not judged worthy. In fact, when the desire to live in our country seizes someone, the guards stop him and take him to the prince who gives him over to people whose responsibility it is to consider him over the course of three months to see if he knows something that makes him worthy of being received among us. After that, he must swear never to leave the country without the per-mission of the prince (who rarely gives it), and he is required to promise to observe inviolably all our customs. Then he is given wealth in proportion to his status and merit."

"But when one of your countrymen wishes to travel," continued Sapho, "must he have the prince's permission as well?" "Yes, Madam," replied Clirantes, "and it is difficult to obtain. And once obtained, when one returns to our country, he must submit to the same three-month examination to see if his manners have been corrupted during his absence. This restriction is certainly somewhat irksome," he added. "In fact, about a century ago it caused an uprising that ended only after a small civil war, but finally the prince who ruled then banished all the rebels from his state. They founded a large colony near a river called the Danube where they established the very customs that had provoked their rebellion: they made a desert all around their state just like ours. But Madam, so as not to bore you with too long a saga about politics and the government of my country, I must tell you one thing only concerning the present state of our court. We are governed by a young queen, one of the most accomplished princesses in the world, who has only one son. Don't imagine that our court is lacking in civility, for all the arts and sciences are to be found among us," he added, "and since we are almost always at peace, gallantry shines its brightest among us. We even have special laws concerning love, and there are punishments for unfaithful lovers as well as for rebel subjects. Fidelity is so venerated among us that it is expected even after death. In fact, those who marry for love are not free to remarry and must declare themselves publicly. We even console separated lovers as you do those in mourning, and they are so censured if they are seen at some place of amusement while their mistresses are away that no one dares."

"We know persons here who would be hard put to observe that custom," interrupted Sapho, blushing. "It is so generally obeyed," replied Clirantes, "that were such persons among us they would observe it. Since the founder of our state wanted his subjects to be committed to their country, he wished them to be bound by love. So gallantry is preserved among us because it is a result of politics, and all the customs of lovers are as old as our state and are almost as inviolable as those of religion. A man can't change his mistress without explaining the reasons for his inconstancy, and a lady can't abandon her lover without declaring the reason for the change. Since peace, leisure, and plenty are always ours, we talk about love in all our conversations so that those who visit our country, which they can only do by way of the ancient Sarmatae, are so astonished after having seen such a savage, brutal people to find such civility and gallantry, that they can't help but show their surprise. What's more, since our founder was Greek, we have preserved the Greek language virtually uncorrupted. Of course it isn't the language of the people, but there isn't a person of quality who doesn't know it. We even have persons at court who write verse that perhaps the beautiful Sapho would not find unworthy of her praise."

"You portray your country in such a delightful way," replied Sapho, "and you witness so well by your very presence all that you say in its favor, that if it were not so far away I think that I should leave my own country to go live there." After that, the entire company joined the conversation, and Clirantes acquitted himself so admirably that he won the esteem of everyone present. Since Sapho knew with an uncanny cleverness what transpired in the hearts of those she cared to observe, she predicted from this first visit that Clirantes would fall in love with Phylire and that Phylire would not at all hate Clirantes if he spent some time on their island. And in fact, from what happened, it was easy to see that Sapho was not mistaken.

In the meantime, although the reconciliation of Sapho and Phaon had been sincere, there remained in Sapho's mind the inclination to suspect Phaon of not loving her in exactly the manner she wished to be loved. And since Athys, Alcæus, and Nicanor were continually trying to undermine him, they often provoked quarrels because he couldn't go anywhere without their telling Sapho how gay he appeared in her absence—either they told her, or they had someone else tell her. Given the fact that it was impossible for him to change, he thus continued to be as he had always been, which is to say, everything amused him and nothing bored him. He was without a doubt happiest when at Sapho's side; joy was so bright in his eyes that you could easily see that it was deep in his heart, but regardless, when he didn't see her, he did not despair and he was in fact able to do without her. There being so many spies interested in observing him and serving him badly, it was no longer possible for him to hide and so Sapho could get no rest. From the moment Phaon was away from her, she wondered what he was doing, and, having informed herself and having learned that usually he amused himself somewhere else, she experienced such sadness that I don't know how to describe it even though my sister told me in part what Sapho said in complaining of Phaon.

"Who has ever lived a fate like mine?" said Sapho one day to Cydnon. "For though people say I should be extremely happy to be loved by the most courteous and worthy man in the world, nevertheless, I would be happier if he hated me because, on my honor, I am persuaded that his hatred would cure me of the love I feel for him; but in the state to which I am condemned, I can neither hate him nor love him with untroubled pleasure. And what is most cruel, there is no remedy. For if Phaon didn't love me at all, I could imagine that one day he might love me as I wish; if he were in fact unfaithful,

I could hope that he would return to me; and if he hated me, I could still more believe that his hatred would not be forever. But Phaon surely loves me as much as he is capable of loving, and if he were the same when I am out of his sight as he is when he sees me, I would have nothing to wish. Yet, with all this ardent love that is manifest in all his actions, in all his words, and in his every look, I am so little satisfied with him that I am the unhappiest person on earth. What causes my sadness can never change, so it follows necessarily that I will always be unhappy."

"But since as long as you see Phaon you are happy, see him always—marry him so as never to be apart," Cydnon said to her. "Oh, Cydnon," Sapho replied, "had I not promised myself never to marry, Phaon's behavior would certainly drive me to such a promise, for if I am not able to make him unhappy when he is away from me in our present situation, imagine how he would be if perhaps I could no longer make him happy to see me." "Well, what remedy do you propose?" asked Cydnon. "I propose," she said, "to make Phaon as unhappy as I am. And that desire is so deep in my heart that if I am able to succeed in making him feel pain, I will feel indescribable joy." "I have seen him so susceptible to jealousy," replied Cydnon, "that if you want to make him suffer, I assure you, you will have all the pleasure you seek." "Two days have already passed," replied Sapho, "since I made up my mind to do so." And she added, carried away by her passion, "I want to begin this very day to treat Nicanor so well that, since Phaon can't manage to be unhappy when he doesn't see me, he will be when he does."

And truly, Madam, the beautiful Sapho resolved to enact her plan and managed it with such skill that Phaon began in fact to be jealous and to be as unhappy as she had desired him to be. At first she felt a strange joy, and all his complaints were so gratifying and sweet to her that she couldn't bring herself to end them quickly. Meanwhile, Nicanor couldn't believe his good fortune, and Alcæus was so surprised that Sapho had changed—but not to her advantage—that he rededicated himself entirely to Athys. Jealousy tormented Phaon, who couldn't imagine whence came this change in Sapho. I told him that it was a whim that caused it, but he didn't believe me, and he came to hate Nicanor so horribly that he couldn't tolerate him. And so that poor lover was hated by his rival without being loved by his mistress, and his unhappiness was the greater since he was extremely perceptive and could tell that in fact Sapho didn't love him at all, but still loved Phaon. He considered the favors she showered on him a stratagem to increase the love of his rival, so he was more vexed at Sapho than at Phaon. There has never been anything like this mix of feelings and their piquant effects in the hearts of all three. But in the end the two suffering rivals, being unable to endure it any longer, quarreled and fought, and no one could say really who had won because they were separated before their fight ended.

Because Pittacus was a wise prince and because the sorrow that he felt at the recent death of Prince Tisander made him quite angry at their quarrel, which had divided the entire city, he banished them both for a year in order to prevent further consequences from this troublesome affair. Since Phaon had traveled more in Sicily than anywhere else, he decided to go there to pass the time of his exile, and Nicanor planned to go to Phrygia. Phaon begged me so urgently to arrange with Cydnon for him to see Sapho alone that I did what I could to satisfy him. It wasn't even difficult because the violent passion Sapho felt in her soul made her repent of the jealousy she had caused Phaon, and she wished passionately to pardon him even though it was hardly to her advantage, because knowing his temperament, she believed nothing was more dangerous to her than absence. But finally, having begged Cydnon to use all her influence with Sapho, and having forced me to admit that his beloved did not care for Nicanor except to increase his love, when I told my friend this agreeable and important secret, he at first didn't want to believe it. But since it is never impossible to let oneself be persuaded of what one wants to believe, he thought at least that it was possible, and he resolved to enlighten himself by means of Sapho's beautiful eyes.

This meeting took place at Cydnon's and renewed their friendship in the tenderest manner in the world. "And so, Madam," said Phaon, approaching her, "having seen me the most jealous and most unhappy of men, do you believe at last that I am the most in love of all lovers? And if the joy that I had at being loved by you did not persuade you, are you persuaded by the sorrow I felt at being abandoned?" "If you had been abandoned," she replied, "you would have had no chance to protest, because I would have refused ever to see you. But Phaon, if you have suffered, reflect upon it, for had you known how to love well, I would not have had to teach you how in so unpleasant a way as jealousy." "In truth, Madam," he told her, "you have made use of a cruel plan to make me suffer; but at least tell me clearly that you never loved Nicanor and that you treated him favorably only because you loved me as always." "Let me tell you only half of what you demand," she replied, blushing, "and I will be content for you to guess the rest."

After that, Madam, the two vexed angry lovers made up completely, telling one another all the endearments a pure and innocent love would allow. Joy did not return to Sapho's heart, however, because the thought of Phaon's long and cruel absence so worried her that she could not rejoice fully in the sweetness of their reconciliation. "What can I expect from you," she said to Phaon, "given your temperament, you, I say, who are strongly moved only by what you see and who are not touched by what you don't see? For though it is possible that you may be faithful during this long separation, it is impossible you should suffer as I will suffer. And if you are capable of joy and pleasure two days after you leave me, what will you be after entire months apart? Should I not fear that the moment I am out of your sight I may lose you? For I know that during a long absence, only sorrow can be the sure safeguard of a lover's heart. Customarily, love is born in pleasure and joy is the first requirement for its birth, and since you will find it again no doubt as soon as I am out of your sight, have I no reason to be apprehensive that a new love will seize your heart and drive me out?"

"Since I have never loved anything as I have loved you, Madam," replied Phaon, "because I have never found anyone to be so delightful as to merit all my affections, I promise—and I speak the truth—that before I met you, I had had little experience of love. In fact, I had felt my passion ebb time and time again, had felt it abandon me even in the very presence of those I thought I loved. Some days I was a stranger to myself from the hour I went into company until the hour I left, until I no longer knew myself. I tell you that I sometimes saw my desire be born and die the same day without knowing exactly why I had felt desire in the first place, nor why I no longer did. But with you, Madam, it isn't like that. I love you quite differently, and if I am any judge of what I will feel when I no longer see you, judging by what I feel when I do see you, I must be prepared to be the most unhappy of men. Because after all, this harsh absence doesn't resemble at all those that you feel I didn't feel sufficiently. When you were in the country, I always knew your return was so near that it wasn't odd that that expectation diminished in part my sadness and that the knowledge that you loved me gave me enough pleasure to prevent despair. But Madam, I am leaving for a year, and I leave anxious that you are not sufficiently persuaded of the magnitude of my love. Truly I do not love you as I loved before I met you, because then my feelings were so strange that my mind and spirit rebuffed even favors if they were not bestowed gracefully and in such a way as to make them agreeable. But now, Madam, my feelings are quite changed because even your smallest kindnesses give me inordinate joy when I receive them; sometimes you even do indifferent things that gratify me because my passion interprets them to my advantage. That is why, Madam, I ask that you please not judge me by the past, because truly, I have never loved as I love now. Yes, divine Sapho," he added, "I love you more than I loved you before and more than I ever believed it possible to love."

"I believe it," she said, interrupting him, "but after all, judging from the past, you will love me less than you think you do once you have been away from me for a fortnight." After that, Phaon spoke his feelings and made a thousand protestations of his fidelity to the beautiful Sapho, and he did it in so passionate a manner that she fooled herself into believing that Phaon's heart had changed and that he would feel this long absence painfully. And so all the tenderness of their love was renewed in their hearts and they said to one another all that the most delicate passion could inspire and all that the most heartfelt sorrow could devise for two lovers who were about to be parted.

So Sapho and Phaon separated, infinitely content with one another. Phaon embarked the next day and Sapho left for the country with my sister, but she went not so much to enjoy the sweetness of delightful solitude as to hide the sorrow in her soul and to avoid saying good-bye to Nicanor. He knew only too well that he was right in thinking that the attention he had received did not rightly belong to him. Following Phaon's departure, Madam, Sapho felt only regret; it's true that on her return to Mytilene, she and Clirantes became close friends. He had fallen so in love with Phylire that you could hardly imagine anyone being more in love. But meanwhile the conversation at Sapho's was not as amusing as it once had been because she was melancholy and avoided, as much as politeness allowed, all pleasurable occasions. And so this amiable and fine company soon began to disband— Alcæus finally married Athys who, after her marriage, saw less of Sapho; Erinne came down with a languishing malady; my sister was in Phrygia with my mother; and Amithone went to the country, so I was almost the only person with whom Sapho could speak with confidence.

Sapho had, however, a woman friend who was very dear to her, whom I didn't mention to you at the beginning of my story, for she had hardly been in Mytilene during the long period of Sapho and Phaon's love. But she returned the day my sister left and took my sister's place—certainly she was worthy of the friendship Sapho felt for her even though her fortune and circumstances were not quite those of Sapho's other friends. She was called Agelaste because of her melancholy temperament, and she had many excellent qualities: her person was more pleasing than many women more beautiful than she. It is true she isn't tall, but she is nevertheless shapely; she has ash-blond hair, soft blue eyes, a somewhat long face with a high nose, an agreeable mouth, a clear complexion, though a little pale, beautiful teeth, a lovely bosom, well-made hands, very beautiful arms, and an expression so wise and modest that upon seeing her everyone thought well of her. Agelaste also played the lute extraordinarily well, but what I most esteemed in her was her intelligence, her discretion, her tenderness, and her loyalty, which was so great that one could confide in her completely. What's more, although she was naturally melancholy, she nevertheless made conversation agreeable, principally for her particular friends, because with others she spoke little and she was so incapable of wishing to put herself forward that she often preferred to let appalling things be said by people who couldn't do otherwise than to interrupt them to say agreeable and decorous things herself.

So Agelaste and Sapho became inseparable once Sapho's friends had deserted her, and Phylire saw her less than she had before. And it is true that Sapho needed consolation just then, because Cynegire, to whom she owed so much, had died, and she discovered only a few days later that her brother, of whom she had had only vexing news for quite some time, had become enamored of a slave named Rhodopis whom Aesop had also loved. Charaxus' passion was so great that, having freed her, he completely ruined himself for her love. Sapho knew as well that Rhodopis, who had become famous in Egypt more for her beauty and wiles than her virtue, had sent him back to Mytilene in a most piteous state. In addition, since the death of Tisander had brought great changes to the court of Pittacus, life in our city was not what it once was. Sapho was very happy, then, to be able to find solace in herself without searching for it in another. Since her major concern was Phaon's absence, she was sometimes forced to endure my speaking of him, even though she deplored both male and female confidants alike, because it was through me that she received news of him and could respond. Nevertheless, since it wasn't possible to receive letters, often her disquiet only grew.

Sometime after that her anxiety redoubled, however, when, receiving a packet from Phaon that I brought to her promptly, she found, in addition to a letter from her lover, one addressed to him in a woman's hand and written so badly that one could easily see that whoever had written it had hardly any wit or intelligence. Nevertheless, it appeared that Phaon must have written her several letters and that he had spent no little time with her and had even serenaded her. In fact, Madam, I learned afterwards that although Phaon still loved Sapho dearly, he had not failed to find consolation in the company of the beautiful fool whom he had previously loved while in Sicily. There was no comparison between the feelings he had for Sapho and those he felt for this beautiful Sicilian, for he felt an ardent passion for the former whereas the relation he had to the latter might rather be termed an amusement than real affection. Nevertheless, he didn't fail to entertain himself as if he were not separated from the most marvelous person in the world, a person who loved him with unimaginable tenderness.

But to return to Sapho, you can imagine, Madam, her surprise at finding in the packet from Phaon a note addressed to him, and what's more, the most stupid and flirtatious missive in the world. In fact, I don't think there has ever been one like it: the handwriting was quite beautiful, but that only made it the more ridiculous, because the spelling was so bad, the meaning so puzzling, the expressions so vulgar, and the syntax so confused and so opposed to all the rules of eloquence and reason that one could hardly understand how it was possible that a lady could write in such a way. But what was ironic was that the letter Phaon wrote to Sapho was so elegant, so courtly, so passionate, that it was unbelievable that a man who could write so well could have anything to do with a woman who wrote so badly. It appeared from this note that Phaon saw her frequently, that he had written to her more than once, and that he had serenaded her, as I have already mentioned.

I can assure you that Sapho suffered a painful shock from this cruel adventure, and being unable to hide her pain, she showed the letter to Agelaste and to me. "Who has ever seen such weakness as your friend's," she said to me, "because really, I know very well when I see him that he loves me as much as it is possible to love, and I even know that he believes then that he will be incapable of taking any pleasure in intercourse with anyone else. Nevertheless, from this note it appears that he is involved in some sort of affair with the stupidest woman in the world and at the same time he receives letters from me, which at least set down my feelings in an orderly fashion, and which he doubtless puts in the same place and saves with the same care as the letters of this new friend or mistress." Since I knew Phaon's character better than Sapho did, I tried to defend my friend as best I could and to persuade this admirable young woman that her lover's heart had no share in the sort of pleasures in which he indulged when he was away from her. It was simply to amuse himself, to be entertained, that Phaon lived as he did.

"Ah, Democedes, a wretched lover shuns amusement, and the most delightful serenades would hardly entertain Phaon if he loved as I do," she said. "Far from serenading others as he has done, he would find it tedious to be obliged to be where others were offering serenades. I am resolved," she added, "to do everything I can to stop loving him and instead to hate myself if I am unable to hate him." In vain I protested that Phaon's love had not changed and that it was merely his way and that his heart had almost no part in his actions; but given the pain she felt, she didn't want to believe me, and she responded to Phaon in a very particular way. She returned the note that he had sent to her unknowingly, and though she had contemplated a long complaint reminding him of his duty, she wrote to him only these words:

Sapho to Phaon

Because you have joined yourself in friendship with the woman whose letter I am returning to you, resolve to break ours off, because I would consider it unworthy of me were I to suffer a man who has deprived me of his heart in order to give it to a person so unworthy of him to remain any longer in mine.

Sapho

Without a doubt this letter was well calculated to cause Phaon pain, but to tell the truth, I wrote him another that succeeded in making him even more miserable, for I reproached him so roundly for his thoughtlessness and I impressed upon him so forcefully that he might well lose Sapho's affection that from the moment he had both her letter and mine, he changed. In fact, when he came to realize that Sapho might drive him from her heart, he no longer had any trouble giving up common pleasures in order to safeguard one so very great. Since he could imagine no other way of healing Sapho's heart than by leaving Sicily and coming to her side, he decided to come to Lesbos in disguise and boarded a merchant ship that left him at a port on the tip of our island. There he hid at the house of a friend who had a place not far from Sapho's country house. But once there, having informed himself where she was and where I was, he knew that I had gone away for a fortnight and that Sapho was at home with no other company than her dear Agelaste. Not wishing to lose so good a chance, and knowing the hours she usually spent beside the delightful spring that I have described to you, he hid himself in the little wood that surrounded it until she arrived there.

But Madam, he had hardly waited a quarter of an hour when he saw Sapho appear with her friend. She was so sad that, however incapable he was of feeling sorrow, his heart was moved. It's true that the certainty of being loved so tenderly by the most admirable woman in the world gave him at least as much joy as Sapho's melancholy made him sad. Meanwhile, he wanted to give her time to sit down before revealing himself and to recover himself a little from the turmoil this sight had caused in him. Chance had it that these two young women had sat down on a grassy seat with their backs to him so that he could approach them and hear what they said. The wood was very thick just there, and he trod so softly that they couldn't hear him approach. They had hardly sat down when Sapho spoke: "But my dear Agelaste, what you tell me seems so unlikely that I don't know if I ought to believe you, so I want to know all the particulars."

"They are easy enough to tell," she replied, "because just after noon when I was leaving Mytilene I learned from Phylire herself that Clirantes, who is extremely well born and a cousin of the queen of the new Sarmatae, is so in love with her that he wants to marry her if she will follow him and go to live in his country. Since Phylire loves him at least as much as he loves her, and is accountable to no one except her brother, who wants her to marry Clirantes, she has made up her mind and is ready to follow him to this renowned Sarmatae. But because she doesn't want it to be known until she has left, since she has some relations who might wish to oppose it, she confided her secret to me and made me promise to ask if you will lend her your house to marry Clirantes. From there, she will leave immediately for that agreeable country where they have such severe laws against unfaithful lovers."

"Might it please the gods," replied Sapho, "that the unfaithful Phaon were there to be punished for his fecklessness. But Agelaste," she added, sighing, "since I know you have no attachment to Mytilene and that the many things that have happened in your life have made you no more attached to one place than another, can we not follow Phylire to Clirantes' happy country? Because I assure you, I can't endure Mytilene any longer." "As long as Phaon is in your heart," replied Agelaste, "I would not advise you to go to a place where he could not be received." "Since I am so little in Phaon's heart," answered Sapho, "I ought to be easy about being in a place where I will never hear him spoken of. That is why, my dear Agelaste, if you are able to follow my fortune, we will follow Phylire's, because there is nothing in Mytilene that doesn't displease me. Charaxus is coming back to persecute me; everyone I see bores me; I will never see Phaon there, or if I see him, I will see him unfaithful and as worthy of my hatred as I believed him worthy of my affection."

"Ah, Madam," he cried, bursting out of the place where he was hiding and throwing himself on his knees before her, "don't treat the most faithful of men with such injustice. To prove to you that I speak truly," he added, taking her hand (she couldn't stop him she was so surprised to see him), "permit me to go with you to this happy country where unfaithful lovers are so rigorously punished, because since I will never be absent from you there, I will not fear laws made against those who amuse themselves in the absence of their mistresses." "What, Phaon," she said, pulling her hand free from his, "you have the audacity to speak as you do after your latest crime?" "Yes, Madam," he said. "The love that I have in my soul makes me so bold that I dare beg you to do for me what I have just learned Phylire wishes to do for Clirantes. For isn't it true that as long as I am with you, I am the most faithful lover on earth? Take me, therefore, to this place from which I may never leave, and where you will never be out of my sight, and you will find in me the most faithful lover in the world. I don't agree," he added, "that my weakness makes me deserve the name *faithless*, for truly, Madam, since I met you there has never been a moment when I didn't adore you. I admit that I have a soul that seeks pleasure and flees pain, but from the moment I knew that I might lose you, I dropped everything that you believe steals my heart away from you and came back to ask, on my knees, your consent that I never leave you again. I know that I dare not be seen in Mytilene and that I am banished for a long time, but if it is true that you love me, you will follow me into exile out of love. I will tell you what I feel, Madam: I want never to be apart from you again. I am so determined, that if I knew Pittacus would have me arrested tomorrow, I would not leave today. Really, I would rather be his prisoner than no longer be your slave. There is no torment I would not choose rather than risk losing you. See, Madam," he said, "if you are capable of such a bold resolution: I left Sicily without a thought so that I might justify myself to you in person; therefore leave Lesbos without looking back, for you can rely on me. We can go anyplace on earth, Madam," he added, "for there is no place I could not live happily at your side as long as I might see you and as long as you remain to me what you have been always been and what I want to hope you still are in spite of all my weaknesses."

"But Phaon, is it possible that you mean what you say? Can I believe that a man who would have anything to do with a woman as foolish as the one whose letter I returned to you could still feel tenderness for one so unlike her? Speak, Phaon. Did you love me? Have you ceased loving me? Do you still love me? Or have you begun to care for me again? Ought I to see the love in your eyes as true love, or feigned love, or a love restored to life?" "Consider it, Madam," he replied, "an immortal love that sometimes hides itself when you do not see me, but which never ends. That is why, to reassure you, and to make me happy, I beg you, be with me always and let us join our lives forever." After that, Sapho said much else to him and Agelaste joined in as well and asked him to speak to her openly of his latest fault by telling her all about what had happened in Sicily. And he told it with such sincerity that Sapho was satisfied.

"Yes, Madam, I admit that I found there someone I had loved before you and that I found her no less receptive the second time than the first, that I spent some time with her, and that I could not tell her that I had changed in my feelings for her. Because truly, Madam, she never made me feel anything but imperfect pleasures before and my heart was never engaged. Occasionally I even received, I am sorry to say, tender enough signs of affection, but I was always ready, the moment you called me back, to leave her without pain. I was weak, Madam, but without being unfaithful. Doubtless my eyes have found that you are not the only beautiful woman in the world, but my heart has found nothing that it could love truly except the admirable Sapho. Come back to me, Madam, as I have come back to you, and give back to me this illustrious heart that once you gave as a precious gift to me, but give it back, I beseech you, with all its tenderness. And to guard against my weakness, choose if you will a deserted island where we will go live together, where I can love nothing but the sound of springs, the song of birds, and the gleaming meadows. As for me, I swear you are everything to me, and that as long as I have you before my eyes, there is nothing else I desire. I could even be blind," he added, "and still be happy. Were I only to hear you speak, my felicity would be great enough; the charm of your mind alone, without the aid of your beauty, would still make me happy. Judge, then, Madam, if seeing you and hearing you, I will not have reason to be the happiest lover in the world if only you permit me to see and hear you always. All the other women I have known are so poor at the art of pleasing that their greatest favors are less sweet than your smallest kindness. You know so well how to make your graces felt by those whom you wish to feel them that no one else can compare with you. You ready hearts for joy by first making them feel trifling cares; you skillfully make known the difficulty of doing what you do, so as to redouble the obligation; and you even know how, for a few moments, to withdraw hope of a favor you wish to grant so that one is all the more agreeably surprised when finally you grant it. I want to believe, Madam, that that is why you have not yet told me you forgive me, so as to surprise me more sweetly by forgetting completely my frailty."

After that, Phaon said other tender, touching things to the admirable Sapho, who for a long time responded like someone who did not intend to forgive, but finally her anger faded despite herself, and it was impossible to make him despair completely. So, taking the middle ground, she allowed him to hope she might be appeased and she promised him that the next day he might see her at the same time and in the same place. But why keep you in suspense concerning the end of this adventure, Madam? Sapho spent the night considering with Agelaste what she ought to do, and after having thought carefully, she concluded that she could not live happily without Phaon's love and that she should never be assured of his affection if she were separated from him. So after having also considered her own situation and that in Mytilene, she resolved to require of Phaon a powerful proof of his love by obliging him to follow her in her plan to go with Phylire. Furthermore, she would oblige him to do so knowing that she would never marry him and would have to content himself with the innocent signs of her affection she had given him during the time they had been together.

And since time pressed because Phylire was to be married at her house in only a week's time and leave the day after her wedding, the next day Sapho told Phaon all she had to tell him. He joyfully accepted her proposal to go with her to the country of the Sarmatae, but he promised, with considerable reluctance, never to press her to marry him. Nevertheless, since she allowed him to love her tenderly, and she promised as well to love him, in the end he promised all she asked so that Sapho considered herself the happiest woman in the world and Phaon also believed himself the happiest lover on earth.

Since Agelaste had neither father nor mother and had lost everything that could make Lesbos agreeable to her, she followed Sapho's fortune. Sapho left her country with such joy that Phaon was also glad to leave it, for in deciding to go, they gave one another such a powerful proof of love that the joy they felt in knowing how much they loved one another enabled them to leave without pain. Or so the valiant Mereontes assured me when he told me what I've just told you, for I wouldn't have known it without him since I wasn't in Mytilene when this happened. My sister was in Phrygia, and even had we been with Sapho, I think she would not have told us of her plan for fear that we might have opposed it. What convinced her most forcefully was knowing that there was only one city in Sarmatae's little state and that it would not be easy for Phaon to be often apart from her. So, being satisfied with his love when with her, she supposed that there she would always be content with him because he could never be long absent. Meanwhile, Agelaste told Phylire and Clirantes the lovers' plan and they were overjoyed. That well-known Sarmate knew that of all people, none were more apt to be well received in his country, and what's more, he knew that the queen who then governed that state respected him, and so he was sure that he could see to it that their entire charming group would be favorably received. So Clirantes went to Sapho's to arrange for them to join in their plan, and Phaon, who was always with his friend Clirantes, who lived near that admirable young woman, went with him. Such a beautiful friendship had grown up between these two lovers and Sapho, Phylire, and Agelaste as well that there had never been anything like it.

What made the voyage they undertook so convenient was that they had no need to concern themselves with how they would live, for not only did Clirantes assure them that he had more than enough to support them with reputation, and he could never be suspected of lying—Phylire's brother knew with certitude that what he said was true—there was as well the custom of the country, as I have already mentioned, for the prince to give foreigners whom he received in his state as much wealth as they needed to support them according to their condition and merit. Therefore, since Sapho departed planning never to return, she disposed of her wealth as if she had died and left papers in the hands of an older relative in which her will was explained with instructions that it not be opened for one month. After this, the wedding of Clirantes and Phylire took place secretly, and the next day this charming band set sail, planning to pass through the Bosphorus of Thrace and then to cross the Black Sea, so as to land above the Sea of Azov.

They had hardly embarked when a storm arose that changed their course considerably, for having buffeted them from headland to headland and from shore to shore, it cast them up at Epirus at the foot of a huge cliff forged by the sea at Leucas on which was built a temple to Apollo. This cliff was quite remarkable, because it was said that there Deucalion, when he was in love with Thessaly, threw himself into the sea and was cured of his passion. After their lovely troupe had given thanks to the god who was worshiped there, and their ship was refitted, they embarked again and continued happily on their course, so Mereontes told me. But Madam, before I finish telling you what I learned from him, I must tell you how surprised all the ladies and gentlemen of Mytilene were when Sapho's relation opened the will in which she declared how she wished to dispose of her estate. For when she left, she had represented her journey as the fulfillment of a vow that she had made to Neptune who had a temple some three days journey from Lesbos. But when it became known that she had bequeathed her estate as would someone who would not return, they didn't know what to think. To show her generosity, she left almost everything to Charaxus, even though they did not get along at all, but she gave all that was in her study to her friends without saying anything about her plans or where she was going, so that each person thought and said whatever seemed right to him or her.

Since it had been rumored that she wasn't happy with Phaon because he had fallen in love in Sicily, and no one knew that he had returned to her, some people believed that she had gone to find him. Others believed that she had been shipwrecked, which was what most people thought, though the story as told in Mytilene was unbelievable. For people knew that Sapho had been at her house in the country before she set sail, so those who love the astonishing and the marvelous and believe such things sometimes more easily than what is credible said that when she had been seated on the bank of the delightful spring I described to you, where she was lamenting Phaon's infidelity, a naiad had appeared to her and told her to go to Epirus and throw herself into the sea in the same place where Deucalion had once thrown himself and that she would be healed of her passion as he had been healed of his. And they added that Sapho had at that very moment obeyed the naiad, gone to Epirus, been shipwrecked, and had in fact been cured of her love by death.

But honestly, rational people did not believe so improbable a tale. We knew that Sapho was too wise to do such a thing, and besides, when I got back to Mytilene, I questioned Phaon's friend, at whose house he had hidden for several days, so closely that in the end he confided to me that Phaon had been with him and had seen Sapho often and had left with her. But he didn't know any more than that, so I knew very little of my friend's plan. I did have the satisfaction of knowing, though, that Sapho wasn't dead and that Phaon was happy, for I concluded that they would not have departed together had they not been fully reconciled. But what was quite surprising was that Phylire, her brother, and Agelaste had also disappeared with Sapho, though no one spoke of it, for Sapho's whereabouts so occupied everyone's minds that they spoke of nothing else.

Meanwhile poor Nicanor turned this conjecture to his advantage, for when people said that Sapho had been shipwrecked because she knew Phaon had been unfaithful, he was cured of his passion. It seemed to him that he ought not to love the memory of someone who had loved someone else so much. For her part, Damophile was the only one who rejoiced at Sapho's loss because she believed that at last she would be the only learned lady in Mytilene. But in the end, Madam, when my sister returned from Phrygia, we discovered as well that Clirantes had married Phylire before they left, and we remembered having heard Clirantes's admirable description of the laws of his country, and so we thought that Sapho, Phaon, and Agelaste had gone there. We were so sure that I decided to find out for myself and undertook the voyage with Leontidas. This voyage was both a success and a failure, because I learned from the valiant Mereontes that Sapho and Phaon had been received more honorably than any other foreigners had ever been by the queen of the Sarmatae and that this admirable young woman was staying in the queen's palace and that Phaon was with Clirantes in his. The two of them were enjoying the pleasures of the court and Agelaste had won the hearts of both the gentlemen and the ladies. But most important, I learned that Phaon is now the most faithful lover in the world and Sapho the happiest woman on earth because in this court she is at last adored: it is she who distributes the queen's favors to others, and Phaon's passion is lasting.

They did have, though, a little matter that came up after they arrived. Since there were laws concerning love, and judges who knew only things having to do with that passion, Phaon sued to oblige them to charge Sapho to allow him to hope that one day he might marry her. According to the country's laws, Sapho was required to plead her case and Phaon his, which they both did admirably. But in the end, Sapho made people understand so skillfully that to love always, with an equal ardor, one must never marry, that the judges ordered Phaon not to press her further and declared that only she might grant such a favor. In the meantime, he should consider himself the happiest and most honored lover on earth to be loved by the most perfect person in the world, a person who refused him her hand only because she wished always to possess his heart. Since then, they have lived as peacefully as ever could be imagined, and they enjoy all the sweets a gallant, delicate, and tender love can inspire in the hearts of those who possess it. But what is cruel to me is that Mereontes told me that Sapho and Phaon were so afraid that someone from Mytilene might trouble their happiness that they made the queen prohibit strangers from entering the country for ten years, so it was useless for me to pursue my journey and I returned without being able to prove to Mytilene that Sapho wasn't dead. As for her plan not to be troubled in her felicity, I think I ought not to say what I know about it for fear that some of her former lovers might seek her there or people might say things against her worse than what they are saying already. So while Sapho enjoyed the good fortune she deserved, all Greece believed her dead, and still do, because the vessel that carried her was lost on its return voyage. While this admirable poet of Lesbos doubtless spends her days writing gallant and passionate verses, those who are renowned throughout Greece write epitaphs to her glory.

THE TWENTIETH HARANGUE
FROM *LES FEMMES ILLUSTRES, OU, LES HARANGUES HÉROÏQUES*

Sapho to Erinne

Argument

Soon you will hear speak that renowned woman who has been so talked of across the centuries that Plato himself admired her; whose image has been graven like that of a great nation; who left us a kind of poetry called saphics because it was she who invented the meter; and whom two great men of ancient Greece and Rome have called the tenth Muse. I have made her take this occasion to exhort her friend also to write poetry so as to show both that women are able to do so, and that they are wrong to neglect so agreeable an occupation. Such is the argument of this oration, which I offer to the glory of that fair sex, just as I have offered this whole volume to the glory of women.

> Come see herein a thing so rare
> The wonder of the universe
> Remember prose cannot compare
> To the beauty found within her verse.

Sapho to Erinne

I must this very day, Erinne, overcome the self-doubt in your soul, the false modesty that prevents you from using your mind to do all it is capable of doing. But before I speak of your own merits, I want to make you see those of our sex more generally so that through that knowledge I can convince you more easily to do as I wish. Those who say that beauty is women's part and that arts and letters and all the liberal and sublime sciences belong to men and that we have no part in them are equally far from both justice and truth. If such were the case, all women would be born beautiful and all men with a keen inclination for learning; otherwise, Nature would be unjust in bestowing her treasures. Yet daily we see ugliness in our sex and stupidity in theirs. If it were true that beauty were the only gift bestowed on us by the heavens, not only would all women be beautiful, but what's more, I believe, they would be beautiful until they die; time would respect in women what in fact it destroys each instant. If they were put on this earth merely to display their beauty, they would be beautiful for as long as they remained on earth: it would be a strange destiny to live for an age with only one thing to recommend us for all those many years that lead to the tomb and to have only five or six years of glory.

Those things Nature seems to have made only to adorn the universe almost never lose their beauty once it is bestowed. Gold, pearls, diamonds all preserve their brilliance as long as they exist; they say even the phoenix dies with its beauty only to return to life beautiful again. Tell me then, since we see neither roses nor lilies that the rigors of a few winters don't wither in the faces of even the greatest beauties; since there are no eyes that don't become cloudy, even though they were once brighter than the sun; no eyes, having once made a hundred brilliant conquests, that don't find themselves at last almost unable to see even the conquests of others; since every moment, despite ourselves and all our efforts, we are robbed of all that is most beautiful; since time carries away our youth and those golden threads that ensnared so many hearts one day turn to silver; and finally, since this air of beauty that combines so agreeably all the features of a beautiful face, where one sees manifest a glimmer of the divine, is not strong enough to conquer sickness, time, and age, we must conclude of necessity, I say, that we have other advantages than beauty alone.

It is reasonable to say that beauty is to our sex as valor is to theirs, but since that attribute doesn't prevent them from loving the study of arts and letters, our beauty doesn't prevent us in the least from study and learning. If there are differences between men and women, they are only in those things having to do with war: it is for the beauty of my sex to conquer hearts and for the valor and strength of men to conquer kingdoms. Nature's intention seems so clear in this regard that one cannot oppose it: I agree, therefore, that we ought to leave the taking of cities, the pitching of battles, and the business of arms to those who were born to it; but as for things that require only imagination, a lively mind, memory, and judgment, I will not allow us to be dispossessed of them.

Men, as you know, are almost all either our slaves or our enemies; nevertheless, when the chains we make them wear seem too heavy or when, having broken them, they are the most angry at us, still they do not dispute the beauty of our imaginations, the liveliness of our minds, or the strength of our memories. As for judgment, some are unjust enough to maintain that they have more of it than we do. I sometimes think that the moderation and modesty of our sex are quite enough to demonstrate that we do not lack judgment. But if it is true that we are possessed of these former advantages to a high degree, then it is almost impossible that we should not possess the other. Because if our imaginations let us see things as they are, if our minds let us know them perfectly, and if our memories serve us as they should, how can our judgments fail us? A vivid imagination is so faithful a mirror, a bright mind penetrates so to the heart of things, and a skilled and cultivated memory teaches so powerfully by example, that it is impossible that judgment should not be formed.

Believe me, Erinne, when the sea is calm, it is difficult to be shipwrecked: even the worst pilot can enter the harbor. There are no dangers that cannot be avoided if one sees them and the waves are not stirred up. For my part, I declare to you that I don't understand those who allow us imagination, intelligence, and memory and then pride themselves on having more judgment than we have. When their imaginations don't show them things as they are, when their minds have not a perfect understanding, and when their memories are not accurate, how should their judgment be just, given such false foundations? No, Erinne, it isn't possible, and to be more reasonable than many of them, let us admit that among them and among us there are those with imagination, intelligence and wit, memory and judgment. It isn't that I could not, if I wanted to, show by powerful and rigorous argument that our sex might well boast of being richer in the mind's treasures than men. Consider, Erinne, the almost universal law one sees in the animal kingdom, among those who live in forests and caves, that those who are born with strength and courage are often less adroit and intelligent than the weak, who ordinarily have a sixth sense and are closer to reason than those to whom Nature has given other advantages. You can see how, according to that principle, since Nature has given more strength and courage to men than to women, she must also have given more intelligence and judgment to us. But once again, Erinne, let us allow they have as much as we do, as long as they remain agreed that we have as much as they.

You will say, perhaps, that having won this admission from all men, I cannot also persuade you that knowledge of the liberal arts is appropriate or suitable for a woman because, according to conventions established by men for fear, perhaps, of being surpassed by us, study, like war, is forbidden to women. To write verse is the same thing as to do battle, if one is to believe them, and if truth be told, it seems we are only permitted that which should rather be forbidden us. Erinne, have we a lively imagination, a perceptive mind, a good memory, and solid judgment only in order to do our hair and choose some ornament that adds to our beauty? No, Erinne, that would be to waste the favors the heavens have bestowed on us. Those born with eyes made to conquer have only to join deceit to Nature's gifts—what a disgraceful use of our minds to spend our lives only in such occupations.

One might even say that if things were ordained as they should be, the study of arts and letters ought rather to be permitted to women than to men because men are in charge of the universe—some are kings, others governors of provinces, some are priests, other judges, and in general, all are heads of their households and consequently taken up either with public affairs or their own, so no doubt they have little time to give to that sort of study. They have to steal time from their subjects or their friends or themselves; but our leisure and sheltered life give us all the opportunity we might wish. We steal nothing from the public or ourselves; on the contrary, we enrich ourselves without impoverishing others; we bring renown to our country in making ourselves illustrious; and without doing wrong to anyone, we acquire great fame. It is just, it seems to me, since we leave governing to men, that they should leave us at least the liberty to know all things of which our minds are capable. Desire of the good ought not be forbidden us, and thus it follows that it is not a crime to pursue good. The gods have made nothing useless in all of Nature; everything has its place: the sun shines and heats the universe, the earth gives us fruits and flowers every year, the sea offers all its riches, the rivers water our meadows, the woods lend us their shade—everything serves the social good. Therefore, why should we be the only rebels, ungrateful to the gods? Why should our minds be trivially employed or eternally useless? What decorum could there be in scorning what is right and honest? What sort of reason could agree that what is infinitely praiseworthy in itself could become wrong and blameworthy in us?

Those who own slaves educate them for their own convenience, but those whom Nature or custom gave as our masters want us to extinguish in our souls the lights Heaven put there and to live in the deepest shadows of ignorance. If they want to obtain our admiration more easily, they don't succeed, because we do not admire in the least what we do not know. And if it is to make us more subject to them, that is hardly generous; and if it is true that they have some power over us, there is little glory in having power over the stupid and ignorant. You will say, perhaps, that all men are not so severe and that some consent to our using our minds to study the arts, literature, and history as long as we don't get involved in wanting to write such works ourselves. But those who hold that opinion should remember that if Mercury and Apollo are of their sex, Minerva and the Muses are of ours. Nevertheless, I admit that, having received so much from the gods, we ought not to engage in such things lightly. There is no shame in writing poetry, only in writing bad poetry, and if mine had not had the good fortune to please, I would never have shown it a second time. Such shame is not unique to us; anyone who does badly something that he or she has freely undertaken deserves to be blamed regardless of sex. A bad orator, a bad philosopher, a bad poet gains hardly more glory than a woman who acquits herself in all these subjects with bad grace. Regardless of sex, one deserves censure when one does something badly and esteem when one does something well.

But to concede something to custom and to the corruption of our century, let us leave the thorny sciences, Erinne, to those who prefer to seek glory the hard way. I don't wish to lead you in disagreeable directions; I don't wish you to spend your entire life in a troublesome search for secrets that can't be found; I don't wish you to apply your intelligence uselessly to find out where the winds hide after having caused shipwrecks; finally, I don't want you to spend the rest of your days speculating indifferently about everything. I care about your tranquility, your glory and your beauty together: I don't urge you to those sorts of study that turn your complexion sallow, that dim your eyes and sink your cheeks, that furrow your brow and make your disposition gloomy and anxious. I don't want you to avoid company or daylight; I simply want you to follow me to the shores of Permessus:[1] it is there, Erinne, that I wish to lead you; it is there that you will surpass me from the moment you arrive; it is there that you will acquire a beauty that time, the years, the seasons, age, and death itself can never take

---

1. A spring flowing from Mount Parnassus, a mountain sacred to Apollo and the Muses and associated with literary endeavor and achievement.

from you; it is there, finally, that you will know perfectly that our sex is capable of everything we wish to undertake.

Perhaps you will say that in wishing to lead you to poetry, I break my word because it seems that beauty is incompatible with the frowning concentration attributed to those who write verse. But know, Erinne, that this is nothing but an invention of men who would have us believe that, just as we see those who deliver oracles troubled by the presence of the god who speaks through them, so divine poesy will trouble those who practice it. But even if this were true, your eyes would be no less bright, for just as after the oracle has spoken and the priest's earlier tranquility returns, so no sooner will you have put down your pen than you will find your earlier graces have returned. And anyway, I don't think you will ever fill your mind with such dread images that something dreadful might spring into your eyes. You will be absolute mistress of the subjects you wish to treat, and given all the beauties there are in Nature, you can choose whatever moves you. The description of a wood or spring, the lament of a lover or his mistress, praise of some virtue, all of these will give you ample subjects to demonstrate the talents the heavens have given you. You were born with such glorious gifts that you would be ungrateful to those who gave them if you did not know how to use them well.

You will ask me as well, perhaps, if it is not glory enough for a beautiful woman to be praised in verse by all the great poets of her time without getting involved herself in creating her own portrait. You will ask me, I know, if her glory is not better founded in this way than in the other, but I tell you in reply that whatever praises may be offered you, it will be more glorious to have written verse for the illustrious persons of your century, if you write well, than it would be to have them write for you. Believe me, Erinne, it is better to give immortality to others than to receive it from someone else, better to find glory within yourself than to wait for it from elsewhere. The portraits made of you of that kind might some day be considered by posterity as tableaux made for amusement. The poet's imagination would be admired more than your beauty, and the copies would eventually pass for the originals. But if you leave traces of yourself from your own hand, you will live forever honored in the memory of all men. Those of your own time who praised you will seem truthful, and those who didn't will seem stupid or envious. Yet I don't claim that you should draw your own portrait or that you yourself should speak of your beauty, your virtue, and all of your rare qualities. No, I would not impose such a hard task on your modesty. Poetry has many other privileges: you have only to let others speak of you to make yourself known to posterity; you have only to speak with good grace and you will be well enough known. Yes, Erinne, you have only to use your pen to condemn the vices of your time, and the world will not fail to praise you.

Consider once more, I beseech you, how weak and transitory is fame founded on beauty. Of the infinite number of beautiful women who doubtless have lived in times past, we hear of only two or three, but we see the fame of many men solidly established by the writings they have left. Erinne, allow time, age, and death to steal only roses from you; don't let them carry off all your beauty. Triumph over these enemies of all that is beautiful; make yourself, by your example, uphold the glory of our sex; make our common enemies admit that it is as easy for us to conquer by the force of our minds as by the beauty of our eyes; make the whole world see through the beautiful paintings of your imagination, through the noble efforts of your mind, through the beautiful effects of your memory, through the beautiful signs of your judgment, that you alone have the power to reestablish the glory of all women. Don't scorn what I say to you, for, if out of false modesty you decide not to heed my advice and you consign all your glory to your beauty, you will lament the loss of that beauty while you live. You will be spoken of as if you came from another century, and you will find that I was right to say to you today what I believe I have said before in some of my verses:

> Lilies, carnations, roses—all
> the beauties that color your face,
> Your bright eyes, your radiant skin,
> All will lose shape and form,
> And you will die, utterly,
> If, to conquer Fate and death you
> do not, through study, seek immortality.

THE EFFECT OF THIS ORATION

It cannot be said that this oration had no effect if we attend literally to the letter, for it seems that the one to whom it was addressed was moved in the desired direction: a Greek epigram tells us that Sapho surpassed Erinne in lyric poetry as much as Erinne surpassed Sapho in hexameters. If we leave aside the literal sense and consider my intentions, I will be renowned if I am able to persuade our ladies of what this beautiful Lesbian persuaded her friend, and more, if I can persuade the whole world that the fair sex is worthy of our adoration so that one day temples and altars will be dedicated to women just as now I dedicate to them this TRIUMPHANT ARCH THAT I HAVE RAISED TO THEIR GLORY.

VOLUME EDITOR'S
BIBLIOGRAPHY

THE TEXT

The most convenient edition of the French text is the Slatkine Reprints facsimile from the1656 edition of *Artamène, ou, Le Grand Cyrus*, which appeared from Droz (Geneva, 1972). The original edition appeared in 10 volumes (Paris: Augustin Courbé, 1649–1653). As I have already indicated, there has been no modern edition, nor is there a modern edition of *Les femmes illustres, ou, Les harangues héroïques* (Paris: Antonin de Sommaville and Augustin Courbé, 1642) from which the twentieth harangue, Sapho to Erinne, is taken.

STUDIES IN ENGLISH

Aronson, Nicole. *Mademoiselle de Scudéry*. Boston: Twayne, 1978.

Bayley, Peter. "Fixed Form and Varied Function: Reflections on the Language of French Classicism." *Seventeenth-Century Studies* 6 (1984): 6–21.

Beasley, Faith E. *Revising Memory: Women's Fiction and Memoirs in Seventeenth Century France*. New Brunswick, N.J.: Rutgers University Press, 1990.

DeJean, Joan. "No Man's Land: The Novel's First Geography." *Yale French Studies* 73 (1987): 175–89.

———. "Female Voyeurism: Sapho and Lafayette." *Rivista de litterature moderne e comparate* 40 (1987): 201–15.

———. *Fictions of Sapho, 1546–1937*. Chicago: University of Chicago Press, 1989.

———. *Tender Geographies: Women and the Origins of the Novel in France*. New York: Columbia University Press, 1991.

Davis, Natalie Zemon. "'Women's History' in Transition: The European Case." *Feminist Studies* 3 (1976): 83–103.

Goldsmith, Elizabeth. *Exclusive Conversations: The Art of Interaction in Seventeenth-Century France*. Philadelphia: University of Pennsylvania Press, 1988.

Harth, Erica. *Ideology and Culture in Seventeenth-Century France*. Ithaca, N.Y.: Cornell University Press, 1983.

———. *Cartesian Women. Versions and Subversions of Rational Discourse in the Old Regime*. Ithaca, N.Y.: Cornell University Press, 1992.

Lougée, Carolyn. *Le Paradis des femmes: Women, Salons and Social Stratification in Seventeenth-Century France*. Princeton: Princeton University Press, 1976.

Popkin, Suzanne. "Taking Compliments: J. L. Austin with Madeleine de Scudéry." *differences: A Journal of Feminist Cultural Studies* 10 (1998): 82–118.

Showalter, English. *The Evolution of the French Novel (1641–1782)* Princeton: Princeton University Press, 1972.

Stanton, Domna. "The Fiction of Préciosité and the Fear of Women." *Yale French Studies* 62 (1981): 107–34.

STUDIES IN FRENCH

Bassy, Alain-Marie. "Supplément au voyage de Tendre." *Bulletin du bibliophile* 1 (1982): 13–33.

Conrart, Valentin. *Mémoires*. Edited by. L.-J.-N. Monmerqué. Geneva: Slatkine Reprints, 1971.

Cousin, Victor. *La Société française au XVIIᵉ siècle d'après "Le Grand Cyrus" de Mademoiselle de Scudéry*. 2 vols. Paris: Didier, 1858.

DeJean, Joan. "La Fronde romanesque: De l'exploit à la fiction." In *Actes du dix-huitième colloque du Centre Mériodional de Rencontres sur le XVIIᵉ Siècle*, edited by R. Duchêne and P. Ronzeaud, 181–92. Marseilles, 1989.

Godenne, René. *Les Romans de Mademoiselle de Scudéry*. Geneva: Droz, 1983.

Lever, Maurice. *La Fiction narrative en prose au XVIIᵉ siècle*. Paris: CNRS, 1976.

Mongrédien, Georges. "Bibliographie des oeuvres de Georges et Madeleine de Scudéry." *Revue d'histoire littéraire de la France* 40 (1933): 225–236, 413–25, 538–65.

———. *Madeleine de Scudéry et son salon*. Paris: Tallendier, 1946.

Pelous, Jean Michel. *Amour précieux, amour galant*. Paris: Klincksieck, 1974.

Steiner, Arpad. "Les idées esthétiques de Mademoiselle de Scudéry." *Romanic Review* 16 (1925): 171–90.

Timmermans, Linda. *L'Accès des Femmes à la Culture (1598–1715)*. Paris: Éditions Champion, 1993.

SERIES EDITORS'
BIBLIOGRAPHY

PRIMARY SOURCES

Alberti, Leon Battista. *The Family in Renaissance Florence.* Translated by Renée Neu Watkins. Columbia, S.C.: University of South Carolina Press, 1969.

Arenal, Electa, and Stacey Schlau, eds. *Untold Sisters: Hispanic Nuns in Their Own Works.* Translated by Amanda Powell. Albuquerque, N.Mex.: University of New Mexico Press, 1989.

Astell, Mary. *The First English Feminist: Reflections on Marriage and Other Writings.* Edited and with an introduction by Bridget Hill. New York: St. Martin's Press, 1986.

Atherton, Margaret, ed. *Women Philosophers of the Early Modern Period.* Indianapolis, Ind.: Hackett Publishing Co., 1994.

Aughterson, Kate, ed. *Renaissance Woman: Constructions of Femininity in England: A Source Book.* London and New York: Routledge, 1995.

Barbaro, Francesco. "On Wifely Duties." Translated by Benjamin Kohl. In *The Earthly Republic,* edited by B. Kohl and R. G. Witt, 179–228. Philadelphia: University of Pennsylvania Press, 1978.

Behn, Aphra. *The Works of Aphra Behn.* 7 vols. Edited by Janet Todd. Columbus, Ohio: Ohio State University Press, 1992–96.

Boccaccio, Giovanni. *Famous Women* (The I Tatti Renaissance Library). Edited and translated by Virginia Brown. Cambridge, Mass.: Harvard University Press, 2001.
———. *Corbaccio or the Labyrinth of Love.* 2d rev. ed. Translated by Anthony K. Cassell. Binghamton, N.Y.: Medieval and Renaissance Texts and Studies, 1993.

Bruni, Leonardo. "On the Study of Literature (1405) to Lady Battista Malatesta of Moltefeltro." In *The Humanism of Leonardo Bruni: Selected Texts,* translated and with an introduction by Gordon Griffiths, James Hankins, and David Thompson, 240–51. Binghamton, N.Y.: Medieval and Renaissance Studies and Texts, 1987.

Castiglione, Baldassare. *The Book of the Courtier.* Translated by George Bull. New York: Penguin, 1967.

Cerasano, S. P., and Marion Wynne-Davies, eds. *Readings in Renaissance Women's Drama: Criticism, History, and Performance 1594–1998.* London and New York: Routledge, 1998.

Christine de Pizan. *The Book of the City of Ladies.* Translated by Earl Jeffrey Richards. New York: Persea Books, 1982.

————. *The Treasure of the City of Ladies*. Translated by Sarah Lawson. New York: Viking Penguin, 1985.

Clarke, Danielle, ed. *Isabella Whitney, Mary Sidney and Aemilia: Renaissance Women Poets*. New York: Penguin Books, 2000.

Crawford, Patricia, and Laura Gowing, eds. *Women's Worlds in Seventeenth-Century England: A Source Book*. London and New York: Routledge, 2000.

Elizabeth I: Collected Works. Edited by Leah S. Marcus, Janel Mueller, and Mary Beth Rose. Chicago: University of Chicago Press, 2000.

Elyot, Thomas. *Defence of Good Women: The Feminist Controversy of the Renaissance* (Facsimile Reproductions). Edited by Diane Bornstein. New York: Delmar, 1980.

Erasmus, Desiderius. *Erasmus on Women*. Edited by Erika Rummel. Toronto: University of Toronto Press, 1996.

Female and Male Voices in Early Modern England: An Anthology of Renaissance Writing. Edited by Betty S. Travitsky and Anne Lake Prescott. New York: Columbia University Press, 2000.

Ferguson, Moira, ed. *First Feminists: British Women Writers 1578–1799*. Bloomington, Ind.: Indiana University Press, 1985.

Gethner, Perry, ed. *The Lunatic Lover and Other Plays by French Women of the 17th and 18th Centuries*. Portsmouth, N.H.: Heinemann, 1994.

Glückel of Hameln. *The Memoirs of Glückel of Hameln*. Translated by Marvin Lowenthal. New York: Schocken Books, 1977.

Henderson, Katherine Usher, and Barbara F. McManus, eds. *Half Humankind: Contexts and Texts of the Controversy about Women in England, 1540–1640*. Urbana, Ill.: Indiana University Press, 1985.

Joscelin, Elizabeth. *The Mother's Legacy to her Unborn Childe*. Edited by Jean leDrew Metcalfe. Toronto: University of Toronto Press, 2000.

Kaminsky, Amy Katz, ed. *Water Lilies, Flores del Agua: An Anthology of Spanish Women Writers from the Fifteenth through the Nineteenth Century*. Minneapolis, Minn.: University of Minnesota Press, 1996.

Kempe, Margery. *The Book of Margery Kempe*. Translated by Barry Windeatt. New York: Viking Penguin, 1986.

King, Margaret L., and Albert Rabil, Jr., eds. *Her Immaculate Hand: Selected Works by and about the Women Humanists of Quattrocento Italy*. 2d rev. ed. Binghamton, N.Y.: Medieval and Renaissance Texts and Studies, 1991.

Klein, Joan Larsen, ed. *Daughters, Wives, and Widows: Writings by Men about Women and Marriage in England, 1500–1640*. Urbana, Ill.: University of Illinois Press, 1992.

Knox, John. *The Political Writings of John Knox: The First Blast of the Trumpet against the Monstrous Regiment of Women and Other Selected Works*. Edited by Marvin A. Breslow. Washington, D.C.: Folger Shakespeare Library, 1985.

Kors, Alan C., and Edward Peters, eds. *Witchcraft in Europe, 400–1700: A Documentary History*. Philadelphia: University of Pennsylvania Press, 2000.

Krämer, Heinrich, and Jacob Sprenger. *Malleus Maleficarum* (ca. 1487). Translated by Montague Summers. London: Pushkin Press, 1928 (reprint, New York: Dover, 1971).

Larsen, Anne R., and Colette H. Winn, eds. *Writings by Pre-Revolutionary French Women: From Marie de France to Elizabeth Vigée-Le Brun*. New York and London: Garland Publishing Co., 2000.

de Lorris, William, and Jean de Meun. *The Romance of the Rose.* Translated by Charles Dahlbert. Princeton: Princeton University Press, 1971 (reprint, University Press of New England, 1983).

Marguerite d'Angoulême, Queen of Navarre. *The Heptameron.* Translated by P. A. Chilton. New York: Viking Penguin, 1984.

Myers, Kathleen A., and Amanda Powell, eds. *A Wild Country out in the Garden: The Spiritual Journals of a Colonial Mexican Nun.* Bloomington, Ind.: Indiana University Press, 1999.

Russell, Rinaldina, ed. *Sister Maria Celeste's Letters to Her Father, Galileo.* San Jose, Calif., and New York: Writers Club Press, 2000.

Teresa of Avila, Saint. *The Life of Saint Teresa of Avila by Herself.* Translated by J. M. Cohen. New York: Viking Penguin, 1957.

Weyer, Johann. *Witches, Devils, and Doctors in the Renaissance: Johann Weyer, De praestigiis daemonum.* Edited by George Mora with Benjamin G. Kohl, Erik Midelfort, and Helen Bacon. Translated by John Shea. Binghamton, N.Y.: Medieval and Renaissance Texts and Studies, 1991.

Wilson, Katharina M., ed. *Medieval Women Writers.* Athens, Ga.: University of Georgia Press, 1984.

———., ed. *Women Writers of the Renaissance and Reformation.* Athens, Ga.: University of Georgia Press, 1987.

Wilson, Katharina M., and Frank J. Warnke, eds. *Women Writers of the Seventeenth Century.* Athens, Ga.: University of Georgia Press, 1989.

Wollstonecraft, Mary. *A Vindication of the Rights of Men and a Vindication of the Rights of Women.* Edited by Sylvana Tomaselli. Cambridge: Cambridge University Press, 1995.

———*The Vindications of the Rights of Men, The Rights of Women.* Edited by D. L. Macdonald and Kathleen Scherf. Peterborough, Ontario: Broadview Press, 1997.

Women Critics 1660–1820: An Anthology. Edited by the Folger Collective on Early Women Critics. Bloomington, Ind.: Indiana University Press, 1995.

Women Writers in English 1350–1850. 15 vols. Oxford: Oxford University Press,

Wroth, Lady Mary. *The Countess of Montgomery's Urania.* 2 parts. Edited by Josephine A. Roberts. Tempe, Ariz.: Medieval and Renaissance Texts and Studies, 1995, 1999.

———. *Lady Mary Wroth's 'Love's Victory': The Penshurst Manuscript.* Edited by Michael G. Brennan. London: The Roxburghe Club, 1988.

———. *The Poems of Lady Mary Wroth.* Edited by Josephine A. Roberts. Baton Rouge, La.: Louisiana State University Press, 1983.

de Zayas Maria. *The Disenchantments of Love.* Translated by H. Patsy Boyer. Albany, N.Y.: State University of New York Press, 1997.

———. *The Enchantments of Love: Amorous and Exemplary Novels.* Translated by H. Patsy Boyer. Berkeley, Calif.: University of California Press, 1990.

SECONDARY SOURCES

Akkerman, Tjitske, and Siep Sturman, eds. *Feminist Thought in European History, 1400–2000.* London and New York: Routledge, 1997.

Backer, Anne Liot. *Precious Women.* New York: Basic Books, 1974.

Barash, Carol. *English Women's Poetry, 1649–1714: Politics, Community, and Linguistic Authority.* New York and Oxford: Oxford University Press, 1996.

Battigelli, Anna. *Margaret Cavendish and the Exiles of the Mind.* Lexington, Ky.: University of Kentucky Press, 1998.

Beilin, Elaine V. *Redeeming Eve: Women Writers of the English Renaissance.* Princeton: Princeton University Press, 1987.

Benson, Pamela Joseph. *The Invention of Renaissance Woman: The Challenge of Female Independence in the Literature and Thought of Italy and England.* University Park, Penn.: Pennsylvania State University Press, 1992.

Blain, Virginia, Isobel Grundy, and Patricia Clements, eds. *The Feminist Companion to Literature in English: Women Writers from the Middle Ages to the Present.* New Haven, Conn.: Yale University Press, 1990.

Bloch, R. Howard. *Medieval Misogyny and the Invention of Western Romantic Love.* Chicago: University of Chicago Press, 1991.

Bornstein, Daniel, and Roberto Rusconi, eds. *Women and Religion in Medieval and Renaissance Italy.* Translated by Margery J. Schneider. Chicago: University of Chicago Press, 1996.

Brant, Clare, and Diane Purkiss, eds. *Women, Texts and Histories, 1575–1760.* London and New York: Routledge, 1992.

Briggs, Robin. *Witches and Neighbours: The Social and Cultural Context of European Witchcraft.* New York: HarperCollins, 1995.

Brink, Jean R., ed. *Female Scholars: A Tradition of Learned Women before 1800.* Montreal: Eden Press Women's Publications, 1980.

Brown, Judith C. *Immodest Acts: The Life of a Lesbian Nun in Renaissance Italy.* New York: Oxford University Press, 1986.

Cervigni, Dino S., ed. *Women Mystic Writers.* Annali d'Italianistica 13 (1995) (entire issue).

Cervigni, Dino S., and Rebecca West, eds. *Women's Voices in Italian Literature.* Annali d'Italianistica 7 (1989) (entire issue).

Charlton, Kenneth. *Women, Religion and Education in Early Modern England.* London and New York: Routledge, 1999.

Chojnacka, Monica. *Working Women in Early Modern Venice.* Baltimore: Johns Hopkins University Press, 2001.

Chojnacki, Stanley. *Women and Men in Renaissance Venice: Twelve Essays on Patrician Society.* Baltimore: Johns Hopkins University Press, 2000.

Cholakian, Patricia Francis. *Rape and Writing in the* Heptameron *of Marguerite de Navarre.* Carbondale and Edwardsville, Ill.: Southern Illinois University Press, 1991.

———. *Women and the Politics of Self-Representation in Seventeenth-Century France.* Newark: University of Delaware Press, 2000.

Davis, Natalie Zemon. *Society and Culture in Early Modern France.* Stanford: Stanford University Press, 1975.

———. *Women on the Margins: Three Seventeenth-Century Lives.* Cambridge, Mass.: Harvard University Press, 1995.

DeJean, Joan. *Ancients against Moderns: Culture Wars and the Making of a Fin de Siècle.* Chicago: University of Chicago Press, 1997.

Dixon, Laurinda S. *Perilous Chastity: Women and Illness in Pre-Enlightenment Art and Medicine.* Ithaca, N.Y.: Cornell Universitiy Press, 1995.

Dolan, Frances E. *Whores of Babylon: Catholicism, Gender and Seventeenth-Century Print Culture.* Ithaca, N.Y.: Cornell University Press, 1999.

Donovan, Josephine. *Women and the Rise of the Novel, 1405–1726.* New York: St. Martin's Press, 1999.

De Erauso, Catalina. *Lieutenant Nun: Memoir of a Basque Transvestite in the New World.* Translated by Michele Stepto and Gabriel Stepto. Boston: Beacon Press, 1995.

Erickson, Amy Louise. *Women and Property in Early Modern England.* London and New York: Routledge, 1993.

Ezell, Margaret J. M. *The Patriarch's Wife: Literary Evidence and the History of the Family.* Chapel Hill, N.C.: University of North Carolina Press, 1987.

——. *Social Authorship and the Advent of Print.* Baltimore: Johns Hopkins University Press, 1999.

——. *Writing Women's Literary History.* Baltimore: Johns Hopkins University Press, 1993.

Ferguson, Margaret W., Maureen Quilligan, and Nancy J. Vickers, eds. *Rewriting the Renaissance: The Discourses of Sexual Difference in Early Modern Europe.* Chicago: University of Chicago Press, 1987.

Fletcher, Anthony. *Gender, Sex and Subordination in England 1500–1800.* New Haven: Yale University Press, 1995.

Frye, Susan, and Karen Robertson, eds. *Maids and Mistresses, Cousins and Queens: Women's Alliances in Early Modern England.* Oxford: Oxford University Press, 1999.

Gallagher, Catherine. *Nobody's Story: The Vanishing Acts of Women Writers in the Marketplace, 1670–1820.* Berkeley, Calif.: University of California Press, 1994.

Gelbart, Nina Rattner. *The King's Midwife: A History and Mystery of Madame du Coudray.* Berkeley, Calif.: University of California Press, 1998.

Goldberg, Jonathan. *Desiring Women Writing: English Renaissance Examples.* Stanford, Calif.: Stanford University Press, 1997.

Goldsmith, Elizabeth C., ed. *Writing the Female Voice.* Boston: Northeastern University Press, 1989.

Goldsmith, Elizabeth C., and Dena Goodman, eds. *Going Public: Women and Publishing in Early Modern France.* Ithaca, N.Y.: Cornell University Press, 1995.

Greer, Margaret Rich. *Maria de Zayas.* University Park, Penn.: Pennsylvania State University Press, 2000.

Hackett, Helen. *Women and Romance Fiction in the English Renaissance.* Cambridge: Cambridge University Press, 2000.

Hall, Kim F. *Things of Darkness: Economies of Race and Gender in Early Modern England.* Ithaca, N.Y.: Cornell University Press, 1995.

Hampton, Timothy. *Literature and the Nation in the Sixteenth Century: Inventing Renaissance France.* Ithaca, N.Y.: Cornell University Press, 2001.

Hardwick, Julie. *The Practice of Patriarchy: Gender and the Politics of Household Authority in Early Modern France.* University Park, Penn.: Pennsylvania State University Press, 1998.

Haselkorn, Anne M., and Betty Travitsky, eds. *The Renaissance Englishwoman in Print: Counterbalancing the Canon.* Amherst, Mass.: University of Massachusetts Press, 1990.

Herlihy, David. "Did Women Have a Renaissance? A Reconsideration." *Medievalia et Humanistica,* NS 13 (1985): 1–22.

Hill, Bridget. *The Republican Virago: The Life and Times of Catharine Macaulay, Historian.* New York: Oxford University Press, 1992.

A History of Women in the West. Volume 1: From Ancient Goddesses to Christian Saints. Edited by Pauline Schmitt Pantel. Cambridge, Mass.: Harvard University Press, 1992.

A History of Women in the West. Volume 2: Silences of the Middle Ages. Edited by Christiane Klapisch-Zuber. Cambridge, Mass.: Harvard University Press, 1992.

A History of Women in the West. Volume 3: Renaissance and Enlightenment Paradoxes. Edited by Natalie Zemon Davis and Arlette Farge. Cambridge, Mass.: Harvard University Press, 1993.

Hobby, Elaine. *Virtue of Necessity: English Women's Writing, 1646–1688.* London: Virago Press, 1988.

Horowitz, Maryanne Cline. "Aristotle and Women." *Journal of the History of Biology* 9 (1976): 183–213.

Hufton, Olwen H. *The Prospect before Her: A History of Women in Western Europe, 1: 1500–1800.* New York: HarperCollins, 1996.

Hull, Suzanne W. *Chaste, Silent, and Obedient: English Books for Women, 1475–1640.* San Marino, Calif.: The Huntington Library, 1982.

Hunt, Lynn, ed. *The Invention of Pornography: Obscenity and the Origins of Modernity, 1500–1800.* New York: Zone Books, 1996.

Hutner, Heidi, ed. *Rereading Aphra Behn: History, Theory, and Criticism.* Charlottesville, Va.: University Press of Virginia, 1993.

Hutson, Lorna, ed. *Feminism and Renaissance Studies.* New York: Oxford University Press, 1999.

James, Susan E. *Kateryn Parr: The Making of a Queen.* Aldershot and Brookfield, UK: Ashgate Publishing Co., 1999.

Jankowski, Theodora A. *Women in Power in the Early Modern Drama.* Urbana, Ill.: University of Illinois Press, 1992.

Jed, Stephanie H. *Chaste Thinking: The Rape of Lucretia and the Birth of Humanism.* Bloomington, Ind.: Indiana University Press, 1989.

Jordan, Constance. *Renaissance Feminism: Literary Texts and Political Models.* Ithaca, N.Y.: Cornell University Press, 1990.

Kelly, Joan. "Did Women Have a Renaissance?" In *Women, History, and Theory.* Chicago: University of Chicago Press, 1984. Also in Renate Bridenthal, Claudia Koonz, and Susan M. Stuard, eds., *Becoming Visible: Women in European History.* 3d ed. Boston: Houghton Mifflin, 1998.

—————. "Early Feminist Theory and the *Querelle des Femmes*" In *Women, History, and Theory.* Chicago: University of Chicago Press, 1984.

Kelso, Ruth. *Doctrine for the Lady of the Renaissance.* Urbana, Ill.: University of Illinois Press, 1956 (reprint 1978).

King, Carole. *Renaissance Women Patrons: Wives and Widows in Italy, c. 1300–1550.* New York and Manchester: Manchester University Press and St. Martin's Press, 1998.

King, Margaret L. *Women of the Renaissance.* Chicago: University of Chicago Press, 1991.

Krontiris, Tina. *Oppositional Voices: Women as Writers and Translators of Literature in the English Renaissance.* London and New York: Routledge, 1992.

Kuehn, Thomas. *Law, Family, and Women: Toward a Legal Anthropology of Renaissance Italy.* Chicago: University of Chicago Press, 1991.

Kunze, Bonnelyn Young. *Margaret Fell and the Rise of Quakerism*. Stanford, Calif.: Stanford University Press, 1994.

Labalme, Patricia A., ed. *Beyond Their Sex: Learned Women of the European Past*. New York: New York University Press, 1980.

Laqueur, Thomas. *Making Sex: Body and Gender from the Greeks to Freud*. Cambridge, Mass.: Harvard University Press, 1990.

Larsen, Anne R., and Colette H. Winn, eds. *Renaissance Women Writers: French Texts/ American Contexts*. Detroit, Mich.: Wayne State University Press, 1994.

Lerner, Gerda. *The Creation of Patriarchy* and *Creation of Feminist Consciousness, 1000–1870*. 2 vols. New York: Oxford University Press, 1986 (reprint 1994).

Levin, Carole, and Jeanie Watson, eds. *Ambiguous Realities: Women in the Middle Ages and Renaissance*. Detroit, Mich.: Wayne State University Press, 1987.

Levin, Carole, et al. *Extraordinary Women of the Medieval and Renaissance World: A Biographical Dictionary*. Westport, Conn.: Greenwood Press, 2000.

Lindsey, Karen. *Divorced Beheaded Survived: A Feminist Reinterpretation of the Wives of Henry VIII*. Reading, Mass.: Addison-Wesley Publishing Co., 1995.

Lochrie, Karma. *Margery Kempe and Translations of the Flesh*. Philadelphia: University of Pennsylvania Press, 1992.

Love, Harold. *The Culture and Commerce of Texts: Scribal Publication in Seventeenth-Century England*. Amherst, Mass.: University of Massachusetts Press, 1993.

MacCarthy, Bridget G. *The Female Pen: Women Writers and Novelists 1621–1818*. New York: New York University Press, 1994. Originally published by Cork University Press, 1946–1947.

Maclean, Ian. *Woman Triumphant: Feminism in French Literature, 1610–1652*. Oxford: Clarendon Press, 1977.

———. *The Renaissance Notion of Woman: A Study of the Fortunes of Scholasticism and Medical Science in European Intellectual Life*. Cambridge: Cambridge University Press, 1980.

Matter, E. Ann, and John Coakley, eds. *Creative Women in Medieval and Early Modern Italy*. Philadelphia: University of Pennsylvania Press, 1994.

McLeod, Glenda. *Virtue and Venom: Catalogs of Women from Antiquity to the Renaissance*. Ann Arbor, Mich.: University of Michigan Press, 1991.

Mendelson, Sara, and Patricia Crawford. *Women in Early Modern England, 1550–1720*. Oxford: Clarendon Press, 1998.

Merrim, Stephanie. *Early Modern Women's Writing and Sor Juana Inés de la Cruz*. Nashville, Tenn.: Vanderbilt University Press, 1999.

Miller, Nancy K. *The Heroine's Text: Readings in the French and English Novel, 1722–1782*. New York: Columbia University Press, 1980.

Miller, Naomi J. *Changing the Subject: Mary Wroth and Figurations of Gender in Early Modern England*. Lexington, Ky.: University Press of Kentucky, 1996.

Miller, Naomi J., and Gary Waller, eds. *Reading Mary Wroth: Representing Alternatives in Early Modern England*. Knoxville, Tenn.: University of Tennessee Press, 1991.

Monson, Craig A., ed. *The Crannied Wall: Women, Religion, and the Arts in Early Modern Europe*. Ann Arbor, Mich.: University of Michigan Press, 1992.

Newman, Karen. *Fashioning Femininity and English Renaissance Drama*. Chicago and London: University of Chicago Press, 1991.

Okin, Susan Moller. *Women in Western Political Thought*. Princeton: Princeton University Press, 1979.

Ozment, Steven. *The Bürgermeister's Daughter: Scandal in a Sixteenth-Century German Town.* New York: St. Martin's Press, 1995.

Pacheco, Anita, ed. *Early [English] Women Writers: 1600–1720.* New York and London: Longman, 1998.

Pagels, Elaine. *Adam, Eve, and the Serpent.* New York: HarperCollins, 1988.

Panizza, Letizia, ed. *Women in Italian Renaissance Culture and Society.* Oxford: European Humanities Research Centre, 2000.

Panizza, Letizia, and Sharon Wood, eds. *A History of Women's Writing in Italy.* Cambridge: Cambridge University Press, 2000.

Perry, Ruth. *The Celebrated Mary Astell: An Early English Feminist.* Chicago: University of Chicago Press, 1986.

Raven, James, Helen Small, and Naomi Tadmor, eds. *The Practice and Representation of Reading in England.* Cambridge: Cambridge University Press, 1996.

Richardson, Brian. *Printing, Writers and Readers in Renaissance Italy.* Cambridge: Cambridge University Press, 1999.

Riddle, John M. *Contraception and Abortion from the Ancient World to the Renaissance.* Cambridge, Mass.: Harvard University Press, 1992.

———. *Eve's Herbs: A History of Contraception and Abortion in the West.* Cambridge, Mass.: Harvard University Press, 1997.

Rose, Mary Beth. *The Expense of Spirit: Love and Sexuality in English Renaissance Drama.* Ithaca, N.Y.: Cornell University Press, 1988.

———, ed. *Women in the Middle Ages and the Renaissance: Literary and Historical Perspectives.* Syracuse, N.Y.: Syracuse University Press, 1986.

Rosenthal, Margaret F. *The Honest Courtesan: Veronica Franco, Citizen and Writer in Sixteenth-Century Venice.* Chicago: University of Chicago Press, 1992.

Sackville-West, Vita. *Daughter of France: The Life of La Grande Mademoiselle.* Garden City, N.Y.: Doubleday, 1959.

Schiebinger, Londa. *The Mind Has No Sex?: Women in the Origins of Modern Science.* Cambridge, Mass.: Harvard University Press, 1991.

———. *Nature's Body: Gender in the Making of Modern Science.* Boston: Beacon Press, 1993.

Shemek, Deanna. *Ladies Errant: Wayward Women and Social Order in Early Modern Italy.* Durham, N.C.: Duke University Press, 1998.

Sobel, Dava. *Galileo's Daughter: A Historical Memoir of Science, Faith, and Love.* New York: Penguin Books, 2000.

Sommerville, Margaret R. *Sex and Subjection: Attitudes to Women in Early-Modern Society.* London: Arnold, 1995.

Spencer, Jane. *The Rise of the Woman Novelist: From Aphra Behn to Jane Austen.* Oxford: Basil Blackwell, 1986.

Spender, Dale. *Mothers of the Novel: 100 Good Women Writers before Jane Austen.* London and New York: Routledge, 1986.

Sperling, Jutta Gisela. *Convents and the Body Politic in Late Renaissance Venice.* Chicago: University of Chicago Press, 1999.

Steinbrügge, Lieselotte. *The Moral Sex: Woman's Nature in the French Enlightenment.* Translated by Pamela E. Selwyn. New York: Oxford University Press, 1995.

Stuard, Susan M. "The Dominion of Gender: Women's Fortunes in the High Middle Ages." In *Becoming Visible: Women in European History*, edited by Renate Bridenthal, Claudia Koonz, and Susan M. Stuard. 3d ed. Boston: Houghton Mifflin, 1998.

Summit, Jennifer. *Lost Property: The Woman Writer and English Literary History, 1380–1589*. Chicago: University of Chicago Press, 2000.

Teague, Frances. *Bathsua Makin, Woman of Learning*. Lewisburg, Penn.: Bucknell University Press, 1999.

Todd, Janet. *The Secret Life of Aphra Behn*. London, New York, and Sydney: Pandora, 2000.

———. *The Sign of Angelica: Women, Writing and Fiction, 1660–1800*. New York: Columbia University Press, 1989.

Wall, Wendy. *The Imprint of Gender: Authorship and Publication in the English Renaissance*. Ithaca, N.Y.: Cornell University Press, 1993.

Walsh, William T. *St. Teresa of Avila: A Biography*. Rockford, Ill.: TAN Books and Publications, 1987.

Warner, Marina. *Alone of All Her Sex: The Myth and Cult of the Virgin Mary*. New York: Knopf, 1976.

Warnicke, Retha M. *The Marrying of Anne of Cleves: Royal Protocol in Tudor England*. Cambridge: Cambridge University Press, 2000.

Watt, Diane. *Secretaries of God: Women Prophets in Late Medieval and Early Modern England*. Cambridge: D. S. Brewer, 1997.

Welles, Marcia L. *Persephone's Girdle: Narratives of Rape in Seventeenth-Century Spanish Literature*. Nashville, Tenn.: Vanderbilt University Press, 2000.

Whitehead, Barbara J., ed. *Women's Education in Early Modern Europe: A History, 1500–1800*. New York and London: Garland Publishing Co., 1999.

Wiesner, Merry E. *Women and Gender in Early Modern Europe*. Cambridge: Cambridge University Press, 1993.

Willard, Charity Cannon. *Christine de Pizan: Her Life and Works*. New York: Persea Books, 1984.

Wilson, Katharina, ed. *An Encyclopedia of Continental Women Writers*. New York: Garland, 1991.

Woodbridge, Linda. *Women and the English Renaissance: Literature and the Nature of Womankind, 1540–1620*. Urbana, Ill.: University of Illinois Press, 1984.

Woods, Susanne. *Lanyer: A Renaissance Woman Poet*. New York: Oxford University Press, 1999.

Woods, Susanne, and Margaret P. Hannay, eds. *Teaching Tudor and Stuart Women Writers*. New York: Modern Language Association, 2000.

40445357R00113

Made in the USA
Middletown, DE
27 March 2019